Remembering Yesterday

DENNIS GALLEMORE

This is a work of fiction. Names, characters, organizations, places, events, and incidents are either products of the author's imagination or are used fictitiously.

DEDICATION

This collection of stories is dedicated to all of the members of Racine Christian Church, (RCC), in Racine, Missouri. Special thanks go to the members of RCC's Kindred Spirits life group, who not only endured listening to early versions of these stories, but actually encouraged me to write more.

CONTENTS

ACKNOWLEDGMENTS

First, and foremost, I would like to thank the Holy Spirit for guidance. I would also like to express deep appreciation for Joanne Sher, who edited a number of these stories. Thanks also go to Beetiful Book Covers, (Beetifulbookcovers. com), designer of the cover, which, by the way, inspired the opening story.

REMEMBERING YESTERDAY

Reece Brennan, PhD, gazed at the diploma on his office wall, a reminder of his days as a clinical psychology grad student at UCLA. Sighing, he sipped his coffee. He had graduated, with honors, ten years before, after what had seemed like a lifetime of study. Ready to take on the world, he had been certain he would use his training to heal anyone and everyone. After practicing enthusiastically for years, his enthusiasm had waned, as had his faith, after seeing so much pain and suffering. He had thought of himself as a servant, one who was simply doing what he was called to do. That thought, over time, had faded into oblivion. Now, he simply went through the motions.

He picked up a bible that had been on his desk for years; once upon a time, he had used the book for guidance, for both his personal and professional live, but no longer. He shrugged, opened a desk drawer, and tossed the bible inside.

He glanced at the wall clock. 4:45; close enough to five that he felt he could slip out a little early. His office door opening, he glanced up to see Patty, his assistant, step in. He frowned; this couldn't be good. "Great; I'm just about ready to leave and my amanuensis steps in."

She groaned. "Stop calling me that, Reece. I never should have given you a copy of *Roget's Thesaurus for Intellectuals*. It was a bad idea for a birthday gift."

He laughed. "I won't call you 'secretary,' and 'personal assistant' sounds too mechanical. I had to find another synonym." He shrugged. "Be that as it may, what's up?"

"A Deputy Bill Owens, from the Baxter County Sheriff's department, called and scheduled an appointment for tomorrow morning at nine."

He leaned forward, his interest piqued. "For himself or for someone else?"

"No, not himself." She smiled. "He said that the Department received a call yesterday from a farmer out on Maple Tree Road. Seems the farmer was

1

working on a fence near the railroad; when he spotted a boy walking down the track all by himself."

"Who was he? Why was he walking down a railroad track alone?"

"No one knows. The farmer called out to him but he didn't answer; didn't even look at him, even though he was only thirty feet away. He just kept on walking." She leaned toward him. "It gets even stranger. The boy was dressed in clothes that would have been in fashion at the beginning of the 20th century, complete with a newsboy hat. Guess what else?"

"What?"

She grinned. "He was holding the strings of five red balloons. Balloons the color of holly berries, according to the farmer. How weird is that?"

An image bubbled up in his memory, an image of a boy with red balloons. He shook his head. "Very strange, indeed. What happened next?"

"The farmer walked up the railroad embankment, stopped a few feet in front of the boy, and waited. The boy, looking down at the track, walked right up to the farmer, stopped, looked up, and said 'Excuse me, sir; I seem to have lost my way. I'm looking for someone, but I don't remember who.'"

Reece leaned back in his chair. "Looking for someone? Fascinating!"

"Yeah; I thought so too. Deputy Owens said they couldn't find any records of him. He thought you might be able to help out since the poor kid can't remember who he is or where he came from." She glanced at the clock. "Time to head home. I don't know about you, but I'm looking forward to tomorrow morning." She turned and stepped out the door, a "Good night, Reece" floating back over her shoulder.

"Good night, Patty." Shaking his head, Reece stood, turned the office light off, and stepped out.

Reece was sitting at his desk the next morning when Patty opened the door. "Dr. Brennan, Deputy Owens is here along with the young man I spoke to you about last evening."

Reece smiled. "Thanks, Patty; please send them in."

A smiling young man in a tan Baxter County Sheriff's Department uniform stepped in, closely followed by the boy. About eight years old, he was dressed in jeans and a white t-shirt. Seeing Reece's puzzled expression, the deputy grinned. "Yeah, the old-time clothes needed laundering." He extended a hand. "Good morning, Dr. Brennan; I'm Deputy Owens and this is the lad that I asked you to speak to."

Reece rose and shook hands with the deputy. "Pleased to meet you, Deputy." He leaned over the boy. "Hello, young man! I'm Dr. Brennan. Deputy Owens asked me to talk to you. Why don't you sit down on the couch?"

Without replying, the boy lowered himself onto the couch and sat gazing at the hardwood floor. Patty and the deputy excused themselves and stepped out of the office.

Reece settled himself in a chair next to his young client. "Do you have any memory at all of your name or where you are from? Do you remember anything about where you were before you started walking on the railroad track?"

Without looking up, the boy slowly shook his head. "Nah, not much. I think there were other people there."

"Do you remember your mother or your father? Do you think they were there?"

The boy's head snapped up "Mother? Father?"

"Your parents. Do you remember them?"

"Nah." He frowned. "I do remember someone, a man. He gave me six red balloons."

Reece leaned forward. "Do you remember what he looked like?"

The boy glanced around the room as if searching for inspiration. His eyes rested upon a spot above Reece's desk.

Reece swiveled to see what had grabbed the boy's attention. Surprised, he turned back to the boy. "He looked like Him? Like Jesus?"

The boy, transfixed by the sight of the crucifix, nodded slowly. "Yeah, but he…" He shrugged. "He was different. He didn't look tired and sad. He looked happy."

"Did the man have long hair like Jesus?"

"I think so."

"Do you know why the man gave you the six balloons?"

Smiling, the boy nodded. "Six balloons for six people."

Eyes widening, Reece sat back in his chair. "Six balloons for six people. Were you supposed to give the balloons to six different people?"

The boy shook his head. "Nah; they were supposed to take them from me."

"Will the six people take the balloons from you because they are mean?"

The boy shook his head. "Oh no, they aren't mean. One was lonely; one was sad; one was afraid; one was in danger; one was or will be sick; and one, the last one is…" He hung his head. "I don't remember the other one."

Reece studied the boy. "You had five balloons with you when you were found on the railroad track. Had someone already taken one of the balloons from you?"

The boy nodded. "Yes, Sir. The one who was or will be sick took it from me."

Reece's mind whirled. "Do you mean that someone who was sick took the balloon from you?"

The boy thought for a moment, then shrugged. "I guess so."

The silence was broken by the opening of the office door. Patty stepped in and glanced at Reece. "Would you like a cup of coffee, Dr. Brennan? She looked down at the boy. "How about you, young man; would you like a cup of hot chocolate? With marshmallows?"

Reece nodded. "Sure; coffee is just what I need about now." He turned to the boy. "How about it? Patty's hot chocolate is the best anywhere!"

The boy looked up. "It's not the best anywhere; it can't be better than... back there. I bet it's really good though!"

Eyebrows raised, Patty stepped back. "Uh, okay. I'll be right back." She headed out of the office.

The boy looked to Reece. "I was on a *journey* when I lost my way. I was on the right track; I'm sure of that. I was going *down* the track, not up; but I had to stop and let the present one take a balloon. I'm here, but I don't remember who needs to take the balloon."

Carrying a tray with three steaming cups, Patty stepped back into the room. "Coffee for you, Dr. Brennan, cup of hot chocolate with marshmallows for you, young man, and a cup of coffee for me."

Eyes on the boy, Reece thanked Patty for the coffee. "Like it?"

Smiling, he looked up, a chocolate mustache on his face. "It's good!" He paused, and looked at Reece over the rim of his cup. "Dr. Brennan, may I ask you a question?"

Reece frowned; the boy's change in tone of voice surprising him. "Please do."

"Why do you no longer pray?"

Nearly falling from his chair, Reece spilled his coffee. "What? How in the world would you know that?" He fought to remain calm. "How do you know that I don't pray anymore?'

The boy shrugged. "I just...know."

Eyes widening, Patty took a sip of coffee, and glanced at Reece. "I didn't know you had stopped praying. You used to pray all of the time."

Reece averted his gaze. "Yes, I have. We need to talk about you, young man, not me."

An hour later, Reece found himself understanding no more about the boy than before. Sighing, he tossed his ink pen on a yellow legal pad, and leaned back in his chair. "Well, young man, I think that we have talked enough for today." He glanced at Patty. "Would you step out and ask the Deputy to come back in?"

Smiling, Patty stood, touched the boy on the shoulder and stepped out of the office. Moments later, the Deputy strode in.

Looking down at the boy, he grinned. "Have you learned anything?" He turned to Reece. "I suppose I should be asking you!"

Reece sighed. "We have made headway; but I have more questions now than before. Can you bring him back at the same time tomorrow morning?"

"Sure thing, doc." He turned to the boy. "Okay, time to head out, pardner." With his charge in tow, the Deputy headed out the door.

Driving home from the office that night, Reece's thoughts drifted back to the boy. Who was he? Where had he come from? What was the significance of the balloons? How had he known he had lost faith? The image of a little boy, dressed in antique clothes, and holding red balloons, flashed through his mind. He had seen that image before, but where? In a movie, perhaps? A book? A painting? A...*photograph*? *That was it!* He was sure of it; he had seen a photograph of a boy dressed in old clothes, holding red balloons. He frowned. Was there someone else in that photograph? Where had he seen that? Smiling, he pressed down on the accelerator a little harder.

Arriving home, he parked his car in the driveway, got out, and raced up the sidewalk. He threw the front door opened, sprinted through the living room, and stopped just inside the hallway. Reaching up, he pulled down the rectangular hatch door, releasing the fold-down staircase to the attic.

"Hey Reece; I didn't know you were home. I didn't feel like cooking tonight, so I stopped and picked up Oriental food for us after I left the campus..." Janice, his wife, stopped as she came in sight of him. "Reece, what are you doing?"

He turned. "Hi, honey! I had a patient today who reminded me of someone; someone I remember seeing in an old photo album in the attic." He turned back and began to climb the stairs.

She shrugged. "Okay; I guess dinner can wait for a few minutes while you rummage around in the attic. If you find a squirrel that has got in the attic again, you can keep him."

Reece's laughter floated down the staircase. "I will; they make good pets!"

He stopped off the ladder onto dusty floorboards. Grasping a pull string, he switched on the bare lightbulb. Carefully stepping past stacks of cardboard boxes, sealed with peeling masking tape, he glanced around, finally seeing the attic landmark he was looking for, a stack of board games. Gingerly stepping over to the stack, he reached behind and picked up a small, dusty box with the words "Photo Albums" scrawled in black ink on the side. Picking the box up, he stepped over to a small window at the end of the attic, sunlight illuminating the box. Looking inside, he found the album he wanted, and pulled it out.

The attic hunt successful, he dusted off the cover of the album. In gold writing, the color of a star on a Christmas tree, were the words "*Remembering Yesterday.*" Remembering the conversation he had with the boy earlier in the day, a cold chill gripped his spine. Shaking himself, he stepped over to the ladder, switched off the light, and descended the stairs, box in hand.

Janice was waiting for him at the foot of the stairs. "Find what you were looking for?"

"I did indeed."

Dennis Gallemore

"We can eat in the living room while you tell me just what in the world is going on."

Over bowls of orange chicken and egg drop soup, he summarized the conversation he had with the strange young boy; the unopened photo album resting on the coffee table.

Dinner finished, he sighed contentedly, and sat back on the couch. "That was delicious, but I can't eat another bite. Let's take a look at the album." He held the album reverently for a few moments, and then slowly opened it as Janice scooted over for a closer look. Turning each page over slowly, he carefully examined each photograph. He stopped suddenly, eyes riveted to the page.

Janice gasped. "That has to be it! A photograph of two boys, both dressed in old-fashioned clothing. Look, one of them is holding four red balloons!"

"That's him; that's the mystery boy," Reece whispered.

"You mean it looks like him?"

Reece shook his head. "No. It *is* him! But, how can that be?" He picked up a magnifying glass and examined the photograph. "The date at the bottom is hard to make out, but I believe it says 'June 16, 1902,'" He handed the magnifier to Janice. "Take a look. What do you think?"

Janice peered through the magnifier. "Yeah, that's what it looks like to me. What's going on here? Is he a look-alike ancestor of the boy? Who's the other boy?"

Reece shrugged. "It's certainly possible; he could be an ancestor, but, if he is, he looks *exactly* like my mystery boy. I don't know who the other boy is, but let's see if we can find out." He carefully removed the photograph from the album sleeve and turned it over. Picking up the magnifier, he examined the back of the photo. "According to the note on the back, that's Quinn Brennan, my great-grandfather. He was ten years old when this photo was taken." Shaken, he set the photo down.

Janice gripped his arm. "What is it, Reece?"

"Grandpa used to tell me stories about his dad, my great-grandfather, when I was a kid. Some of the stories were ones that my great-grandfather told Grandpa about; stories that took place when he was a kid. Seems Great-grandpa was quite a handful as a child; he was always getting into trouble. One of the stories was about a boy who saved him from drowning. He had sneaked out of his house and went swimming in a nearby creek. Swollen from recent heavy rains; the current was too strong for him and he was carried downstream. All of sudden, a boy standing on the creek bank threw a rope to him, and pulled him to safety."

"Let me guess," Janice began, "A little boy with red balloons?"

Reece nodded. "You guessed it. The boy made sure that great-grandpa

6

was alright, and then walked over to a tree where a bunch of red balloons were tied. He untied them, and then he went with my great-grandfather by to his house where the photograph was taken. After the photo was taken, the boy released one of the balloons, told Great-grandpa and his parents that he had to get home before dark, and walked away, never to be seen again." He shook his head. "At least not until now, I'm thinking."

They sat in silence for a time, contemplating the photograph and the story. Finally, Recce turned to his wife. "Janice, there is one thing that I haven't told you about the boy. He asked me why I don't pray anymore!"

Eyebrows raised, Janice leaned closer. "I've noticed that you haven't been praying with me for a while, and you don't seem to want to go to church anymore, but I didn't know you had stopped praying!"

He sighed. "I haven't prayed in months. You know I've become disillusioned with my work. I see so many suffering people in my practice; people who have so many problems, I'm sometimes amazed that they are able to function at all. I have begun to doubt whether God really cares, or if He even exists."

Wrapping him in her arms, she pulled him close. "I'm sorry, Reece, I didn't know. I knew you were discouraged with your work occasionally; I didn't know that it was affecting your faith as well."

"I didn't feel like talking about it. I was thinking about talking to the Minister about it." He shook his head. "In any case, with all of this…"

She smiled. "You're wondering if this is supernatural?"

He nodded. "Yeah. I can't help but wonder."

She kissed him lightly on the cheek. "I'm wondering too!"

The next morning, Reece was back in his office. He glanced at the clock; it was almost time. As if on cue, the door opened, and Patty stepped in, Deputy Owens and the mysterious boy trailing behind.

The deputy grinned. "Morning, Doc! Ready for another round? Our young friend here seems to have regained some of his memory." He glanced at the boy. "Learned a lot, haven't you?" The deputy stepped out, followed by Patty, the boy calmly sitting down on the couch.

Puzzled, Reece glanced at the boy. "What did Deputy Owens mean? What have you learned?"

"A lesson!"

Reece frowned. "A lesson? What kind of lesson?"

"I have often wondered how humans can be on the right track, so to speak, but then lose their way. I have often voiced my puzzlement to others of my kind, and to Him. He said that the only way to understand was to experience getting lost for myself. So, with a little help, I did."

Eyes widening, Reece leaned forward. "Are you saying you're an angel?"

7

The boy nodded. "I am."

Speechless, Reece stared at him. Shaking himself, he continued. "Let me see if I understand this correctly. You were sent to help a person." He paused. "No, you were sent to help *six* people, weren't you? That's what the balloons represented! Six balloons, for six different people!"

He clapped his hands. "Very good, Dr. Brennan! Yes, He sent me to help six people; one up track, one now, and four down track!"

Reece considered that. "I think I see. By 'one up track,' you mean someone in the future, don't you? The four people 'down track' are in the past, aren't they?"

He grinned. "Right as rain, Dr. Brennan! You're on a roll, counselor!"

Reece stood and paced back and forth across his office floor. "You said that He gave you six balloons. Was He…Jesus?"

The angel nodded. "Who else?"

"When you were found on the railroad, you had only five balloons. So you had already travelled to the future, my future, and helped someone?"

"You're batting a thousand! Yes, I journeyed up track and helped the one who…"

Reece cut in. "The 'one who was or will be sick'! That's what you meant yesterday! From your point of view, you had already helped him or her, hence "the one who was…sick.' From my point of view, he or she is 'the one who will be sick,' because he or she is in the future!"

"Right, again, Dr. Brennan!"

"You were the boy in the photograph, the one standing by my great-grandfather! You had only four balloons in the photo because one had been taken from you, in the present, by 'the one who…'" Puzzled, he stopped pacing and stared at him. "You never said who the one in the present is." He fell into the armchair. "It's me, isn't it? I'm the one in the present?"

He smiled. "Yes, Dr. Brennan, the one in the present is you. You are 'the one who is in doubt.'"

Reece laughed. "You're certainly renewing my faith. So, what is your name? What should I call you?"

"Messenger!" He replied with a laugh.

"And the other balloons, the other ones…"

"Yes, in the past; after I helped your great-grandfather, I went back further in time to help the others. Or, I should say, I'm going back now. From your point of view; I have already helped them. From mine, I have yet to do so."

Dazed, Reece shook his head. "It gets a bit confusing for us humans."

Messenger laughed. "Humans seem to be confused most of the time!" He stood, waved a hand, and five red balloons appeared in his hand. He gazed at Reece, eyes sparkling.

Standing, Reece drew in a deep breath. He grasped the string of one balloon. "I take this balloon; my faith restored by Messenger."

The angel shook with laughter. "A bit solemn, but whatever! I must be on my way down track. I have a certain little boy to save from drowning in 1902. Goodbye, Dr. Brennan. Keep the faith!"

Reece watched in wonder as Messenger, holding four red balloons, disappeared.

The door opened, and Patty stepped in. "Deputy Owens got a call a few minutes ago and said he had to leave. I asked him when he would be back to pick up the boy and he just shrugged and said 'it won't be necessary,' and walked out. I called the Sheriff's Department to see what was going on, and guess what?"

Reece smiled. "They never heard of a Deputy Bill Owens?"

She gasped. "How did you know that?" She looked around the office. "Where did our mystery boy go?"

Reece grinned. "Come on in and sit down on the couch. I have a little story to tell you, my amanuensis."

She rolled her eyes. "Stop calling me that!"

ACTUALITY

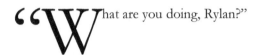"hat are you doing, Rylan?"

Opening my eyes, I glanced up at the Holovid screen to see Cassana's frowning virtual image. "I was praying, my A.I. friend." Cassana is an artificially intelligent being; a super-sophisticated computer program designed to mimic the thought processes and body language of a human, albeit in a virtual manner. "She" controls my ship, *Starfall*, a precious metals survey ship, and serves as a companion on the long, lonely voyages through deep space.

Cassana studied me for a moment; probably searching her information banks on the subject of prayer. "Why are you attempting to communicate with an entity whose existence has never been proven?"

I sighed. "By 'entity' you mean God. True, God's existence has not been proven by the scientific method. I *believe* in God; I have *faith* that God exists. In other words, Cassana, I choose to believe He exists, not based upon the conclusions of the most recent journal articles, but instead upon the bible and the evidence of His creation."

I waved at the Holovid screens around the bridge which displayed various celestial objects. "Consider these wonders we have seen, Cassana; some from a great distance, others up close. Galaxies, red giant stars, ringed planets, comets. I don't believe they were formed out of chaos by mere chance."

Cassana raised a virtual eyebrow. "Rylan, I am surprised. You are not speaking as a scientist; even though I know you hold a PhD in Exogeology from Earth's Harvard University. You were trained in the utilization of the scientific method, not theology."

I nodded. "True. But science has not explained everything. We under-

10

stand much about the nature of the universe. We have theories to explain the origins of life. But there is much about the universe, about life itself, which we don't completely understand. Our theories suggest possible explanations about the origin of the universe, but have they been proven absolutely beyond-a-shadow-of-doubt correct? No, they have not. Science has not been able to answer all questions; I don't believe it ever will."

Cassana frowned. "Let us assume, for a moment, that God does, indeed, exist. How do you know that He will hear your prayer? You cannot see God; you cannot feel God's presence."

"Yes, it's true that I can't see God, but I can feel His presence. No offense, Cassana, but this is a difficult concept to explain to an A.I. I cannot see 'love,' but I know it exists because I can feel 'love.' Often, when I am praying, I can feel the presence of the Holy Spirit."

Cassana pondered that for a moment. "What were you praying about earlier?"

I gestured at the Holovid screens displaying three different planets. "The information we received from our current employer, Stellar Metals, suggested three nearby planets for geological surveys. All three have equal probabilities of possessing valuable metals. So which one do we choose? We have time for only one planet on our current mission. Science has contributed as much as it can in the decision making process. I could trust to luck; instead, I chose to ask God for guidance as to which planet to survey."

Cassana smirked. "And did you receive an answer, Rylan?"

I smiled. "No, I didn't, but I have faith I will."

She rolled her virtual eyes. "Of course you will."

I stood and stretched. "I'm going to the galley to get a cup of coffee."

I stepped off the bridge, and when I returned a few minutes later, the only Holovid screen that was working was Cassana's. "What's going on, Cassana?"

She frowned. "After you left the bridge, there was a power surge in the Holovid circuits. Before you ask, no, I do not know what caused it. I reset the circuit breakers. The screens should come back on...now."

All but one of the screens remained dark. I smiled as I studied the solitary reactivated screen. "There is the answer to my prayer, Cassana. The only screen to relight is showing *one* of three potential planets to survey." I leaned closer to the holographic image and studied the information tag. "Thadus K3V. That's the one. You see; God did answer my prayer."

Cassana hesitated. "Or...I suppose it could be a simple coincidence."

I laughed. "Perhaps, but what if it isn't?"

She sighed. "You win. Setting course for Thadus K3V."

ALL IN GOOD TIME

The chime of a text arriving on his phone woke him. He glanced at the clock and was surprised to see it was only four a.m. *"Who in the world would be texting me this early?"* He reached for his phone on the bedside table. Glancing at the screen, he saw that the call was from an unknown number. The message was simple: *"Come to my house this morning ASAP. I must give you something to keep for me. Uncle Allen."*

Sitting up, Jeff turned on the light. *Why would Uncle Allen not use his regular cell phone? What would he want me to keep?*

Uncle Allen was an eccentric inventor and one-time theoretical physics professor at Harvard. For the last few years, Jeff recalled, his uncle had been working on a method of traveling through time.

He dressed, shrugged his coat on, and headed out the door. He climbed into his Ford pickup. Minutes later, he was headed east, toward Springtown. An hour later, he turned south on U.S. 108 and headed toward the city of Cranston.

As he approached his uncle's cabin just outside Cranston, he saw an ocean of flashing red lights. He parked down the street, fear gripping his spine. Stepping out of the pickup, he walked toward the cabin. Several Cranston police cars and an ambulance were parked in front of his uncle's cabin.

A Cranston policeman stopped him as he approached. "I'm sorry sir, but this is an active crime scene. Do you live around here?"

He shook his head. "No, I'm Jeff Owens; I was coming to see my uncle. What's going on? Is he okay?"

Turning, the officer shouted, "Sargent Brown? This man is Allen Owen's nephew."

Jeff waited as the second officer hurried over. "Mr. Owens? I'm Sergeant Brown with the Cranston Police. I'm sorry to have to tell you this son, but your

12

uncle has been murdered."

Jeff recoiled in shock."Murdered? Who would want to kill my uncle?"

Brown placed a reassuring hand on Jeff's shoulder. "We don't know who or why at this point. Someone evidently broke in to your uncle's cabin during the night and shot your uncle with a silenced pistol. We are treating it as a burglary-murder as several items were taken, a computer for one. I'm going to need you to ride down to the station with me so I can ask you a few questions."

Ten minutes later, Jeff sat across the desk from Brown at the Cranston Police Station. *I have no idea what is going on here. Whatever Uncle Allen wanted me to keep for him; I'm betting that whoever broke into his cabin was looking for it. Whatever it was, whether they found it or not, it got him killed.* He decided to keep the cryptic text message from his uncle to himself for the time being.

Brown flipped open a small notepad. "First of all, what is your full name, address, and occupation?"

"Jeff Owens, 1704 Doe Avenue, Natton, Missouri. I'm a logger."

Brown nodded and scribbled on the pad. "Why were you coming to see your uncle so early in the morning?"

Not knowing who he could trust, he decided to keep the real reason quiet for the moment. "I came down to look at some new logging equipment that I was thinking about buying from a local dealer. My uncle is an early riser; I thought that I would surprise him by stopping by and seeing if he wanted to go to breakfast with me."

Leaning back in his chair, Brown studied him for a moment. "Okay. Why do you think someone would break in, steal a computer, and then murder your uncle? Did he have any enemies that you know of?"

Jeff shook his head. "Not a clue. I don't know of anyone that was enemy of my uncle; in fact, I don't know of anyone that he didn't get along with. Everybody liked him."

Brown nodded. "That squares with what we have been told by his neighbors. According to his neighbors, your uncle was an inventor; what kinds of things did he invent?"

"Mainly laboratory equipment for physics labs, that kind of thing. He was a physics professor at Harvard for quite a few years before retiring to the Ozarks. He grew up around here before he went off to college."

Brown nodded. "Can you stay in Cranston for a couple of days? We will probably have some more questions for you."

"Sure. I normally stay at my uncle's cabin when I'm here but I guess I will get a room down at a motel instead."

"Fine. Give me your cell number and then I'll take you back to your truck."

Brown remained silent during the ride back to his uncle's cabin. He stopped in front of the cabin. "Just one more thing, Mr. Owens. I would like for you to come in the cabin with me and look around, if you don't mind. Maybe you will notice something missing or something out of the ordinary that our CSI guys missed."

Jess sighed. "Yeah, sure. Anything that I can do to help, I will."

Opening the cabin door, Jeff stepped inside, followed by Brown. He flipped on the light switch and a table lamp across the living room came on. He walked slowly through the cabin. The only thing that seemed to be missing was his uncle's computer that had sat on a small desk in the living room. Nothing else seemed to be out of place.

Brown sighed. "Well, it was a long shot. In any case, this certainly doesn't look like a normal break in. I think the perp was after information, not goods to fence."

Jeff nodded. "I would say so too, but as to what information, I have no idea. His inventions weren't that valuable; they made a good living for him, but there weren't anything that anyone would kill for." He decided to keep his uncle's last research area to himself.

They turned off the lights, locked the door, and walked outside. Brown shook hands and drove off, leaving Jeff to his thoughts. He stood in the yard looking back at his uncle's cabin. Tears welling up in his eyes, he got into his truck and headed toward the hotel.

After crashing for a couple of hours at the hotel, he headed to lunch. He sipped coffee while waiting for his burger and fries as he stared out the restaurant's window. *I wonder if he figured out a way to travel back in time? He talked about it a lot, how great it would be to go back and see how everything actually occurred. Who built the pyramids and how? Who really discovered America first?*

He thought about that. It was possible, he decided, that his uncle could have developed a method for time travel. *Would that be something that someone would kill for? Absolutely! You could go back in time, buy up Apple stock when it first listed or be one of the first investors in Amazon!*

It hit him then, an even bigger reason. Someone could travel back in time and change things to benefit themselves or their cause. He shuddered. If he was right, the stakes in this game were very, very high. He suddenly knew what the intruder was looking for. The plans for building a time machine and his uncle must have told him the plans were on the computer. His uncle, for some reason, had known that someone would be after the plans, someone that he didn't want to get them.

With sudden clarity, he saw what his brave uncle had done. He had stored the plans on some other device and had lied to the intruder. He had told the intruder that the plans were on the computer; he probably had some useless fake or incomplete files on the computer to fool whoever was after the plans. The real plans his Uncle had stored…where?

He finished lunch, and drove back to the cabin. Using the key his uncle had given him last year, he unlocked the cabin and walked inside. He knew that CSI had searched the cabin thoroughly so the plans either weren't there or had been carefully hidden. He recalled that, one evening while watching a crime drama on television; his uncle had remarked that the best place to hide something was in plain sight.

He stood in the middle of the living room and slowly turned, carefully observing every item. He finished the circuit and started toward the kitchen when he stopped and turned back toward the living room drapes. *The curtain rod is different than the last time I was here. The knobs on the ends are much bigger and more ornate.*

He walked to the window and stood staring up at the knobs. He carefully unscrewed one and then the other. One of them was lighter, much lighter, than the other. *Hollow?*

He walked to the kitchen, found his uncle's cooking scale, and carefully weighed each finial. The heavier one weighed 13.7 ounces, the other only 4.5 ounces. He removed the end plug from the finial. The inside was hollow and, when he tilted it up, a flash drive fell out onto his hand.

He retrieved his tablet from his truck, went back inside the cabin, and set the tablet on the kitchen table. He plugged the flash drive in and powered on the tablet. He pulled up the flash drive's menu and found it loaded with technical files. He opened the one labeled "Master Directory" and found a listing of files dealing with the theory of time travel and the construction of a time machine.

The cabin door opening, Sergeant Brown strode in. "What are you doing here Jeff?" He glanced at the flash drive which Jeff had pulled and was holding. "What's on that drive?"

Jeff paled. "Plans for how to build a time machine. This is what the intruder was looking for. My uncle had it hidden in one of the curtain rod finials." He explained to Brown how he had come to be there and how he had discovered the location of the hidden drive.

Jeff frowned. "How did you know I was here?"

"We pinged your cell phone. We wanted to keep track of you. We wanted to make sure that you didn't have anything to do with your uncle's murder. Hand the drive over to me and we will take another ride down town."

Jeff shook his head. "I didn't murder my uncle." He held onto the drive. "You know, Sergeant, the files on this drive could, no will change the world, and not for the better."

"How so?" Brown asked.

Jeff grimaced. "If humans, given our nature, go back in time, what would they do? Those in power would make sure that no one else could travel in time.

They would make themselves richer and more powerful. Worse yet, greedy, power hungry men would go back and change time to their advantage. And something else, the worst of all, I think. Men who don't want others to have faith in God; they could go back in time and eliminate all traces, all references to God, all bibles, everything,…"

Brown blanched. "You're right, of course. That could happen, probably would happen…" He shook his head. "But that's not why I am here. I am here to solve a murder."

Jeff shook his head and laughed. "You won't find a shred of evidence. Whoever or whatever was after this flash drive would be able to beat any law enforcement agency."

Brown nodded. "We haven't found any evidence at all. Even the bullets we found don't match any known gun. It's like they were made for a special gun, one that, for all we know, doesn't exist."

Jeff stared at Brown. "There is something that we could do. If God exists, and I believe that He does, he wouldn't want us traveling around in time, mucking things up. We could destroy this drive. No one else would ever know."

Brown stared down at the drive in Jeff's hand. Finally, he looked back up and nodded. "We need to make sure that none of it is left. Burn it and then dissolve the residue in acid, something like that."

Jeff nodded. He built a fire in the fireplace, threw the drive into the flames, and stepped back. He and Brown watched as the drive quickly melted. He scooped the residue into a coffee mug.

"Let's go down to the station. The crime lab will have some acid, sulfuric or nitric." Brown turned and walked out the door.

Jeff took one last look around his uncle's cabin. "Sorry Uncle Allen, but your invention could have destroyed…faith." He glanced upward. "And sometimes, Uncle Allen, faith is all we have."

EASTER EGGS

The minister cleared his throat. "Okay, let's get the show on the road. First on the agenda is the Easter egg hunt. Are we ready?" He glanced around the room at the gathered staff members and volunteers. Heads bobbed all around.

"We're ready boss dude!" The worship minister replied with a grin. "Thousands of plastic eggs stuffed with candy and volunteers lined up to hide them!"

One by one, the others chimed in with their reports of, and support for, the church's annual Easter egg hunt. The minister smiled to himself. *If happiness and pride could be measured by a thermometer, it would be a couple of hundred degrees in here!*

It was there again; that strange feeling that he had experienced over the last few weeks. A feeling that something was going to happen during the Easter weekend, something...joyous. The Holy Spirit was talking to him, trying to tell him something, but what?

He leaned forward. "There's something I should tell all of you. Over the last few weeks, I have been getting these feelings that, well, something incredible is going to happen sometime during the Easter weekend. I think the Holy Spirit has been trying to tell me something. I thought you should know."

The others sat silent for a moment, then burst into a cacophony of voices. The worship minister's voice raised above the others. "What do you think is going to happen?"

The minister shook his head. "I don't know. I guess we'll just have to wait and see. The chatter died down and the minister sensed that it was time to move on. "Next on the agenda..."

***

A blue sedan rolled down the highway. "Mommy, how many eggs do you think I will find this year?" Jamie asked her mother.

Tonia took her eyes off the road long enough to glance over at her precocious, seven year old daughter. She smiled. "At least a dozen honey!" She laughed, picturing Jamie scampering across the church grounds, gleefully searching for the hidden confectionary treasures.

Her thoughts turning to a darker place, she turned back to her driving. *Why did he have to leave us now? Right before Easter. What am I going to do? How can I raise Jamie by myself?* Unbidden, tears flowed down her face.

"It's going to be all right, Mommy," Jamie began, "Jesus will take care of us!"

Tonia glanced at her precious daughter. She wiped the tears from her face as she pulled into the parking lot of the church. "We're here!"

***

The red pickup sailed down the highway. The driver glanced over at his wife. "Jillian, I still don't understand why you want me to go! You and the others don't need any help hiding the eggs."

She turned in her seat. "Because it will do you good to get out of the house and be around other people. You need a change of scenery, Alan."

"You're just trying to rope me into going with you to services on Sunday."

She smiled. "Of course I am. First, I slyly convince you to help hide Easter eggs. Then, mesmerized by the sights and sounds of planting plastic Easter eggs, you will not be able to help yourself. You will march into church Easter morning as if in a trance. All part of my sinister plot to get you to go with me to church."

He snorted. Suddenly, the images swam in front of his eyes. His unit checking out a village in Iraq, the IED, the explosion, and, just like that, three of his buddies dead. *How could God allow that?* The images vanished to be replaced by the church parking lot.

***

Lance slid his yellow sports car into a parking space and switched the engine off. He sat for a few moments gazing silently at the church. He hadn't been there for years. He had gone there a few times with an old girlfriend, but after she left, he really didn't have a reason to go back. He picked up his cell. "Hey Jake, I'm here, right in front."

"Be right there Lance!"

He pocketed the phone and stepped out.

***

Jillian and Alan strolled across the grounds, carefully secreting the colorful plastic eggs. He stopped and stretched. "I have to admit, I am enjoying this. For some reason, I feel good, really good!"

Jillian smiled. "That's great Alan! I knew you would like it!" She eyed the basket. "We're out of eggs…no wait, there's one left." She shook her head. "That's odd. I could swear that was the last of the eggs." She handed the bright red egg to her husband. "Here's your reward for helping hide the eggs!"

He laughed. "Alright! I tell you what; if there is enough candy I will even share it with you!" He twisted the egg open and dumped the contents into his hand. He glanced at Jillian. "It's not candy; it's a piece of gold paper."

She looked at the note. "What in the world? What does it say?"

He unfolded the tiny note. "It says…"Be at peace, for they are with Me." He staggered back against a nearby tree.

Jillian stepped to his side and gently took the note from his trembling hands. She stared at it in wonder.

He pulled her close. "Tell me you didn't do this…you didn't make up that egg for me."

She shook her head. "No, Alan, I didn't. I really don't think anyone did. It's…it's a message for you Alan, a message from…Him."

***

Lance and Jake angled across the grounds, dropping the plastic eggs helter-skelter. "Jake; tell me again why I am doing this?" Lance called after his friend.

Stopping, Jake turned to his friend. "Because you lost the bet Bro! I told you I could bench 400 pounds! 'No way,' you said. We had a deal! If I was right, you had to help hide Easter eggs and if you were right, which you weren't, I would have to mow and trim your yard."

Jake held up the sack. "It doesn't matter anyway; the sack is empty. No, wait; that's weird, there's another egg left. I know that sack was empty. What gives?" He upended the sack and dumped the egg into Lance's hand. "A consolation prize for you for being such a loser."

Lance opened the yellow egg and dumped the contents. He stared at the gold note in surprise. "What's this? Aren't the eggs supposed to have candy in them?"

Jake moved closer and peered at the note. "Yeah, some have money though, but what's that?"

Lance opened the note and read aloud. "Luke 15: 11-32. That's all it says."

Jake grabbed the note in disbelief. "It's the story of the prodigal son…"

19

***

Hand in hand, Tonia and Jamie skipped across the church grounds, Jamie happily scooping up the hidden treasures. She picked up another one with a squeal of delight. She carefully counted the eggs in her basket. "Twelve, Mommy, I have twelve eggs now!" She frowned. "Where did that egg come from? It's a blue egg and I didn't pick up any blue eggs." She carefully counted the eggs again. "Thirteen. Mommy there are thirteen eggs now." She plunged her hand into the basket and pulled out a bright blue egg. She handed it to her mother. "Here Mommy, this one must be for you!"

Tonia laughed, carefully opened the egg, and tamped out its contents into her hand. To her surprise, instead of chocolate, a gold note fluttered out. "What's this?"

She opened the note and read. Swaying, she swayed sank slowly to her knees.

"Mommy, what's wrong?"

Tonia drew her daughter close.

"What does it say Mommy?"

Tonia drew a ragged breath. "It says...'He may have forsaken you, but I never will...'"

***

The minister strolled across the grounds as the Easter egg hunt swung into high gear. Glancing around, he was startled to see a woman sinking to her knees. Recognizing her, he rushed to her side. "Tonia, what's wrong? Are you alright?"

Tears streaming down her face, Tonia looked up and silently handed the note to him.

He glanced at the note in shock. Suddenly, shouts and cries erupted from all over the churchyard. The minister gazed around in disbelief. People were laughing, people were crying, many were hugging others. Some were kneeling, others stood with arms held high.

The minister went from person to person. In each case, the story was the same; an extra egg, a golden note, and a special message of hope and promise.

His friend, an elder, rushed up. "What's happening, Reverend?"

The minister looked up into the brilliant blue sky. "Easter! Easter is happening!"

THE ALCHEMIST

S abrina sat on a stool overlooking a table filled with chemical glassware. She sighed, jotted some notes in a weathered, brown journal, and slipped off the stool. She yawned and stretched; time for bed. She slipped her shoes back on and gently blew out the candles that cast a soft yellow light in the room. She opened the door and stepped into one of only two remaining rooms in her small house.

She checked to make sure that the windows were carefully covered by the wooden shutters. Satisfied that they, and the only door to her small home in Salem Village, Massachusetts, were securely locked, she lay down in her small bed. As she drifted off to sleep, she wondered what the New Year, sixteen hundred and ninety-two, would bring.

***

Silas Morenton sauntered down the street. The people of Salem Village scurried out of his way, a fact which made him quite proud. He considered the village's inhabitants to be of the lowest class of people while he, a minister, was of the highest class possible; only one step below the beloved inhabitants of the heavenly realm.

Making his morning rounds, he checked with every shop owner each day to make sure that the town's center of commerce was strong in the word and work of the Almighty God. He entered the last shop on his itinerary, Josiah's Candle Shoppe. "Good morning, Josiah. How are you on this fine, February morning?"

Josiah Weaver stood quietly dipping a rack of slender white taper candles. Frowning, he looked up. He was a serious man and he hated to be interrupted, even if it was by the parson. He considered himself to be a Godly man, but his work, the making of quality candles, was his life.

"Good morning ,Parson. I'm fine, thank you." He hesitated with what he hoped would be obvious reluctance. "And you?"

Silas ignored his reticent reply. "Fine, man, fine. Today is a gift from God, as is every day; but today is a special day. God's work will be done today, Josiah, it will be done!"

Josiah sighed. He was well accustomed to the parson's long-winded exhortations concerning the degree of Godliness of each and every day of the week. "And what work would that be parson?" As soon as he had spoken the words, he mentally kicked himself squarely on his rear end. Now the rant would last even longer.

Silas smiled in satisfaction, a smile that did not quite reach his eyes. "Ah, Josiah, there has been evil work done in this village, the work of the Evil One himself! A certain young woman, without husband mind you, without husband, has been practicing the Dark Arts!"

Josiah grimaced. Silas believed that everybody and their dogs practiced dark arts. "Which young woman are you speaking of parson, and what exactly has she done?"

Silas, much to Josiah's chagrin, grabbed a chair and sat down. "Sabrina Smythe is the young woman of which I spoke, and as to what she has done, well…" At this he leaned close to Josiah and dropped his voice to a whisper. "She has, and still is, for that matter, attempting to transmute base metals into gold." He finished with a flourish and leaned back with a deeply satisfied smile.

Josiah grunted. He really didn't care and he really didn't think that there was anything dark about attempting to convert lead into gold. He really wished he could do it himself; but he kept those thoughts confined to his own mind. "Is that so, Parson?" There, that was a completely non-committal reply; hopefully Silas would continue on his way and quit bothering him.

Silas nodded. "Yes, it is God's own truth. I, God's humble servant, will bring her to justice. She will be tried for what she is, a witch!"

Josiah blanched. Ranting was one thing, accusing a young woman of being a witch was another. The Massachusetts Colony had a history of sanctimonious parsons ferreting out supposed witches and then, after farcical trials, hanging them. "I beg your pardon, Silas, but do you know for sure that Sabrina is a witch? I have heard that she has attempted a time or two to change lead into gold, but look at all of the good she has done for this village! She uses herbs and plants to help heal the folks of the village when they are sick or hurt. Would a witch do that?"

Smirking, Silas shook his head. "Josiah, my friend, do you not see? Witches are like the Roman god, Janus. They can present one kind and friendly face while they hide the evil face that Satan would be proud of!"

Josiah studied Silas' face for a moment before responding. "Everyone can present two faces, Silas, everyone."

"I will bring her darkness into the light, Josiah, mark my words!"
Josiah shook his head in disbelief. Silas had, once again, completely missed the mark. "Silas, I greatly enjoy our daily conversation, but I really must finish these candles…"

Silas nodded. "I must get on with the day's work. Idle hands are the devil's playground, so the Good Book says." He turned and strode out the door.

Silas nodded as the door closed behind the parson. "The Good Book also says beware of wolves in sheep's clothing." He turned to finish the batch of candles, but his mind was on Sabrina Smythe.

***

Kneeling, Sabrina applied salve to the boy's scraped knee. She smiled up at his cherubic, albeit smudged, face. "All done, Johnathon. Your knee will heal just fine now. You should listen to your mother and be more careful. Jumping off tall haystacks may be fun, but if you land on a sharp rock, you are going to get hurt. She stood, tussled his hair, and turned to the boy's mother, who stood nearby, watching apprehensively. "He will be fine, Jane, just fine."

"Thank you, Sabrina. I do not have any coins to pay you with but I brought a sack of apples from our orchard. They will make a delicious pie." Without meeting her eyes, she handed the bag to Sabrina, grabbed the boy's hand, and pulled him out the door.

Surprised, Sabrina's eyes followed the two as they walked away from her house. She shook her head at the woman's sudden and distracted departure. She thought about spending some time on her study of alchemy but it was late and she was exhausted. She blew out the candles and collapsed into the bed and was asleep in moments.

She awoke with a start, heart pumping and her breath coming in gasps. The nightmare had been horrific; she had been chased by pitchfork-wielding, torch-carrying villagers, all screaming for her blood. Their chants of "Kill the Witch!" still echoing in her mind.

Getting out of bed, she poured herself a drink of water. Sitting at the kitchen table, she drank the water, silently willing her heart to slow its incessant beating. The words "Run with him!" suddenly floated through her mind. In wonder, she looked around her home for the source of the words. "Who's there?" She received no answer.

***

Josiah awoke. Getting out of bed, he lit a candle, and sat at the table. He pondered the dream that he had just awakened from. He and a young woman, hand in hand, had been running for their lives, chased by a shouting, angry mob. The woman, he realized with a start, was Sabrina Smythe.

"Save her. You must flee together. Save her!"

Standing abruptly, Josiah knocked his chair over backward. "Who's there?" He picked up the candle holder and waved it around the room. "Show yourself!"

The flickering candle threw dancing shadows on the walls, but no intruder showed himself. Realizing he was quite alone, he picked up the fallen chair and sat down. The urge to act was overwhelming. He stood, quickly threw some salted venison and a few of his precious candles into a pack, grabbed his walking stick, and bolted out the door. "Yes, it has finally happened. I have completely lost my mind…"

***

Sabrina nearly fell out of her chair when the door suddenly shook from someone hammering on the outside. Recalling her traumatic dream, she looked around for a weapon. Finding nothing suitable, she stood, raised her chin, and strode determinedly to the door. She opened it, resigned to her fate, but determined to meet it squarely in the eye.

Josiah, chest heaving from his sudden exertion, stood holding an oaken walking stick with a traveling pack on his back. "Sabrina Smythe, you must come with me. Now. You are in great danger. I have been sent to protect you."

Sabrina stared at the apparition at her door in wonder. Taking a deep breath, she stepped aside. "Come in, then, and protect me. Josiah, isn't it?"

He looked, she thought, as if he had expected her to scream and slam the door in his face. He stood for a moment shifting his weight from foot to foot, an uncertain look upon his face.

He shook his head and stepped over the threshold. She closed the door behind him.

"You are in great danger, Sabrina. I was told by---I was *informed* that you will be accused of being a *witch*."

Sabrina nodded. "I see. Very well; I had a dream in which I was chased by murderous villagers, and I heard a voice tell me to flee with a man. I listen when He speaks. I believe that *you* are that man."

Surprised that she had accepted so easily, he nodded numbly. "If you would quickly prepare, my lady, we should leave in great haste."

She turned, picked up a cloth bag, and filled it with herbs and potions. She opened a small box, pulled out a leather-bound book, and placed it into the bag

Josiah opened the door and stepped out. Sabrina, with one last look around her cabin, blew out the candle and followed. The two were quickly on the simple road out of the village.

After walking for hours, they stopped to make camp beside a stream flowing through a forest of oak, hickory, and ash trees. As the morning sun rose, Josiah built a small fire while Sabrina retrieved water from the stream. The two sat fireside, chewed pieces of smoked venison, and drank the sweet, cold water.

Josiah studied Sabrina's fiery red hair that curled gently around her face. She's pretty, he thought; pretty and mysterious. "Sabrina, are you a witch?"

Sabrina nearly choked on a mouthful of water. She placed her tin cup on the ground and stared at him in silence.

Josiah cleared his throat. "I do not believe that you are, Sabrina, but the other villagers…"

She nodded then. "I am."

It was his turn to choke. "What? You…you are? You really are a witch?"

"Yes. In fact…" She reached into her poke. "It is time to turn you into a toad." She slowly pulled out…

He froze.

…a weathered bible, and a small, wooden cross.

She laughed gleefully. "You thought that I was going to pull out my magical wand and turn you into a toad. How delightful!"

He let out a breath he did not realize he had been holding. "You, my lady, are not a witch! I knew it! You are definitely not a witch!"

She snorted. "Of course you knew it. Which is why you just wet yourself."

He instinctively glanced down at his waist.

She laughed again. "You, my new friend, are quite gullible!"

His face reddening, he sputtered, "You are a Believer? Not a witch?"

She smiled. "I am guilty as charged; of being a follower of Christ that is, and not a witch!"

He took her hand. "Where should we go?"

Her laugh was reminiscent of silvery bells. "Away from Salem, my dearest Josiah, away from Salem!"

HALF-OFF

"**M**y boyfriend is such a jerk! How in the world did I end up with him anyway?" Strolling down the street, she shook her head in disgust. Chagrined, she realized that she had verbalized her thoughts. She walked faster, putting distance between herself and her boyfriend. She walked on down the street, glancing occasionally at the small shops along the way. Delis, fashion boutiques, and art galleries passed by in a continuous blur of windows, displays, and garish lights.

She had just left him at the deli; a lunchtime meeting had, once again, turned into an impromptu argument. He had denied, yet again, that he was seeing someone else. She knew better; she had known for some time. She couldn't understand why she stayed with him. "*What is wrong with me?*" she asked herself for the millionth time.

She was on her way back to her crummy job after the less than enjoyable lunch. Working at the Fast and Friendly Dry Cleaner was certainly not what she had envisioned when she entered the working world. She had always wanted to be a songwriter, had even written a few songs, but it didn't pay the bills. She sighed and continued the forced march back to work.

She glanced at the storefront as she marched by. "Destinations Unlimited," The marquee proudly proclaimed. She stopped, turned around, and walked back to the shop. *When did a travel agency go in there?* For some reason, she didn't recall seeing that store there before. She shrugged it off; there were dozens of stores along the street that she walked.

She glanced at her watch; she still had 15 minutes before she needed to be back to work. *I could really use a vacation and I do have a week's vacation time accumulated.* As she studied the travel agency's front window, the digital sign, which had stated "Great Vacations," changed to "Vacation Packages Half-Off Today Only."

Opening the door, she stepped inside. Two large, walnut desks faced her, a man sitting behind one, a woman behind the other; both middle-aged, both with friendly faces.

The man stood. "Welcome, young lady, welcome. I am Derrick and this is…" he hesitated, "my associate, Erica."

Erica smiled, rose, and walked to stand before her. She held out a hand. "Nice to meet you…?"

She smiled in return and clasped the woman's hand. "Tiffany, Tiffany Owens. It's nice to meet you two as well."

"Please have a seat," Erica offered as she turned a chair toward Tiffany.

Derrick sat on one corner of his desk. "What can we do for you Tiffany?"

"I was passing by and I saw your sign, the half-off sign that is. I could really use a vacation, but, well, I don't have a lot of money."

"You've come to the right place," Derrick replied. He waved a hand at Erica. "I'm training Erica to be…," he hesitated again, "to be a travel agent. I will let her help you while I observe."

Tiffany seated herself as Erica returned to sit behind the desk. With a glance at Derrick, she began. "First, Tiffany, tell us a about yourself."

Surprised at the question, Tiffany shrugged. "Okay; well, I'm 26 years old and single. I share an apartment with two other women. I work at a dry cleaner down the street. That's about it."

Erica nodded. "Tell me about your relationships. Are you close to your family? Are you involved in a romantic relationship?"

"My relationships? What does that have to do with a travel package?" Tiffany asked, surprised and irritated.

Erica smiled. "Our methods are a little unorthodox, but we have our reasons. In order to more completely help you with your destination, we would like to know about your life. Then we can put together a more complete package."

Tiffany relaxed slightly. "Okay, I guess. I'm close to my parents and my sister. I have a boyfriend…" She trailed off, suddenly fascinated by the floor in front of Erica's desk.

"I take it that your relationship with your boyfriend is not the best," Erica replied.

Tiffany stiffened. "I don't see that is any of your business!"

Erica glanced at Derrick before continuing. He nodded at an unspoken question from Erica.

"Tiffany," Erica continued, "I'm just trying to help you. I don't mean to pry."

Tiffany shook her head. "It's okay, I guess. You're right; it isn't the best relationship. In fact, I really need to end it with him. I was thinking that a vacation might help with my life, but, well…"

Erica nodded. "A vacation can help, but often, changes in one's life help more. That being said, we can help you with a travel destination that can help with both."

Tiffany looked up. Derrick and Erica were staring at her. "What destination could possibly do that?"

"Erica," Derrick began, "I think that we should talk about Tiffany's favorite past times."

Erica nodded. "Tiffany, do you have any hobbies?"

Tiffany had grown accustomed to the off-beat questions. "Actually, I do. I write songs."

Erica smiled. "Excellent. Now, one more question. Where do you attend church?"

"I don't," Erica replied in surprise

Erica scribbled on a yellow legal pad. She tore off the top page and handed it across to Derrick.

He scanned the page. "Yes, that would do nicely, Erica. Well done. Please continue."

Erica opened a desk drawer, retrieved a small package wrapped in gold wrapping paper, and handed it across the desk to Tiffany. "Here is your ticket. Instructions are included."

Tiffany took the package. "Where am I going? We haven't discussed a destination and we haven't discussed the price!"

Eric smiled. "The price, as advertised, is one-half the normal price. Since the normal price is free, the reduced price is also free. Half of free is still free."

Tiffany sat in shocked silence.

Erica continued. "Your final destination is up to you. Your ticket will help to get you there. Follow the instructions included and you will find your way."

Tiffany felt that, like the literary Alice, she had fallen down the rabbit hole, and it was very deep. She stood and, without a single word, walked out the door.

Erica sighed. "What do you think Derrick? How did I do?"

Derrick, his eyes following Tiffany as she left, replied "You did fine. The seed has been planted. Now we will see if it will grow."

Tiffany, dazed and confused, made her way to the dry cleaner. She made it through the day and hurried home. Upon entering her apartment, she hurried to her bedroom, sat down on her bed, and carefully unwrapped the package.

Stunned, she found a small bible, a golden envelope inside the front cover. She opened the envelope and unfolded the letter within. In a beautiful flowing script, she found the words "Bakerton Christian Church, 2700 South Clemons Avenue. Second Service, 10:30 a.m., Sunday morning." Lost in thought, she sat and held the letter for a long time.

The next Sunday morning, Tiffany sat quietly in the back of the Bakerton Christian Church. She hadn't been in church for years, not since she had lived at home. It was a beautiful church; the people were friendly, the worship band was great, and the sermon was intense.

The minister paused as he summarized the events for the upcoming week. He turned to the worship minister. "Alex, I believe that you have something to add?"

The guitar-playing worship minister bobbed his head. "Yes, indeedy. Folks, it's time for our annual songwriting contest. Those who are interested have one month from today to turn in an original song for our band to perform. The song selected will be performed for the entire church and the video will be posted to You Tube. Last year we had 28 entries; this year we expect even more."

Tiffany sat, eyes riveted to the stage. She glanced down at the bible in her hands. She recalled Erica's words. "*Your final destination is up to you…*" The service over, Tiffany hurried back to her apartment.

When her house-mates returned from their Sunday morning trip to Starbucks, the startled friends found Tiffany hard at work writing a new song.

On Monday morning, she walked down the street on her way to work. Intending to stop in at the travel agency, she found, to her shock, the business gone, replaced by yet another art gallery.

She stepped inside. "Excuse me," she said to the lady behind the counter, "How long have you been here?" Puzzled, the lady replied, "We opened our doors five years ago."

***

The reporter sighed. "Okay, Tiffany, how did you really get your start as a songwriter?"

Tiffany smiled. "I'm sorry you don't believe my story, but that's exactly what happened five years ago." She glanced at the man sitting next to her. "If you don't believe me, ask my husband, Alex!"

LET IT GO

"She did it again!" Jade muttered to herself, as Ashley, the department chair, walked away. "Two more grad students for me to supervise! She must think that I live to mentor students. Great! I was already snowed under; just what I need, more work to do."

She glanced at the clock above her desk. "Fifteen to five. I'm supposed to be here until five today, but I think I'll call it a day." She powered down her computer, shrugged her coat on, and headed out the door. Stalking down the hallway past her fellow professors' offices, she glared at Ashley's office door as she breezed past. *"TGIF"* she thought; *"At least I won't have to see the Ice Witch until Monday!"*

She walked outside into another cold, dreary day. February, in Fairbanks, Alaska, was predictably cold with lots of snow. Today was no different. As she walked past, she glanced at the department sign outside the building: "University of Southern Alaska, Arctic Engineering Department. Her family and friends down in the lower 48 states often laughed when she told them she was an arctic engineer. She had once tried to explain to her giggling niece that arctic engineering was, yeah, a real thing, and no, she didn't build snowmen. Actually, she had informed her, she taught engineers how to build structures and equipment that could survive in extremely cold environments.

Jade made her way to her SUV, careful to not slip on the icy sidewalk of the campus. She slipped in and carefully eased into the traffic on Valiant Drive. Rush hour traffic was in high gear as she drove homeward. Suddenly, a blue van pulled out in front of her; she slammed on the brakes and skidded on the icy pavement right up to the back of the van. She sat still for a moment, chest heaving and pulse racing from the adrenaline flow. She lowered the window, stuck her head out, and yelled "You're lucky I didn't ram into you! Watch where you're going!

With a sheepish wave of apology, the driver sped off. Still fuming, she rolled the window back up and raced down the street. By the time she got to her apartment building, she had calmed down, but not by much. She angrily punched in the front entry security code and walked to the elevator. She rode it up to the fifth floor and walked down the hallway to her apartment. As she was unlocking the door, her neighbor, Faith Keystone, peeked out of her apartment.

"Jade, my dear, how are you?" Faith asked. "You look a little frazzled, girl!"

Jade couldn't help but smile in return at her older neighbor and friend. "Hi Faith; yeah I guess I am a bit irate. Rough week."

Faith chuckled. "Sorry to hear that. Say, I just made dinner, eggplant parmesan, and, as usual, I made too much for one person. Why don't you come over in ten minutes and we can have dinner together?"

"I would love to," Jade replied, "See you in a bit."

Jade sat quietly as Faith placed a plate of eggplant parmesan and steamed vegetables in front of her. Faith retrieved another plate from the kitchen and sat down across the table from Jade. Just as Jade picked up her fork, Faith bowed her head. Jade sheepishly put the fork down and bowed her head as well.

"Lord, bless this meal, bless this food, bless those who are about to eat. In the name of Jesus, the Lamb of God, amen."

Jade hastily added "amen" and picked up her fork. "Faith, I can't tell you how much I appreciate this dinner. It really has been a tough week and, oh I don't know, but I always feel more relaxed, calmer, when I get a chance to talk to you."

Faith laughed. "Just like I feel when I talk to the Lord in prayer." She eyed Jade thoughtfully over a forkful of spaghetti. "You know Jade, life has a way of throwing obstacles in our paths, some little, some big. But the Lord is bigger than any of them. What obstacles have irritated you so much this week?"

Sighing, Jade leaned back. "Problems at work, mainly. Ashley, I've told you about her, gave me two more grad students to look after."

Faith sipped her iced tea and eyed Jade speculatively. "Well, well. Would two more be too much for you to handle?"

"She just wants to heap more on me. I don't know what the problem is." Faith remained silent.

Jade continued. "She doesn't load up anyone else in the department like that. Why me?"

"I noticed," Faith began, "that you didn't answer my question. Would two more graduate students overload you?"

Jade slowly shook her head. "To be honest, no. Yeah, I probably could handle two more grad students. It's just that I feel like I am being singled out for punishment by the Ice Witch."

"The Ice Witch?" Faith asked with a smile. "Is she really that cold?"

Jade grimaced. "I call her that because she doesn't seem to have any emotions at all. She dumps more and more on me without ever asking if I can handle more. She's stone cold."

Faith studied her. "Hmmmm. Have you tried talking to her? You know, to warm her up a little? Maybe find out why she is giving you more work?"

Jade shook her head. "No, I haven't. She just rubs me the wrong way."

"What exactly has she done to you?" Faith asked.

"She just gives me more work to do, more assignments, more responsibilities, more grad students…"

"You know Jade," Faith began, "things are not always what they seem to be. Perhaps there is another reason for what Ashley is doing."

"I don't know what it would be," Jade replied. "In any case, there isn't much I can do about it. I like teaching at the department; I don't want to go elsewhere."

Faith cleared the dishes and placed bowls of strawberry gelato on the table. Before she sat down, she picked up her worn, red leather bible. She flipped through the pages. "Jade, it says in 1 Peter chapter 3 that we should be of one mind and have compassion for one another. I know you feel that Ashley is dumping on you, but you may not know the whole story. Often, when something irritates, or even angers us, we need to try to understand the other person's position. It's easy to feel resentful, or even to lash out, but acting like that doesn't help you to understand the other person, in this case, Ashley. The Lord works in mysterious ways; He may be preparing something for you."

Jade mulled that over as her thoughts drifted back to the driver who pulled out in front of her. *What if he really hadn't seen her coming? Maybe he was in a hurry to get home because a family member was sick? Who knows?*

Jade sighed. "Maybe I don't know the whole story. I know I can handle the extra work; I actually enjoy supervising the grad students, well most of them anyway."

Faith smiled. "You could talk to Ashley about it, in a nonthreatening manner. In any case, harmony is always better than hostility. At some point, of course, you will have to draw the line and accept no more assignments than you can actually handle, but it doesn't sound like you have reached that point yet. My advice to you Jade is to let it go."

Faith watched Jade carefully. "Jade, you and I have talked about you giving your life to Christ. What we are talking about here is a tiny slice of what Jesus did for all of us. He told all of humanity to Let it Go! Everything that we have done or said, everything that we were, we can let go because of Christ's forgiveness. We can let it go, because He did as well. After we surrender to Him, He lets everything we have done or said go; the slate is wiped clean! He lets it go and, as a result, we are free!"

Faith paused for a moment. "Tell you what, Jade, why don't you go to church with me on Sunday and learn more about it?"

Jade nodded slowly. "I think that I will, but on one condition."

"What's that?" Faith asked.

Jade finished the last bit of the gelato. "You invite me to dinner again next weekend!"

On Monday morning, Jade walked down the hall to Ashley's office and knocked on the door.

"Come in," Ashley called from inside.

Ashley looked up as Jade walked in. "Jade! Great! I was just getting ready to call you!"

"You were?" Jade replied.

"Yes. Have a seat, Jade. She waved a hand at one of the guest chairs in front of her mahogany desk. "Congratulations! You are the new department chair!"

Jade's jaw dropped. "What?" *"Did Ashley just smile at me?"*

Ashley handed a letter across the desk to her. "Frank Bannington has officially retired as the dean of the college of engineering. I have been slotted to replace him. You are moving up to be the department chair of arctic engineering!"

The impact of Ashley's words hit Jade like a thunderbolt. "All this time, the extra work, the added responsibilities…"

Ashley nodded. "Were to get you ready. You accepted every assignment that I gave you and never said a word. That proved to me and the department that you were ready to take over for me."

"Faith was right," Jade thought, *"There was more to the story."*

"One more thing," Faith continued, "I want you to design a program for teaching harmonious relations to the department's staff. Not everybody here is a team player like you are. If the program works well, I will implement it throughout the college of engineering."

Dazed, Jade nodded. She stood, thanked Ashley, and headed to her office. Pulling out her phone, she called Faith. "Faith, do you recall your conversation about how God works in mysterious ways? Well…"

LIFT

He parked his pickup in Mercy Crest Hospital's employees' lot, switched off the engine, and sat for a time as the first rays of morning sunshine washed over his bronze skin and jet black hair. He was one of the Dine`, "The People" in the Navajo language. He thought of his childhood on "The Big Rez," the Navajo reservation, an area of land encompassing over 27,000 acres in Arizona, Utah, and New Mexico. It had been a time of love, peace, and the simple joy of understanding and appreciating nature and his fellow Dine`. He had been in *hozro*, the Dine's word for being harmony with everything.

When he was ten, his father, a sales manager, had received a promotion that had resulted in him and his family moving from Big Sky country to the Midwest. Before he left the Big Rez, Father Begay, a kindly Catholic priest, had given him a silver cross. He had placed it on a chain and had worn it ever since.

His thoughts returned to the present. He glanced at his watch and sighed. Time to clock in. He stepped out of the truck, crossed the parking lot, and entered the hospital through the ER entrance. He waved at a security guard just inside the entrance. "Morning Jake. How's the coffee this morning?"

"Actually pretty good for a change, Jesse. Want a cup?"

Jesse nodded. "Sure. I have to get my heart pumping before I can spread my wings and fly."

Jake turned and stepped back into the security office. He emerged with a steaming cup of coffee and a donut which he handed to Jesse. "Caffeine and sugar. If that don't get you airborne, Windwalker, nothing will."

Jesse laughed at the moniker his friends at Mercy Crest had bestowed upon him five years ago when he had joined the air ambulance crew. It was, he thought, an appropriate nickname for a Navajo air ambulance pilot who had taken The Jesus Road.

He walked into the Medair ready room and found Adam and Beth, the on-shift flight paramedic and RN, sitting at the break table, quietly sipping coffee.

Jesse set his own coffee and donut on the table, pulled a chair out, and sat down. "Morning folks. You two look bushy-eyed and bright- tailed this morning."

Beth snorted. "You see how great you look after being up half the night with a colicky baby."

Adam sighed. "What can I say; I'm definitely not a morning person. I'm not like you Navajos; you guys get up before the crack of dawn just to watch the sun come up."

Jesse opened his mouth for a retort just as the phone rang. He picked it up. "Air Ambulance, this is Jesse."

"Jesse, this is Michelle in Dispatch. Bilmont General has requested a transfer of a cardiac patient to Mercy Crest for direct admit to CCU."

"Sure. We will be there in 20 minutes." Jesse hung up the phone and turned back to Adam and Beth. "Cardiac transfer from Bilmont to here. Wheels up in ten minutes. Let's ride."

Adam sighed, took one last sip of coffee, stood, and cleared his throat. "'Ride like the wind…"

They trotted out to the helicopter parked on the helipad outside the ER entrance. After completing the pre-flight checklist, Jesse switched the engine on. Revving the engine, he pulled back on the collective as the chopper lifted from the pad. After lifting thirty feet, he pushed the cyclic forward, and the helicopter headed away from the hospital. Gaining altitude, he angled the cyclic left and veered southwest, toward Bilmont. He leveled off at 6,000 feet and cruised through the beautiful blue sky.

Jesse never tired of flying. Cruising through the sky with the Earth below and Heaven above, he felt close to God; he felt that he was in *hozro*. He reached inside his shirt, pulled out his silver cross and held it. So began a personal ritual that he had practiced on every flight since his days as a medevac pilot in Afghanistan. "Jesus, as I wind walk through the sky, I pray that you will guide me. Help me to keep my passengers safe, and may your love and power give lift to us as we go about your work. Amen."

He glanced back at Beth and Adam. As usual, they had joined him in the prayer.

"May we have lift, brother," Adam said as he fist bumped Jesse.

The flight was uneventful, for which Jesse was grateful. He gently landed the helicopter; Beth and Adam quickly retrieved the patient, an older woman with an oxygen mask on, skin ashen. They loaded the cart into the chopper and strapped in for the return flight. Less than ten minutes after touching down, they were airborne again and heading back toward Mercy Crest.

Five minutes into the flight, Jesse glanced at the altimeter and was alarmed to see that the chopper's altitude was dropping. He scanned the instrument panel, but found no indications of mechanical failure. He re-checked the altimeter; the helicopter was continuing to lose altitude.

"Heads up guys," Jesse said into his helmet microphone, "We are losing altitude and I don't know why yet. Prepare for possible hard landing."

As Adam and Beth double-checked the patient and strapped themselves back in, Jesse turned his attention to the instrument panel. He still saw nothing amiss. He turned to the passenger bay. "Could be one of the gear boxes. I don't know for sure. In any case, we're still dropping." He turned back to the altimeter. "Four thousand and dropping…three nine zero zero…three eight zero zero…"

He switched radio frequencies. "Dispatch, this is Mercy Crest One; we are going to execute an emergency landing. GPS coordinates to follow." He rattled off a string of numbers.

"Mercy Crest One, this is Dispatch. Copy that. I will dispatch ground ambulances and any available air ambulance. One moment…Addison Airport's Emergency Response Unit has been notified as well. Good luck Mercy One."

He checked the altimeter. "Two five zero zero…"

He glanced back at his passengers and keyed his mic. "Hang on guys, we'll get through this." He pulled out his silver cross. "Jesus, my savior, give me strength. Please Lord. I must not fail my passengers, Beth, Adam, and…" He trailed off as he realized that he didn't know the patient's name. He never took the time to find out. *"If we get through this, I will never make that mistake again, Lord!"*

He swiveled his head and keyed his mic. "What's the patient's name?"

Adam looked up at Jesse. "Why do you want to know that now? Fly the ship, man, fly the ship!"

At Jesse's hard stare, Adam shook his head. "I don't know why that would make any difference now, but it's Alice, Alice Pearson."

Jesse nodded and turned back to the instrument panel. "…and Alice, Lord. I cannot fail them!"

"Eight zero zero feet…seven zero zero…" He glanced up and froze. "Oh dear God, no. Bannerton Lake." Focusing on the loss of altitude, he had forgotten that the helicopter would be flying directly over the lake. It was too late to turn; they were already over the edge of it.

"We're going down in the lake! Get ready!" He switched frequencies. "Dispatch, we're going to splash in Bannerton Lake. Repeat: we are going to splash!"

He checked the altimeter. "Two zero zero…" He turned to his charges. "I'm sorry…"

He turned back to watch the dark waters rush toward them. "Dear God, help us...please lord, save us..." He stared helplessly out the windshield.

The helicopter dove toward the lake as the Windwalker and his passengers called out to God...and the helicopter, less than fifty feet from the surface of the lake, lifted.

Jesse pulled back on the collective as the chopper shuddered, rose, and veered back toward the edge of the lake. Finally over land, he gently dropped the collective, and the chopper settled onto a cleared shore of the lake. It was then that he noticed the helicopter's rotors were not spinning. Turning to his passengers, he shouted, "We're down! Everybody alright back there?"

Adam pumped his fist in the air. "Way to go, Windwalker!"

Unstrapping herself, Beth checked the patient. "Alice is stable; she slept through the whole ride!"

Stunned, Adam looked out the window. "Jesse...why are the rotors still? They should still be spinning..."

Jesse grinned. "Yeah, they should be. The fact is the rotors quit spinning when we were over the lake. One of the gearboxes must have completely frozen up or a shaft broke. I don't know. All I know is that we should have gone down in the lake. Instead, we gained altitude and turned back toward land, *and flew hundreds of feet while the rotors were not turning.*"

Beth looked up. "But that's impossible, unless..."

"Unless," Adam continued, "God lifted us up!"

One month later, Jesse walked out to the helipad to find Beth and Adam waiting for him beside the chopper. Grinning, they stood back, revealing just-added artwork to the side of the helicopter. In bright blue letters, was the word "Windwalker." Below the moniker was a freshly-painted white cross.

Jesse turned as the ER crew brought a patient out for transfer. He walked to the cart, took the elderly woman's hand, and looked into her eyes. "Hello, Janice. I'm Jesse Nakai, born to the Bitter Water Clan, and born for the Crystal Rock People. I walk The Jesus Road, and I fly The Jesus Sky. My friends call me...Windwalker!"

POINT OF VIEW

Phoenix drifted through the hatch into the commons area of Space Visions One, a small space habitat in orbit around Earth. He grabbed a wall-mounted hand hold and pulled himself down into a recliner. Strapping himself in, he activated the chair's com. "Jayden, baby, I'm finished with the propulsion system check. How about lunch?"

The com crackled. "Great! I'll be there in a sec."

Phoenix Jackson had been on the prototype mini space station for six months. Jayden Sanders had joined him three months prior, but their relationship had been on-going for two years. They had joined the commercial space program together, and their friendship had quickly blossomed into romance.

Jayden drifted in from the control center. "Any problems with any of the systems?" She drifted over to a supply cabinet, retrieved two meals, and slipped them into the microwave. "How about the altitude-control subsystem?"

Phoenix shook his head. "No problems. The ACS is working just fine, thank you very much. We have green lights across the board."

The microwave beeped and Jayden retrieved the lunches. Crossing to Phoenix, she handed one lunch to him and then strapped herself into her own recliner. "Well that's good news. So far on this mission we have had really good luck; I just hope it continues."

Phoenix pealed back the cover from the lunch tray. "Hey, what do you know? Salisbury steak!" He took a bite and smiled.

Jayden shook her head. Phoenix was the most appreciative man she had ever known. He managed to find the upside of everything, including tasteless microwave meals. It was one of the many things about him that had endeared him to her.

Jayden took a bite of the steak and swallowed. She glanced at Phoenix. "Are you ready for the spacewalk tomorrow?"

He nodded. "You bet. The first time for both of us to venture outside! I can't wait!"

She laughed. "Only you could be so positive as to look at something as dangerous as a spacewalk and talk about it like we were kids getting ready to ride our new bikes for the first time!"

"Yeah, it's dangerous," he replied, "But, you have to admit, it will be exciting! Just think; we get to step outside this habitat and literally stand in the middle of space with no protection other than our space suits!"

She blanched. "That's what worries me!"

He smiled. "Hey, it will be fine! Just think how romantic it will be! How many couples get to look at the stars while literally surrounded by them?"

Lunch finished, Phoenix unbuckled from his recliner and drifted over to Jayden. He floated by her chair as Jayden watched him in surprise. "What are you doing now, Phoenix?" she asked with a laugh.

Phoenix unzipped a pocket on his shirt, and pulled out a small package. He carefully opened the package to reveal a silver ring. His face became uncharacteristically solemn. "Jayden, I love you with every ounce of my being. Will you do me the honor of becoming my wife?"

Jayden sat unmoving, shocked into complete silence.

Phoenix smiled. "Surprise!"

Jayden laughed. "How could I possibly say no? Of course I will marry you! Someone has to take care of you and, well, I don't trust any other woman to do it!"

Phoenix carefully slipped the engagement ring onto her finger. "Actually, I have another surprise. I've arranged for Reverend Jones to be available via radio tomorrow when we spacewalk. If you're willing, we can be the very first couple to be married during a spacewalk!"

Jayden stared. "Tomorrow?"

Phoenix smiled. "I don't believe in long engagements!"

The rest of the day and the next morning went quickly as the two prepared for their spacewalk. When the time came, the two suited up, attached tethers to the backs of each other's suit, and opened the airlock. The tethers unspooled as they used their suits' micro-jets to push away from the habitat. At a distance of 100 meters from the habitat, they stopped.

"We're in position, Jayden," Phoenix announced. "Maneuvering micro-jets off." The tethers securely anchored them to the habitat; without them, they would have continued to drift off into space.

Jayden and Phoenix stared in rapture at the panoramic images around them. Earth, in all its beauty, lay underneath them. Stretching to infinity in all directions was an ocean of brilliant stars.

After several minutes, Jayden broke the silence. "It's beautiful. Words cannot begin to describe its beauty."

"It's incredible!" Phoenix whispered.

"All of my life," Jayden began, "I have studied and trained to be here, to be in space. I have always had a scientific mind, even when I was a child. I never really thought about God being here today, and seeing this beautiful, majestic universe; I see, not forms of matter and energy, but the handiwork of God!"

Phoenix turned to Jayden. "Jayden, I have run from God all of my life. I never believed in Him either, until now. But there is no way that I can look at the wonders of the universe and not believe that God is real and He did create them!"

Phoenix's radio beeped. "Hello Phoenix, this is Reverend Jones. Can you hear me?"

Phoenix smiled. "Loud and clear, Reverend, loud and clear."

"Phoenix, did you talk to Jayden about our deal?"

"No, I didn't. I know you agreed to marry us only on the condition that we begin weekly radio discussions with you about Jesus, but I didn't discuss it with her. I don't think that it will be an issue anymore."

"Why not, Phoenix?"

"We didn't go looking for God; He found us."

"Ah, yes. I can see that, once you have spacewalked, it would be very difficult to not believe in Him! Does Jayden feel the same way?"

"Yes, I do, Reverend."

"I'm sorry Jayden, I didn't realize that you were listening."

"No worries," she replied.

"Well, then," the Reverend continued, "let's begin. Do you Phoenix take Jayden to be your wife?..."

THE CIRCUIT RIDER

"It's going to be another hot one, Jake!"

Turning, I smiled a greeting at the customer. "Indeed it will be Jeremy, indeed it will. What can I get for you today? Coffee? Flour? Ammunition?"

"Ammunition." Unholstering his pistol, he set it down on the counter. "For this."

Picking it up, I eyed it appreciatively. "Nice. Two boxes?"

"Yeah, should do it. I've got varmints hanging around the herd again. Lost three calves over the past three weeks."

Now most folks hereabouts would prefer a long gun in such a situation but Jeremy was partial to short ones. I knew better than to ask him if he needed ammo for a rifle. "What else, my friend?" I didn't want to push, but I'm a businessman, after all.

He glanced around the store. "I could use some coffee. Three pounds."

"Regular or decaffeinated?"

"Whaaat?" He shook his head. "Jake, you always were a joker."

I pulled a can from the shelf and dropped it in a sack along with the ammunition. "That will be two and a half, Jeremy."

"Thank you, kindly." Handing the money to me, he picked up the bag, and strode out.

"Good hunting!" I called after him.

Walking out onto the porch, I glanced down the street. Quite a few folks were going about their morning business. Ambrose, the town barber, walked out of his shop across the street, and waved.

41

"Morning, Jake, going to be another hot one!"

"Now how did I know you were going to say that, Ambrose?"

He laughed. "You're a mind reader, I reckon! Say, when are the new supplies do in? I'm running out of necessities! I can't open up my shop in the morning if I don't have a cup of coffee first!

I shook my head. "They're overdue. I'm hoping that they will get here today but..." I shrugged. "The way things are, I'm just a praying that they get here someday."

He crossed the street and leaned against the porch rail beside me. He glanced up and down the empty sidewalk. "Supplies for a settlement like ours would be very valuable to the wrong folks. Marshalls are few and far between; there's no way they can protect every shipment. I don't think most folks around here realize just how precarious our situation is."

I nodded. "You're right, of course. The frontier settlements need better protection. The forts are good protection, but there aren't enough of them either. The Calvary troops do a great job but, just like the Marshalls, they're spread mighty thin."

"Yeah, you're right, Jake, they are. We could use more of them."

We chatted a while about the weather, raising livestock on the Frontier, and the trials and tribulations that all small settlement businessmen and businesswomen have.

"I guess I had better get back to the shop. See you later, Jake." The barber crossed the street as my favorite lady in the whole wide world, Lucy O'Connor, glided up the sidewalk.

She stopped in front of me, tossed her shoulder length black hair, and batted her eyelashes. "Jake Fields, as I live and breathe! How are you this fine morning?"

I smiled. "Top of the morning to you, Lucy O'Connor!" I offered her my arm. "Shall I escort you into this fine retail establishment?"

"Yes, Jake Fields, fiancé of mine, you may." She hooked her arm in mine and we strolled inside. "Mattie told me that the Circuit Rider hasn't made it in yet."

I shook my head. "No, for safety reasons, the Church has mandated that the Circuit Riders have to travel with a Marshall. Who knows when a Marshall will be able to bring a Circuit Rider around again?"

She sighed. "Have things gotten that bad?"

"From what I've been hearing, yes." I took her in my arms. "Don't you worry none. As soon as that preacher gets here, we will get married first thing."

A shadow darkened the door. We both turned and there, standing in the doorway, was a tall, dark complexioned man, with a head of fiery red hair.

He looked like he was strong enough to lift a cow with one hand, and he wore a pair of silver-plated pistols around his waist. A Territorial Marshall badge was pinned to his shirt.

Stepping forward, I offered my hand. "Howdy, Marshall! I'm Jake Fields, and this lovely lady is my fiancée, Lucy O'Connor."

Lucy curtsied. "Pleased to meet you Marshall...?"

"Marshall Obediah Kane, ma'am..." He stepped forward and shook my hand.

He had a powerful grip; I could feel bones cracking under the pressure. "We were wondering when you would be able to come by here. If you're here, then perhaps the new circuit rider is with you?" I asked with a glance at Lucy.

He reached inside his shirt collar, and pulled out a cross hanging on a silver chain.

Dumbfounded, Lucy and I stared at him. Lucy found her voice first. "You mean you're a Marshall and a minister? Is that about right?"

He nodded. "I am. I am a Marshall of the Territories, and I am an ordained minister of the Church. I brought a load of supplies with me as well."

True to his word, he brought the supplies to my store and even helped me stock the shelves. After finishing, I was tired and sweating like the proverbial pig. "How about a lemonade Marshall?"

"Thank you friend, but no." He cast a sideways glance at me. "Since you introduced Lucy to me as your fiancé, I'm assuming that you two would like for me to marry you while I'm here?"

I nodded. He was quick witted. Oddly, I noticed that the Marshall wasn't sweating at all and didn't seem to be the least bit tired.

"That's right Marshall, uh Reverend."

"Where and when?" he replied.

"How about tonight at the City Hall Meeting Room? Lucy wants to be married right away; I will let the town folk know this afternoon. Say 7:00?"

He nodded. "I will be there. Well, I have a few other stops to make before this evening, so I better get going." He headed out the door.

As I had expected, everyone in town closed up shop early to prepare for the evening. Everyone in town, all 75 of us, and even a few of the closer ranchers, were in the Hall waiting when the Reverend Marshall strode in.

"Good evening folks," he began, "Looks like we've got a great turnout this evening. Before we get started with the wedding, I need to talk to all of you first." He walked to the podium in front of the Hall as we hastily sat down.

"I want to explain the new situation in the Territory. Due to the increasing boldness of..." He hesitated slightly, "...bandits in the Territory, 25 new Marshalls have been added with more to come."

The audience stirred. That was a big increase in the number of Marshalls.

"In addition, every new Marshall will also be cross-trained in a number of different areas. I, for example, am an ordained minister, as you know. I can also move freight. A few of the new Marshalls are also physicians. I could go on."

Happy murmuring began. Marshalls who could do baptisms *and* splint broken arms? We were a happy group of settlers to say the least.

The wedding began, and in short order, Lucy O'Connor became Lucy Fields. After saying our "I dos" we kissed as literally the entire town cheered. We walked over to the reception table, drank the toast, and fed each other wedding cake.

Billy Fenton played the fiddle while his son Trance played the harmonica. We ate, danced, sang, and ate again. I didn't expect the Reverend Marshall to drink any of our homemade fruit wine, but I was surprised to see that he didn't eat any food.

I strolled over and offered a piece of wedding cake to him. "Reverend, I never saw you try Aunt Bethany's cake. You have got to try this! This is a little slice of Heaven!"

He shook his head. "I'm sorry Jake; I simply can't eat." He waved a hand at a couple of chairs away from the serving tables. "Let's sit down."

We sat. He glanced around. Seeming satisfied that no one was within hearing distance, he continued. "Jake, you seem to me to be a modern man, comfortable with new ideas and new ways."

I nodded. "I am, I suppose, but what in the world does that have to do with you not eating?"

He sighed. "What I am about to tell you is confidential, at least for the time being. I am...not human."

I looked closer at him. He seemed human to me. "What are you saying, Reverend?"

He extended his left arm toward me. With his right hand, he pressed on his left wrist; a section of his skin peeled back to reveal wires and cables underneath. "I'm an android."

I sat back in shock. I had heard, of course, that artificially intelligent robots were beginning to be used on the Frontier, but I had no idea how advanced the systems had become.

Regaining my composure, I leaned forward. "Okay, I can see AIs being used as Marshalls. That makes sense. But ministers? No offense, Reverend, but how can you be a minister? You don't have a soul!

He nodded. "I know. But I believe in God, I pray, I read the Bible, and I am an ordained minister. I may not have a soul, but I can still worship God and I can still be of service to Him."

I sat in silence for a few moments. I shrugged. "I can't argue with you

Reverend, and I certainly can't fault you for wanting to serve the Lord. I take it that this isn't going to be made public for a while? It will take some time for most folks on the Frontier to get accustomed to AI ministers."

He laughed. "Yes, I am sure it will." He stood. "I must be going, Jake. I need to get back to my ship. I would like to be landing on the next territorial frontier planet in two months."

I stood and shook hands. "Godspeed Reverend Marshall, Godspeed."

THE DOOR

lancing around the six by eight feet room, he wondered, once again, how he had managed to keep from losing his mind. A shelf attached to the end wall of the tiny room, and covered with a thin mattress, served as a bed. *"How many nights have I lain awake there, staring up at the dirty-white ceiling?"* His gaze rested next on the stainless steel sink and commode. *"How many times, while sick from anxiety and depression, have I sat on the floor while embracing the toilet like an old friend?"* His gaze landed on the last piece of furniture in the room, a small wall shelf that served as a desk. A grey plastic chair rested underneath.

He scanned the dull walls, which he had covered with nature pictures in a feeble attempt at decorating. Waterfalls, mountains, oceans, beaches, forests, the Grand Canyon. All beautiful, all forever out of his reach. He glanced at a photograph, one of himself as a younger man, dressed in a pair of Levis and a blue chambray shirt; his favorite clothes from days gone by.

He turned to the last of the three walls of the room that he had any control over. He had allowed only one item to adorn that wall, a slightly out of focus 8 x 10 photograph. The image was that of a distinguished older man with white hair and a serious demeanor. He was dressed in a light blue long-sleeved shirt, highlighted with a wide blue tie. A navy blue hat sat atop his head, and a patch, emblazoned with the single word *"Security"* was upon his left sleeve.

He studied the portrait, the same one that was seared into his mind. He had been branded on his innermost self with it and, as a result, he had been branded on his outer self with a label, the worst of all possible labels, *murderer.* Dropping his head, he cried uncontrollably as he had every day, for 12 long years.

Tears finally spent, he staggered to the sink, turned on the tap, and splashed cold water on his face. There was no mirror in the room, but in his mind's eye, he knew what he would see if there were. A 40 year -old man with short black hair and a bright orange jumpsuit with the words "State Prison Death Row 24487" emblazoned upon the shirt.

He stared at his own mental image as if from a great distance. *"How can God love me? How can He forgive me? No one loves me. No one has forgiven me."*

Turning, he gripped the cell door's cold steel bars. *"How can you love me God? I'm a murderer! How can you forgive me? My own mother didn't forgive me. How can you?"*

He screamed then, a primal scream of pure despair and self-loathing. *"How can you love me God? How?"* His chest heaved as sobs racked his body and soul.

The guard appeared at the door, a rare concerned expression on his rugged face. "Okay, Destry, that's enough. You need to settle down." He stared pointedly at Destry, and then turned and walked away.

Staggering back to his bed, Destry fell onto it. Sobbing quietly, he soon fell into a troubled sleep.

The rattling of the cell door awakened him. He sat up on the edge of the bed to see the guard opening the door.

The guard gestured. "You have a visitor." He turned and handed a tray to a smiling middle-aged man who stood in the hallway. "Ten minutes, Reverend." The guard spun and strode back down the hallway.

Pastor Jorge Gomez, the only person to ever visit Destry's cell, walked in, handed the tray to him, pulled the solitary chair from under the desk-shelf and sat down. "Hello, Destry." He smiled gently with kind glittering eyes. "There's your bacon, son, apple-smoked just like you requested."

Destry set the tray on the bed, forked slices of bacon onto the accompanying rye bread, and took a bite. He smiled, the first time in weeks. He glanced at Jorge to catch his questioning look. He chewed, swallowed, and took a drink of the hot, black coffee. "When I was a kid, Momma used to make bacon sandwiches for me. We didn't have much money, so it was a real treat to get one of these." He took another bite and swallowed. "They make me think of her before I..."

The minister nodded. "I understand, Destry." He paused. "Have you thought more about our last conversation?"

"Yes, I have, Reverend. I understand what you have said to me and I appreciate it, I really do." He glanced over at the small Bible resting upon the shelf. "I have read the verses over and over. I nearly have Romans chapter eight memorized." He cleared his throat. "Verses one through four. 'Therefore, there is now no condemnation for those who are in Christ Jesus, because through Christ Jesus the law of the spirt who gives life has set you free from the law of sin and death. For what the law was powerless to do because it was weakened by the flesh, God did by sending his own Son in the likeness of sinful flesh to be a sin offering. And so he condemned sin in the flesh, in order that the righteous requirement of the law might be fully met in us, who do not live according to the flesh but according to the Spirit.'"

Jorge nodded. "Then you understand?"

Destry took in a deep breath. "Yes, I understand the verses, Reverend. I just don't know that I can believe them. I'm a sinner and I committed the ultimate sin. I took another man's life." Tears filled his eyes, and he looked away. His glance fell upon the solitary photograph on the wall. "I planned the bank robbery and I knew that there would be a chance that I would have to shoot the security guard. I knew that it was possible that I would have to kill a man and I planned for it. Premeditated murder, a jury of my peers said, and they were right. I am a *murderer*."

Jorge sighed. "You did commit murder. Nothing can change that. But you have accepted Christ into your life and you have asked for His forgiveness. He shed blood on the cross for all of us, for all of our sins. All who have asked for forgiveness, and truly meant it in their heart of hearts, have been forgiven. All, Destry. Not 'someone there and another one over there, but not the one in the prison cell.' All. We have all sinned, Destry, all of us."

Destry stood, and paced the short length of his cell. "How can God forgive me? The bank guard's family couldn't forgive me and I have asked for their forgiveness in the letters that I have sent for 12 years. If they couldn't, how could God?"

Jorge stood, and pulled Destry to him in a bear hug. "God's ways are not our ways, Destry, and I am thankful for that. His forgiveness is all-encompassing, complete and pure. You are forgiven, Destry, you just have to believe that you are." He released him and stepped back. "I have to go now Destry, but I will be in the room with you when the time comes." He turned and stepped to the door. "Guard, I'm ready to leave now."

After Jorge left, Destry sat on the edge of the bed and stared at the closed cell door. He was still sitting there one hour later when the guard returned. "It's time, Destry." He slid the door open as Destry stood.

Taking one last look at the photograph, Destry stepped out of the cell. He walked down the long grey corridor until they reached the last door. He entered the cold grey antiseptic room, and sat down on the solitary hospital-like bed.

A guard strapped him to the table as Jorge and the prison warden entered the room. Jorge strode to his side and clasped his hand. "Remember what we discussed Destry. You are forgiven."

Destry nodded. "Thank you, Reverend, for everything. I..I hope to see you on the other side."

The physician administered the lethal injection and, at 12:45 a.m., Destry was pronounced dead. The warden pulled the doctor aside. "Did you see that? He was…smiling. I have been present at nine executions and that is the first time that I have ever seen the inmate smile!"

***

Opening his eyes, he found himself back on the bed in his prison cell. *"Was it a dream? Am I still on death row?"*

The cell door rattled open. Sitting up, he stared at the cell door. Glowing bright white, it wavered as if in a dream. Images of snow-capped mountains and effervescent waterfalls drifted just beyond the cell door. A swirling, white fog drifting into the room as the door swung open. In the soft white light, an olive complexioned man stood, jet black hair cascading down to his shoulders. He had the most piercing blue eyes that Destry had ever seen.

"Hello, Destry. You can call me J.C." He handed a stack of clothes to Destry. "You need to change. I thought you might like these better than the orange jumpsuit."

Destry took the offered clothes and, to his surprise, found them to be a pair of Levis with a blue chambray shirt. He quickly dressed while J.C. stood quietly on the other side.

Destry smiled as he walked toward the door. "Do I smell bacon?"

Laughing, J.C. stepped back, away from the prison cell. He held out his hand. "Come."

Prisoner 24487, formerly of State Prison, stepped out of his cell, a prisoner no more.

THE TRAVELER

"*Beep, beep, beep, beep…*" Opening one eye, she glanced at the alarm clock on the bedside table, reached over, and shut it off. Slipping off the covers, she sat up, and stared at the closed bedroom door. *The Outside World* waited on the other side. Praying silently; she prepared herself to meet it.

She stood, slipped on a robe, opened the door, and stepped into the hallway. She made her way to the kitchen, brewed coffee, and toasted a slice of bread. Sitting at the breakfast bar, she nibbled on the toast. She took a sip of coffee and glanced around her silent home. She sighed and closed her eyes in prayer. *"Lord of my heart, when will I find him? When will I ever find true love? Why am I still alone?"* Not receiving an answer, she opened her eyes to begin yet another day.

***

200,000 miles above her, not far from the Moon, space twisted and whirled. With a brilliant flash, a vessel appeared out of the void, a man its single occupant. He opened his eyes as the post-Shift disorientation wore off. He glanced at the Holovid screens above his chair and nodded to himself. "Solomon, ship's status?"

"On course for 21st century Earth with all systems functioning within acceptable parameters," the Timeship's computer replied, "Are you ready for the mission summary, Phoenix?"

The man waved a hand at the computer screens. "I am, Solomon. Please begin."

"I have unsealed your mission directive. You are to precede to Earth, Russian Federation, Moscow. The destination time is April 3, 2020. You are to observe…"

Phoenix waited while his ship's computer electronically collected its thoughts. He frowned. "Solomon, are you alright?" He swiveled in his chair, checking each monitor carefully. Nothing seemed to be amiss, but he was uneasy. He tried again. "Solomon?"

One by one, the Holovid monitors winked out. *"This is not good."* He bowed his head. "Dear God, please have mercy on me. If it be Your will that I perish, so be it, but if not, please save me. In the name of Jesus, my Savior, amen." The ship plummeted into his home planet's atmosphere, finally crashing onto the planet's surface. He blacked out as the ship finally came to a rest, deep in a wooded area.

Hours later, he opened his eyes and stared dejectedly at the blackened, twisted circuitry. Showers of sparks cascaded from the wrecked consoles overhead. "Solomon, are you back online?" No answer came as he pushed off the debris that had fallen on him during the crash. He staggered to his feet, swaying unsteadily. Making his way to the only still functioning console, he punched up the ship's systems' status. The readouts confirmed his worst fears. Propulsion system offline. Communications non-existent. Worst of all, the time displacement system was destroyed. He wasn't going anywhere or anywhen other than where he was, which was, according to the screen, *Earth, United States, Missouri, 2020.*

"I am stranded 150 years in my own past; marooned in a time long before anyone I know was even born." He looked up. *Why Lord?* Receiving no answer, he considered his options. He sighed. Too early for the essential technology necessary to repair the Timeship. He was stranded, which meant there was one last duty to carry out. He felt his way around the darkened consoles until he found the emergency manual self-destruct. Flipping open the cover, he set the timer for ten minutes, hit the manual hatch release, and staggered out into the early morning. He walked through the woods while behind him nanobots methodically dismantled the ship leaving only a fine silvery powder which would wash away with the next rain.

He lurched through the woods as the sun began to rise in the east. He staggered out onto a highway, not noticing the oncoming vehicle. He stood immobile, still dazed from the crash as the vehicle screeched to a halt mere inches from him.

The driver, her chest heaving, gripped the steering wheel and stared at the apparition in front of her car. A broad shouldered man with fiery red hair stood in the middle of the road, blood dripping from his face and arms. She eased the car over to the shoulder, switched the engine off, and stepped out. "Are you alright?"

He glanced around and then focused on her. "Yes, I believe I am."

"We need to get out of the road." She took his arm and walked him back to the car where he sat on the hood. "I didn't see you until I was almost on top of you. Thank God I didn't…" She shook her head, unable to voice her thoughts. "Thank God! We need to get you to a hospital. What happened? Did you have a car wreck?" She looked down the highway. "I don't see a car…"

He shook his head. "No. I do not need to go to a hospital. I just have a few cuts and bruises."

She grimaced. "What happened?"

He looked away. "I was…traveling. On foot. Alongside the highway. Some men in a ground vehicle stopped and robbed me."

"Ground vehicle? You mean a car?"

He turned to face her. "Yes, a…car."

He shifted uneasily. "I fought back but they stole my pack and left me at the side of the road. That is how I came to be injured."

"We need to call the Sheriff." She pulled her cell phone out.

"No, do not report this to anyone. I am fine. The men did not steal anything of value from me."

She frowned. "Alright, but we need to get your cuts bandaged. Hop in and I will drive you back to my house."

Bewildered, he looked at her. "Hop in?"

Laughing, she shook her head. "Get into the car. Are you like from Mars or something?"

***

They sat on the couch while she cleaned and bandaged his wounds. She glanced up from her work. "I'm Tressa, by the way, and you are…?"

He studied her elfin face. "I am Phoenix."

"So, where are you from, Phoenix?"

"I was born in Vancouver." He hesitated. "I have…moved around since then."

She leaned back. "All done. Those clothes you have on were pretty torn up. Let's go to Wal-Mart and get some new ones."

He studied the floor. "I have no money."

"No problem. I will buy some new clothes for you and then you can pay me back later. Let's go."

Later that evening, they sat on the porch overlooking the valley. Tressa turned to Phoenix. "It's really weird. Here I am sitting with a strange man that I have only known for a few hours and, for some reason, I feel completely comfortable. My parents would totally freak out if they knew what was going on."

He leaned over and, as much to his own astonishment as hers, he gently kissed her. "In all of my travels, I have never met anyone like you. I feel that we were meant to be together. *"Dominus operatur arcanis modis."*

He smiled at her questioning look. "The Lord Works in Mysterious Ways!"

***

DEPARTMENT OF TEMPORAL MONITORING, HEADQUARTERS, OFFICE OF THE COMMANDANT, TULSA, OKLAHOMA, UNITED STATES, EARTH, SOL SYSTEM, JUNE 16, 2168

The commandant looked up as her office door slid open and Dominick, her adjutant, hurried in. "What is it, Dominick?"

He grimaced. "Bad news, sir. Survey ship Alpha One Three crashed on Earth, circa 2020." He glanced at the pad in his hand. "Something took control of the ship before landing. The ship was supposed to land in the Russian Federation and observe the beginning of the Second Russian Revolution. Instead, it crashed in the United States. The telemetry cut off as the ship hit atmo so we don't know the status of the pilot."

The Commandant sighed. "Who took control of the ship, how, and why?"

He shook his head. "We don't know. All we know is that, just before the data feed stopped; the last command line of code had a sender tag on it."

She frowned. "I thought you said that you don't know who took control of the Timeship. The sender tag would have the person's name on it. Who was it?"

Dominick frowned. "It didn't have a name on it...it simply said 'I am.'"

THE TREE

S itting on his cabin's porch, he gazed silently at the majestic white oak tree nearby, the creek gently flowing behind, as the sun slowly sank behind the band of hills to the west. Chilled by the early spring Ozark air, he zipped his jacket and sat motionless; exhausted from another Sunday afternoon spent scouring the neighboring hills with a metal detector.

Janelle, his wife, stepped out onto the porch. "Beautiful evening, Jeremy."

"Yeah." He glanced up at her. "Want to sit down?"

She nodded and sat on the pine bench beside him. "Any luck this time?"

He shook his head. "Not unless you count two rusted nails and an old chipped axe head."

She glanced at him before returning her gaze to the mesmerizing sunset. "Cassandra called this afternoon. She wanted to know when we would come and visit."

He shrugged. "Someday."

She sighed. "That's what you said last month. Cassandra has lived in Colorado for two years now, Jeremy, two years. We need to visit our daughter! How can we expect her to keep coming to see us when we never go visit her?"

She glanced at him, but he remained silent. "Jeremy, we can't keep living like this. I know how much this...this quest of yours means to you, but enough is enough. You've been looking for Farnham's gold for five years now. *Five years.*"

He removed his cap and scratched his head. "I know. But how can I stop looking? According to the legend, just before the Civil War, old man Farnham, when a neighbor warned him that bushwhackers were on the way, buried his family's gold somewhere in these hills, gold that today would be worth upwards of a million dollars! Think what that kind of money could do for us! For Cassandra!"

54

She smiled. "I know, Jeremy, but…well…" Seeing the despairing look on his face, she couldn't finish the thought.

Tears filled his eyes as he hung his head. "I've never been able to provide you and Cassandra with the better things in life. I've worked hard all my life but I just haven't made much money." He shook his head and his voice dropped to a whisper. "I don't really want the gold for myself; I want it for you and Cassandra."

She took his hand and held it to her cheek. "I know, honey, I know. But you gave Cassandra and me something much more valuable than gold; you gave us love. And that's all we really need."

She stood, leaned down, and kissed his cheek. "And I love you, and so does Cassandra. I'm going in to fix supper—it will take about half an hour. I'm making your favorite dish---Shepherd's Pie."

She was right, he thought; the quest needed to come to an end. He glanced at the old white oak tree; his praying tree. He walked to the towering tree, and gazed up at the massive branches flowing from the trunk in all directions. He sat down, his back against the rough bark.

Closing his eyes, he raised his arms, palms up. He imagined himself as the tree was, rooted to the Earth but reaching skyward to touch Heaven and, for a moment, he did. "Father God, I pray to you to end my desire for Farnham's gold. I don't know if it was wrong to search for it in the first place, but I am stopping now. My…my quest is over. The knight returns to his humble castle empty-handed. Amen."

He opened his mist-filled eyes and sat watching a hawk soar overhead. Suddenly, the tree warmed against his back. He leaped up and turned to gaze in disbelief at the trunk, which had become shrouded in a golden glow. He watched in awed silence as the glow brightened and then slowly disappeared. He stared at the tree for a moment, attempting to make sense of what he had seen. Suddenly, he turned, ran to the tool shed, and picked up his chain saw and splitting maul.

He was just finishing the first cut at the base of the tree when he noticed Janelle, hands on hips, standing on the porch. He shut the saw off. "Stay on the porch, Janelle, until I drop this tree!"

She threw both arms up. "What in the world are you doing, Jeremy? Why are you cutting that tree down?"

"You'll see! Just stay there!"

He turned and sawed until the old white oak crashed to the ground. He waved at her. "Come on over! It's safe now!"

They stood together and stared at the fallen tree. "It's hollow, Jeremy!" She bent down and looked inside. "There's a box in there, wedged inside the tree!

He looked. "Sure is!" He cut off a section and split it open with the maul. The box fell onto the grass, spilling gold coins.

He knelt and picked up a coin. "Farnham's gold! Call Cassandra! We're coming to visit!"

TO EVERYTHING THERE IS A SEASON

She ran down the street, glancing furtively behind her. She had gained some distance between herself and her pursuers but they were still following. She darted down an alley, stumbling over trash cans as she ran. Emerging from the alley into a parking lot, she saw the riverside park ahead. She was close, very close, to safety.

She sprinted across the parking lot and half-ran, half-fell down the embankment on the other side, bruising her exposed legs on the hillside's jutting rocks. Limping to the edge of the river, she removed the branches that she had hastily thrown over the skiff earlier in the day. Shrugging off her backpack, she tossed it into the skiff, and pushed off. Jumping into the boat, she started the motor, and headed downstream.

Angry shouts from the shore behind her echoed down the stream. Tossing her head back, she laughed, relief flooding her adrenaline-soaked body. She had entered the very belly of the beast and had, once again, emerged unscathed. She patted the backpack. "To the victor, belongs the spoils of war."

Two hours later, she reached the creek, a small tributary of the river, and angled the skiff up it. Two miles up creek, she turned the motor off, grounded the skiff, and slipped the precious backpack on. Carefully covering the skiff with tree branches, she made her way up the wooded hill to the small log cabin. She stood back out of sight while carefully surveying the cabin and the surrounding area. Her practiced eye could discern nothing out of place.

She pulled her pistol from her shoulder holster and held it in front of her in the low ready position, angling from tree to tree as she approached the cabin. Reaching the porch, she climbed the steps, carefully opened the door, and stepped in. The sun was setting but there was still enough light remaining to illuminate the cabin's interior. The main room of the cabin was empty; she opened the door to the bathroom and found it empty as well.

She set the gun down on the table, locked the door, and checked the window locks. The cabin was secure. If anyone approached the cabin during the night, her jury-rigged concertina in the woods around the cabin would alert her.

She glanced in the mirror beside the door. Her mirror image suggested a trim African-American woman of 30 years of age with jet-black hair, cropped short. She picked up an old comb and ran it through her hair. She laughed at her private vanity and tossed the comb on the table.

She sat down in the old blue recliner, one of the very few pieces of furniture in the cabin. Opening her backpack, she carefully removed each precious item. The first was a box of kitchen matches, worth its weight in gold. A package of iodized salt was soon followed by half-dozen bars of soap and five pounds of sugar. She smiled as she pulled out the real treasure, a small case of chocolate bars.

She stood, crossed to the old stone fireplace, and built a small fire from dry, bark-free wood. Years ago, she had discovered that smoke from such wood would be limited and she had rebuilt the chimney so that the smoke exited through the tops of trees, further dissipating the smoke. She didn't want to advertise her presence any more than was absolutely necessary.

She sat by the fire in an old wooden rocking chair and chewed on venison jerky while gazing into the flames, her thoughts drifting back to her childhood. It had been a different world then, one full of love and excitement. She and her parents had lived in the City, surrounded by family and friends.

She picked up the worn bible that rested on the hearth and turned to one of her favorite verses, Ecclesiastes 3:8: "A time to love, and a time to hate; a time of war, and a time of peace." Her childhood had been the "time to love," but it was long gone. Her parents had been Christians before The Troubles began, the "time to hate" of Ecclesiastes. Her parents, along with many other Christians, had been persecuted and then, as time went on, imprisoned.

Orphaned at an early age, she had escaped the city's horrors and had fled to the woods, leaving behind civilization and its accoutrements. The last memory she had of television was a scene from a news program showing a Christian internment center with hundreds of emaciated prisoners staring morosely at the video camera. One young woman had held a crudely made cardboard sign that declared "I am Unto Death a Christian."

The tears flowed then, cascading down her cheeks as the memory of her beloved parents seared her soul. She slipped out of the chair and knelt on the floor in front of the blazing fire. "God, Lord of All, blessed be thy name. I call upon you in my time of need. Give me strength for the season to come. Amen."

She rose, wiped the tears from her face, and opened her notebook. She gazed thoughtfully at the hand-drawn map of the City. Picking up a pencil, she scribbled underneath the map "a time of war."

Two weeks later, she sat on a bench across the street from the glass and steel office building. Across the building's side, in crimson letters, were the words "Department of Internal Pacification-Central Region." Without bowing her head or closing her eyes, she offered up a small prayer for success and for forgiveness for what she was about to do. Taking a deep breath, she started to rise when a young man sat down beside her.

He was about her own age, she guessed, with short brown hair and a friendly face. "Don't do it. You wouldn't get past the front entrance," he said without looking at her.

She turned to him in surprise. "What are you talking about?" It was the first words that she had spoken to another human in months.

"We can't talk here. Meet me in the park by your boat at the picnic tables in one hour." Without so much as a glance at her, he stood and walked away.

She sat in silence as she pondered his words. With a shake of her head, she stood and headed toward the park. She approached the picnic tables, chose one at random, and sat down. She glanced around. No one was around.

An hour later, the man approached, and sat across the table from her. "You had good intentions, I'm sure, but you would have accomplished nothing more than getting yourself killed."

She leaned forward. "Who are you? What exactly did you think I was going to do?"

He laughed. "I'll answer the second question first. You were going to enter the DIP headquarters and shoot as many of them as you could. Don't worry; I'm not a DIP operative. If I were, you would be dead already."

"Fair enough," she replied, "So if you aren't a Pacification agent, then who are you, and how did you know what I was going to do?"

He smiled. "I'm a member of the Christian Underground and we have been keeping an eye on you. We decided that it was time to recruit you."

"Recruit me for what?"

"Asymmetric warfare."

"What's that?"

"It's when a resistance movement, that's us, fights a much larger entrenched military, that's the Pacification Department."

She smiled. "There's a Christian resistance? Tell me more!"

He laughed. "I knew I was right about you. The CR has been growing for years, all over the country. We have a covert training center not far from the City. If you are willing to go with me, we can train you. You've got nothing to lose and everything to gain. What do you say?"

She nodded. "I'm in. When do we leave?"

"Right now. My SUV is parked not far from here. It's a few hours drive to the training camp and I've already picked up some sandwiches for us to eat on the way."

She laughed. "You seem pretty sure that I was going to join up."

He nodded. "I'm rarely wrong about my recruits. There was one though….but that's a story for another day. Let's go."

They walked to the SUV, got in, and drove away. She glanced in the rear view mirror, mentally saying goodbye to the City. Heading southwest, the City receding in the distance, she took a bite of a sandwich and wondered what the future would hold.

DENOUEMENT

Standing on the porch, he gazed down the valley, appreciating its natural beauty for the last time. He had sold the rustic cabin only two days earlier; his neighbor would be arriving in a few hours to help remove the remaining furniture. He sighed, turned, and stepped inside. Glancing around, his eyes rested upon a portrait of himself with Joanne, his beloved wife of forty-two years. The photographer had captured her essence in a single snapshot; beautiful, kind-hearted, and cheerful; the image of her mere weeks before the devastating diagnosis of pancreatic cancer.

Tears threatening to burst forth, he turned to the task of building a fire in the stone fireplace; more to occupy his mind than to warm the chilled cabin. He sat beside the fire in his wing-back chair, carefully adding pieces of split red oak as the flames grew. A lifetime of memories flashed through his mind; a mental mosaic built from decades of love, laughter, joy, sorrow, and pain.

He had gifted her with the cabin on their thirtieth anniversary, and they had stayed in it nearly every weekend for years. She had loved the weekly ritual of trading the hustle and bustle of the city for the solitude of the cabin.

He glanced at the unoccupied wooden rocking chair by the door as a wave of sadness and loneliness washed over him. They had sat fireside, Joanne in the rocker, he in his wing-back, on countless nights, reminiscing about the past; smooth jazz playing on the stereo. She had loved to dance; he, not so much; but after a glass or two of wine, she was able to pull him from his chair. His hand on her back, her hand on his shoulder, their free hands entwined; they swayed back and forth in time to the slow, sensual music. He remembered how she looked; eyes closed, lips slightly parted, her face flushed.

He stood, walked to the stereo, selected a jazz CD, and slid it into the player. Stepping to the refrigerator, he selected a bottle of Riesling, Joanne's favorite. He retrieved two wine glasses from the cupboard, poured wine into one, made his way to the rocking chair, and pulled it next to the fireplace. Stepping over to the couch, he picked up a large, white teddy bear, carried it to the rocking chair, and gently placed it in the seat. He nestled the second wine glass against the bear, and returned to the wing-back. Grasping one arm of the wooden chair, he gently rocked it.

He raised his glass to the teddy bear. "To you, Joanne, the love of my life." Gazing into the flames, he sipped the wine as smooth jazz notes filled the cabin. He finished the glass and set it upon the hearth, a slight smile playing across his face. He stood, turned to the rocking chair, and extended his hand. "May I have the honor of this dance, madam?" The snow-white bear, eyes sparkling, silently gazed back.

He tenderly picked up the bear and moved to the center of the living room. Placing one hand on the bear's back and the other on the bear's silky arm; he waltzed her around the room. Swept away by the soft music, he closed his eyes. "I love you, honey, and I miss you so very, very much."

He opened his eyes as the music ended, the last track finished. He hugged her tightly and then gently placed her in the rocking chair. "Care for another glass of Riesling?" She didn't reply, evidently content with only one glass.

"I know; the second glass makes you sleepy, but I believe that I will have another." He poured himself another glass of wine; sipping occasionally; he studied her. "When will I see you again?" She remained silent.

Sighing, he placed the half-empty glass on the hearth. "When?" He rocked her chair with increasing force. "When?"

The bear slid down in the chair until it was on its back. He followed the bear's upward gaze, which seemed to pierce the cabin's roof as it travelled ever upward. Glancing back down, he picked up the half-full glass of Riesling and studied it. He sipped, enjoying the wine's sweet finish. "Honey, I still have some work left to do here on Earth, but someday, when my glass is finally empty, I will rejoin you, and we will forever dance."

COUNTDOWN

4 YEARS, 6 MONTHS, 3 WEEKS, 6 DAYS, 4 HOURS, 27 MINUTES, 6 SECONDS

The exhausted but joyous mother lay back on the hospital bed as the nurse by her side calmly wiped her perspiring forehead. On the other side of the bed, her husband sat while quietly holding her hand. A second nurse gently handed the newborn baby to the radiant mother.

"Our gift from God!" the mother exclaimed to her husband.

He smiled and nodded, tears of joy welling up in his eyes. He gently kissed the baby's forehead and then his wife's as well. "Soon we will take him home and together, we will be a family."

34 YEARS, 4 MONTHS, 2 WEEKS, 3 DAYS, 16 HOURS, 49 MINUTES, 32 SECONDS

"I don't want to go to church!" the little boy complained once again to his parents. "Do I have to go *every* week?"

His father sighed. "Yes, son, we are going to church. But you don't have to go to church; you get to go to church. In many countries, people are not allowed to go to church; they would be put into jail for worshiping Jesus!"

The boy's mother nodded. "We go to church to worship the Lord. We want you to grow up in God's House."

24 YEARS, 2 MONTHS, 1 WEEK, 5 DAYS, 21 HOURS, 38 MINUTES, 16 SECONDS

College at last. He unpacked his bags as soon as he entered his new dorm room. He pulled out the last item, a Bible his parents had hidden underneath his clothes. He considered opening it but instead shrugged and tossed it into the trash can.

20 YEARS, 7 MONTHS, 3 WEEKS, 17 DAYS, 18 HOURS, 5 MINUTES, 11 SECONDS

He arrived home exhausted from work as usual. He had just stepped into his apartment when the phone rang. His parents again, once more begging him to find a church to attend. He managed to hang up before bursting into laughter.

5 YEARS, 9 MONTHS, 2 WEEKS, 28 DAYS, 11 HOURS, 44 MINUTES, 59 SECONDS

He left her apartment at 2 am. He drove back to his house, quietly unlocked the door, and tiptoed down the hall to the bedroom. Carefully, he slipped under the covers beside his sleeping wife. He smiled into the darkness as the darkness smiled back.

2 YEARS, 1 MONTH, 1 WEEK, 13 DAYS, 5 HOURS, 23 MINUTES, 42 SECONDS

He awoke and glanced at the clock. 10:35 a.m. *So much for the time; what day is it? Oh, yeah, Sunday. Great!* He didn't have to get up. Maybe his wife would fix some breakfast. Wait. She wasn't around anymore. When had she left? Oh, yeah. Two months ago? No: three. He rolled over and noticed a half-empty bottle on the nightstand. *Good; breakfast is served.*

0 YEARS, 8 MONTHS, 2 WEEKS, 5 DAYS, 4 HOURS, 16 MINUTES, 13 SECONDS.

"Mother, for the last time, I will not find a church to attend. C'mon, you have to know that God doesn't really exist! No one believes that crap anymore! Yes, I will come and visit you and Dad. No, I don't know when, maybe when I get back from my assignment in Seoul. No, Mother, Seoul, not soul, as in Seoul, South Korea. I don't know how long I will be there for sure; probably several months. It's a big job. I've got to go and catch my flight. Bye."

0 YEARS, 0 MONTHS, 0 WEEKS, 0 DAYS, 1 HOUR, 9 MINUTES, 21 SECONDS

He hated to ride in coach but there had been no business class seats on the flight from Seoul back to LAX. He had enjoyed his stay. Those Koreans really knew how to party, but he was looking forward to being home soon. *I might actually go visit my parents.*

The guy seated beside him was still talking. Still. Talking. "You said that you haven't accepted Christ as your savior. You really should think about it, you know. My friend, how about now?"

He turned to his tormentor. "Listen, I am not your friend, and I really don't believe in God. End of story. Stop badgering me."

The man shut up, but only for a moment. "Please consider what I have said. The simple truth is this: God *does* exist, Heaven and hell are real, and life is very, very short."

0 YEARS, 0 MONTHS, 0 WEEKS, 0 DAYS, 0 HOURS, 5 MINUTES, 10 SECONDS

"Mayday, mayday, this is Asian Aerospace Flight AL10. We have flameouts in two...oh no... make that three engines...we are going down..."

0 YEARS, 0 MONTHS, 0 WEEKS, 0 DAYS, 0 HOURS, 1 MINUTE, 3 SECONDS

His seatmate grabbed him. Over the screams of the other passengers, he heard his final plea: "Accept Christ into your heart, now! There's still time! Repeat after me: 'Jesus, I believe that you died on the cross to atone for our sins. I accept you as my Lord and Savior...'"

Terrified, he wrenched away from the man, away from the words, and turned to watch out the window as the Pacific Ocean rushed up to meet them...

0 YEARS, 0 MONTHS, 0 WEEKS, 0 DAYS, 0 HOURS, 0 MINUTES, 0 SECONDS

THE BALCONY

George Wright, a tall fifty-something man with black hair peppered with grey, sat quietly in the church balcony, staring down at the sanctuary floor below him. He preferred attending the church's first service; the attendees tended to be older and quieter, much like himself. He sat alone in the balcony, quiet and withdrawn into his own thoughts. The service had begun and the praise and worship band had kicked into high gear. Unlike the worshipers below him, he wasn't moved at all by the music. It wasn't that the music wasn't good: it was. At one time, he had enjoyed the music immensely, but no longer.

Once again, he wondered why he was there: why he even bothered coming. Once he had enjoyed it, even looking forward to it throughout the week. But that was then and this, well, was now.

The song service finished and he, along with those who were below, sat down. The minister arrived on the stage and began sharing prayer requests for the week. George bowed his head and closed his eyes, but he wasn't praying.

Instead, he saw...*her*-- just as he had last seen her: unmoving and lifeless in the cold grey coffin, just before the lid had closed on the only part of his life that really mattered, shutting his wife and his emotions inside a steel case for all of eternity.

Tears came unbidden to his tired eyes. He quickly wiped them, thankful prayer time had ended. The minister began to preach a sermon on the resurrection; Easter was fast approaching. The casual observer would have thought George to be listening intently; but that observer would have been wrong. Once again, his mind had slipped back into the past to that dreadful day in which his beloved wife of thirty years had died. He was, in his mind's eye, sitting in the emergency room waiting room, accompanied by a few friends, waiting for word about her.

66

He had looked up as the ER physician came into the waiting room. The look on her face told him the only thing he needed to know. He had sobbed uncontrollably, his friends trying to console him. His faith withered as his wife had passed away in the cold sterility of that ER.

He had seen the man who had killed her, the man who had run a stop sign on a country road and slammed into her car broadside. The man had spilled a cup of coffee and, his attention diverted, had spilled his wife's blood onto the highway.

His anger, once again, threatened to boil over. It had been months since his wife had died but the anger had never really subsided. He had tried to control it, but to no avail. His church had offered counseling through the Stephen Ministry program but he had turned it down. Once, what seemed like long ago, the minister's sermon would have moved him. The thought that Easter was fast approaching, his wife's second favorite holiday, would have brought a smile to his face, but; no longer. Instead, it fueled his anger; not just his anger toward Overton, the man who had killed his wife, but toward God. *Why would God have allowed his beloved wife, who loved God more than anything, to be so cruelly and casually killed? Why did He allow her killer to remain alive, calmly walking upon the face of the Earth? "Why?"*

He realized that he had spoken out loud. He glanced around the balcony. The handful of others around him carefully avoided looking at him.

The tray bearer approached with the communion trays. Mechanically, he drank a cup of juice and swallowed a cracker. The bearer smiled at him and whispered, "God be with you, George."

He nodded in return, devoid of emotion. That weekly ritual performed, he pulled a few small bills from his billfold and waited for the plate to be passed. When the two-handled bag was offered to him, he contemptuously tossed the bills inside. With a sad shake of his head, the bag bearer continued on across the balcony.

The service ended; he walked quickly down the balcony stairs and out onto the parking lot. He opened the door to his pickup, glanced toward the church, and froze; Jesse Overton walked out the side door of the church, got into a minivan, and drove away.

What was he doing here? He never went to this church before! This was her church, not his! How dare he come here?

The drive home was nothing but a blur. He didn't see the highway; he saw *him*. He saw his wife lying in an ER bed.

All that week, while awake, he saw *him*. Even at night, while asleep, he saw...*him*. He had only met the man once. Several weeks after the accident, Overton had come to his house, to apologize for what he had done. George had told him to go to hell and slammed the door in his face.

He planned all week for the upcoming Sunday morning service. He would find Overton and tell him that in no uncertain terms would he be allowed to come to *her* church. He would make sure that her killer would never darken the door of the church again.

When Sunday finally came, he looked around the church for Overton before going up into the balcony, but he didn't see him. He climbed the steep steps to the balcony and settled himself in one of the chairs nearest the edge. The sanctuary was beginning to fill for the first service as he carefully scanned the audience.

He saw him then. Overton was seated on the right side of the sanctuary three rows back from the front. No one was seated beside him. *Perfect,* he thought.

He walked down the stairs and across the sanctuary. He slipped into the seat beside Overton, who glanced up in surprise. When he saw who it was, Overton froze. He opened his mouth, but no sounds emerged.

"Remember me?" George asked with a mocking smile.

"Please, I don't want any trouble. I just wanted…needed to come to church," Overton replied, tears welling up in his eyes.

"I don't care what you want, or need, for that matter. What I want is for you to leave this church. This isn't your church, this is my church. More importantly, it was *her* church!"

Jesse shook his head. "No, I am not leaving. A church belongs to God, not to people. Look, I know how you must feel, but I didn't mean to hit your wife's car. It wasn't like I was drunk or high; it was an accident. I will have to live with that for the rest of my life! I tried to apologize to you but you slammed the door in my face! What do you want from me? Why don't you just leave me alone?"

George exploded. "Leave you alone? You killed my wife! You may have to live with it, but I have to live without *her* for the rest of my life! You killed me as well as her that day!"

"I'm sorry," Jesse sobbed. "That's all I can say and that's all I can do."

"That's not enough," George rasped. "You can do something; you can stay out of this church."

"No, I…I can't. I have no place to go. You aren't the only one that was affected by the accident. I started drinking…I couldn't deal with the guilt. A month ago, my wife left me; she couldn't take my drinking anymore, said she might come back if I sobered up. I had no one to turn to, so I came here."

George stood. "You've been warned."

He stomped back up to the balcony and sat down. Throughout the service, he stared menacingly down at an unmoving and isolated Jesse. The two men sat, one below in the sanctuary, the other above in the balcony, each lost in his thoughts. Both were alone, both suffering.

Throughout the next week, George thought more and more about Jesse. He found, to his surprise, that his hatred of him had diminished considerably. *I am not the only one who suffered loss.* Until last Sunday, he had never thought about how the accident had affected Jesse Overton. With a start, he realized that it was the first time that he had thought about what had happened as an accident. Shame washed over him. George bowed his head and prayed. He prayed for strength, for healing, and for forgiveness. After praying, he picked up the phone and called the church. "Hello, this is George Wright. Would it be possible for a Stephen Minister to be assigned to me?"

The next Sunday was Easter Sunday and George Wright was not in the balcony. He sat near the back of the sanctuary, watching and waiting. Jesse Overton walked in and, with shoulders slumped, made his way to the second row, where he sat down.

George stood and walked to him. "Jesse, may I sit next to you?"

Astonished, Jesse looked up. "George? I…I guess so."

George sat. "I really miss her, you know, my wife…Olivia." He realized he hadn't said her name out loud for months. "We were married for thirty years. She was a florist. She made such beautiful arrangements. She…Olivia, was a great lady." He turned to Jesse. "What is your wife like?"

Jesse, eyes locked on the stage in front of him, replied, "She teaches English at the community college. We've been married for ten years. I can't stand living without her…" He trailed off into silence.

George took a deep breath. "Jesse, I'm sorry. I never thought about how the accident affected you. I guess I really wasn't doing much thinking of any kind. That's all I wanted to say; I will leave you alone now." He stood.

Jesse turned toward him. "Looks like we both need forgiveness. Why don't you sit down and we can ask Him together."

With tears in his eyes, George nodded gratefully and sat down.

The Easter Service was beautiful and George sang along with the worship service. At the end of the service, the minister made the traditional call to Christ and, being Easter Sunday, many went to kneel before the old wooden cross that stood at the front of the sanctuary, some for the very first time, some to rededicate themselves.

George stood, walked to the cross, and kneeled. To his surprise, Jesse kneeled beside him as he asked Jesus for forgiveness, for strength, and for healing. George felt an arm lift him up. Surprised, he turned to Jesse. "Thank you Jesse. With my bad back I was a little worried about getting back up."

Jesse shook his head. "I didn't help you back up. In fact, I was just getting ready to thank you for helping me stand." The two looked around them. They were the last two at the cross; no one was near them.

"I know that someone lifted me up, "Jesse replied, glancing around, "If it wasn't you, then who was it?"

"I think I know," George replied as he turned his gaze to the cross.

THE GIFT

The little boy walked slowly along the muddy path that served as a street in his village. The path weaved in and out between the small stone houses and shops of his neighbors. The village was tiny; only a few hundred people called it home. Normally the streets would be nearly deserted at that hour but on that night, village streets were crowded. Emperor Augustus, the hated ruler of the Roman Empire, had decreed that a census of the people of Judea was to be taken. Quirinius, the governor of Syria and Judea, had been ordered to carry out the census. In order to be counted, all people of Judea had to return to the towns of their births.

The little boy had never seen the village so full of people. They came from all over Judea, from near and far. Most of the men, women, and children walked but some of the women were fortunate enough to be riding on donkeys. They were a quiet and somber group, exhausted by their long journeys. All were seeking shelter for the night.

He zigged and zagged his way through the river of people until, finally, his home was in sight. He struggled to cross to the other side of the path, nearly falling as he made his way through the mud churned by the stream of people. He had almost made it to the other side when he slipped in the mud and fell onto his backside in the street.

A young bearded man, leading a donkey with a smiling mother-to-be riding on its back, stopped and raised the boy out of the muck. The kindly man smothered a laugh as he brushed mud from the boy's clothing.

"Are you hurt, boy?" he asked with a smile.

"Only a little," the boy replied as he rubbed his elbow.

The woman smiled warmly down at him. "Be careful, little one!"

The little boy waved cheerfully to the two, turned, and made his way to the small stone house that he, his mother, and his father called home.

71

He entered. A cheery fire blazed, casting a mellow yellow glow upon the home's interior. The smell of mutton stew, a rarity in his poor home, made his mouth water. His mother, placing the stew on the table, looked up as he came in. "Ah, Seth, you are home! Come, come, and wash up. Dinner is ready!"

Seth washed his face and hands and sat down at the small, rough-hewn wooden table. The door opened again, and his father walked in.

"Mama, Seth, I am home! Work is done and I am ready to eat. Mutton stew: it smells delicious. God is so good to us!" After washing, he sat down across the table from his son.

She placed a small loaf of bread on the table and sat down beside her husband. All three bowed their heads as the father began to pray. "Blessed are you, Lord God who has sanctified us with your commandments. We give thanks to you for the food for which we are about to eat. Amen."

Dinner completed, the family sat around the fire. "I heard today," the father began, "that every room in town is full. The inn is completely full and every spare room in town is filled with guests. Many are sleeping outside and some, I was told, are even in stables."

The mother nodded. "Our little village is overflowing with people. I have prayed many times today that God will be with them all. There are so many!"

The door suddenly opened. Startled, the three turned to see an older man at the door. "He is here! The Messiah has been born! Come with me to the stable near the inn. Come! Angels have told shepherd boys that our Messiah has been born tonight, here, in Bethlehem. A baby, the baby has been born in a manger. Bring gifts for the baby!"

Before the stunned family could react, the man shut the door and was gone. The mother was the first to speak. "Husband, could this be true?"

"I don't know," he replied, "but we are going to see for ourselves!" He glanced around their simple home for something that would serve as a gift. He turned to his wife with a questioning look.

"I finished sewing a blanket yesterday," his wife began. "It is the only thing we have to give, the only thing that we have to lay before a king, to honor him." She picked up the blanket, folded it carefully, and walked to the door.

Seth did not move from his place beside the fire. He stared morosely at the flames. His father gently squeezed his son's shoulder. "What troubles you, my son?"

Seth, tears flowing down his cheeks, looked up at his father. "Father, I want to give the baby a gift of my own, but I have nothing to give."

"Seth, the blanket will be a gift from all of us."

"But Father," Seth replied, "I want to give a gift that is just from me. Is that being selfish, Father?"

"No, Seth, it is certainly not selfish. You have a generous heart. But I know of nothing that you could give." He glanced helplessly at his wife.

Winking at her husband, she opened a cabinet and pulled out a package carefully wrapped in a purple cloth. She handed it to him with a smile. Joyously, he hugged her. "Have I told you that you are very clever woman?"

She laughed merrily. "Not nearly enough, husband of mine."

He turned to Seth and held out the package to him. Seth wiped the tears from his eyes and reverently took it. He gazed quizzically at his mother and father and then, with dawning comprehension, Seth smiled.

Hand in hand, the three made their way to the inn. They quickly located the stable in back and, upon entering, found it filled with people, gazing quietly at one manger, which glowed with a soft yellow light.

"Father, I can't see the baby!" Seth cried out.

The men and women in front of Seth turned at his proclamation, smiling down at him, and parted. As Seth approached the manger, he came face-to-face with the man who had so kindly rescued him from the muddy street. Kneeling beside him was his wife, her face radiant. She held a baby, wrapped in swaddling clothes. He was the most beautiful baby that Seth had ever seen.

Seth's heart was filled with joy. He glanced shyly around at the others. Carefully, he unwrapped the package that he carried. Surprised, the on-lookers saw that it was a small frame drum.

"Shall I play for you?" Seth asked, his voice cracking with emotion.

Mary, with a small smile, nodded. Seth began to play his drum.

Seth's heart leaped with joy as he played his little drum. He had something to give after all; he gave his music, the love of his life. Smiling, the baby listened...

THE BUSINESS OF PRAYER

She stood and leaned over the smoked-glass top of the board room conference table, the skyline of London visible through the large window behind
her. At 38, Jessica Stansberry was young to be the CEO of a major corpo-
ration, but thanks in part to her technical knowledge and business acumen, she
had made it. She had shattered the glass ceiling.

She looked at each of the members of the board. Bruce Marveton, the
Chairman of the Board, sat to her right, smiling as he awaited her usual glowing
update of the firm's activities. The other directors' expressions were carefully
neutral.

Jessica knew only too well that what she was about to say to this august
group would either ignite a firestorm in the world of British business or would
result in the end of her career with Cain, Ltd.

Three years ago, she had started attending a church near her Paddington
flat. Her faith had grown and strengthened over the years. She had, for a time,
managed to keep the secular business Jessica separate from the spiritual Jessica, but the wall between the two soon came tumbling down. She found that
her drive to reach the top was no longer about herself. It was about making a
difference; she would use her position within the firm to steer it in the direction
that, she thought, would please God.

"Before I begin with the highlights of the third quarter's results, I would
like to announce a new financial direction that I want Cain, Ltd. to take. Beginning on January 1, 2016, we will give ten percent of our pre-tax income to the
church. I have not come to this conclusion lightly; I have prayed for months
and I have thought long and hard about this decision and I know in my heart
that it is the correct one."

Jessica paused and glanced around the table at the six stunned directors,
her heart hammering in her chest. Bruce, the only other Christian of the group,

recovered first. "Jessica, as a Christian, I share your sentiments, but as a businessman, I cannot agree with the application. Tithing is a personal choice, not a corporate one."

Dismayed, Jessica studied the other five directors. As she had suspected, all were nodding in agreement with Bruce. She turned back to him. He was the one she had to convince; the others would fall in line.

"Bruce," Jessica began, "in my opinion, tithing is not limited to individuals. Organizations, as you well know, are treated politically, economically, and legally very much like individuals. Why should they not tithe?"

Bruce studied her for a moment before replying. "Jessica, the question is not why should businesses not tithe but rather why should they? Why should Cain, Ltd. give up ten percent of its hard-earned profit? Other than to please God, why should we?"

Jessica pulled out a slim leather Bible from her valise and opened it. "I want to make sure that I get this exactly right- let's see, yes, it's in Malachi chapter 3, verse ten: -'Bring ye all the tithes into the storehouse, that there may be meat in mine house, and prove me now herewith, saith the Lord of hosts, if I will not open you the windows of heaven, and pour you out a blessing, that there shall not be room enough to receive it.'" She closed the Bible. "That is why, if you want to look at it from a financial viewpoint. Not only is it the right thing to do, but God will bless us for it."

Bruce doodled on the yellow pad on the table in front of him. He looked up. "My understanding is that the Exchequer will allow the deduction of donations to charities. It would decrease our pre-tax income, resulting in lower taxes."

Jessica nodded. "It would indeed. In effect, if we donate ten percent, the tax savings would result in a net effect on the bottom line of considerably less than that, especially if it placed us in a lower tax bracket."

For the next hour, Jessica and the directors pored over spreadsheets. Every conceivable effect tithing would have on the firm was scrutinized. In the end, Jessica was disappointed; no consensus was reached.

Bruce sighed. "In any case, this is not something that has to be implemented now. We have until January to hash this out. I move that we shelve discussion of the issue until our next meeting in November." The director to Jessica's left seconded the motion and Jessica reluctantly continued with more mundane issues.

The following Saturday, Alex and Bernice, her brother and sister-in-law, dropped off Daphne, Jessica's twelve year old niece, for a weekend holiday. Jessica had promised to take her to the fictional home of the great detective Sherlock Holmes, currently a museum. Jessica and Daphne walked to the Paddington tube station and boarded a train on the Bakerloo line. A few stops later, followed by a cheery walk, the two found themselves at 221B Baker Street.

Daphne loved the authentic reproduction of Holmes and Dr. Watson's abode; she had already read virtually every short story by Arthur Conan Doyle. As Daphne cheerfully explored the museum, Jessica's thoughts returned to her recent meeting with the board. Lost in thought, Jessica suddenly realized that Daphne had just asked her a question.

"I'm sorry, Daphne," Jessica replied sheepishly. "What did you say?"

"You seemed to be fascinated with something and I don't think it is Dr. Watson's medical bag!"

Jessica laughed. "I guess I was. I was thinking about my company and how I want it to be blessed by God." Jessica explained her concerns to her extremely bright niece.

"You know, Auntie, you have a mystery on your hands, you know, just like Sherlock Holmes." She picked up a deerstalker hat and a pipe from the souvenir rack, placed the hat carefully on her head, and puffed away at the pipe. Daphne looked thoughtful for a moment. "Elementary, Auntie, Elementary. You can pray!"

With tears in her eyes, Jessica gently hugged her niece. "Love you, Sherlock. Now how can I compensate you for your wise advice?"

With a twinkle in her eye, Daphne replied, "Let's start with this hat and pipe. Oh, and I do believe that we should pick up a Paddington bear at the tube station."

One month later, when Jessica found herself facing the directors again, she was ready. The chairman spoke first. "So Jessica, what is the solution?"

Jessica smiled confidently. "Would all of you join me in prayer?"

The board members looked at her in surprise. They glanced at each other, shrugged, and, one by one, they bowed their heads…

Years later, Daphne stood and leaned over the smoked-glass top of the board room conference table, the London skyline visible through the large window behind her. At 32, she was the youngest CEO in the history of the company. She glanced at the excited faces of the six directors, finally stopping at the Chair.

Jessica leaned back in her chair. "It's your show Daphne; tell them."

Daphne waved a hand and a holographic image of an orbiting space station materialized above the table. "May I present our latest endeavor, our first orbital zero gravity manufacturing facility. Since we began tithing, our company's growth has exceeded ten percent each year. Thanks to God's grace, we will be positioned to expand our business beyond Earth…"

THE JOURNEY

It was time for Journey again- Journey to Bethlehem that is- the annual Christmas event that the little church in the Ozarks puts on. To many in the area, "Journey," as it is affectionately known, is the official start of the Christmas season. It certainly is for my family. A number of my relatives and friends had been involved with the performance since it began over ten years ago.

The outdoor Nativity adventure has three performances over the first weekend in December, on Thursday, Friday, and Saturday nights. Last year, my wife Jerusha and I went on the final night of Journey for the year, and probably the busiest, which some folks didn't like but we sure did. We loved seeing the crowds of people flock in from all over Missouri, Kansas, Oklahoma, and Arkansas. The more the merrier I always say, although some of my friends roll their eyes.

We arrived a little before the doors opened at 6 p.m. There was already a long line of people on the sidewalk in front of the modern single story church. The sun had already set and we could see the lights of the campfires to the west out on the Journey trail. The sweet smell of campfire smoke drifted over to us. Ah, the sights and sounds and smells of Journey!

We finally made it to the front door of the church, and slowly but surely, meandered into the sanctuary. The appearance of the church, both inside and out, surprised many. Despite being out in the boonies, it was quite nice.

While we waited our turn to go out onto the trail, we were entertained by a pre-Journey show, consisting of live entertainment. The band was quite good and the singing reminded us of performances that we had seen in Branson. Not bad for a free event: and there would be cookies and hot chocolate after we had walked the Journey trail.

As we waited, Jerusha and I observed the people around us; twenty to

77

thirty of these worthy souls would accompany us upon our Journey to Bethlehem out on the trail. In the row of seats in front of us, a husband and wife sat quietly talking. From what I gathered from, ahem, discreetly overhearing their conversation, he was not happy about something. I leaned forward slightly to hear, and I quote "...being dragged to the middle of nowhere to walk around outside when the temperature is 25 degrees when I could be home with a nice bottle of Jack and watching *The Guns of Navarone* on TCM." His wife, evidently accustomed to retorts like this, merely snorted and turned her attention back to the stage.

Jerusha sat to my right, which, come to think of it, was the way we sat in church, or anywhere else for that matter. Why was that? On the other side of Jerusha was a forty- something mother with her teen-aged son. He was busy; let's see if you can guess. Yes, that's right, alternating between texting and playing a game on his iPhone.

"Les," his mother said, "why don't you put your phone away and enjoy the show? It's really good..." She trailed off as he continued to text, both thumbs moving impossibly fast.

Les ignored his mother for a time and continued with his texting. Finally, he answered. "Why should I? It's not like God cares about what I am doing. If He did, he wouldn't have let Dad leave."

Les' mother sat back into her seat and lapsed into silence. Jerusha and I glanced at each other and lowered our heads as we silently prayed for them. When in doubt, pray; that's my motto, or at least one of them.

Finally, the time arrived for our "family," the group of about 25 of us who would venture out into the cold night together, to hit the trail. We were given name scrolls to take along on our journey, "our papers" as I liked to call them, and then we were escorted out into a large tent. We sat around on bales of hay while we waited for our guide couple.

A few minutes later a tall man wearing a robe that would have made Moses proud strode into the tent. He smiled broadly as he glanced at each of us in turn. "Family, you have finally arrived! It is so good to see all of you again! If you do not remember me, I am Jeremiah, and my wife Ruth and I will accompany you to Bethlehem. Our humble home is just a short walk away. Let's surprise her- she doesn't know that you have arrived!"

His enthusiasm was infectious and we quickly followed him out of the tent and down the path to his "home," a small hut off to the side of the path with a cheery campfire out front. We happily gathered around the warm fire while Jeremiah called for Ruth to join him outside. She quickly came out and threw the basket of bread into the air in theatrical surprise. She, like Jeremiah, was quick to greet the family with a very realistic sense of joy.

Jerusha and I had been through the Journey a number of times and all of the guide couples were great actors, but there was something different about these two. It was like they weren't acting; like it was real for them.

We left the guide couple's home and headed down the trail, lit softly by torches planted along the side of the trail. Jerusha and I hung back and brought up the rear of our family group.

As we walked along, we were behind the husband and wife who sat in front of us in the sanctuary. His grumbling had ratcheted up a notch. "I can't believe that I let you talk me into this corny way-off Broadway production. I could be home right now in my Lazyboy enjoying some real acting. You haven't seen acting until you have seen Gregory Peck in *The Guns of Navarone.*"

His wife didn't so much as glance sideways at him. "You have seen that movie a dozen times. This is your first time seeing Journey to Bethlehem. Chill, oh husband of mine."

We arrived at the blacksmith shop next, the last stop in Nazareth before we headed out into the great unknown. Jerusha and I loved each stop along the trail, but we really enjoyed the blacksmith shop, as we knew the family who played the blacksmith and his family.

Jeremiah and Ruth interacted with the performers better than any other guide couple I had ever seen. They even spoke several words of what sounded like Hebrew. The blacksmith and his wife glanced at each other, obviously puzzled. What was going on here? They didn't act like they knew this guide couple. As we moved away from the shop, I glanced back and the entire blacksmith family was watching Jeremiah and Ruth walk away. Curiouser and curiouser.

The next stop was a donkey drawn cart that had supposedly broken down along the trail. The family stopped and Jeremiah asked the man standing beside it if he needed any help. The fellow replied that he did and Jeremiah went about the usual Journey routine of picking out a couple of children in the group to help put a wheel back on.

Ruth came up to the front of the family, shepherding a boy and a girl in front of her. "Here you are, Jeremiah. These two can help you!" The kids were positively beaming. Jeremiah helped them put the wheel on then he knelt down in front of the kids and said something to them. I couldn't make it out. Whatever Jeremiah said lit those kids up like a Christmas tree. I looked over at Jerusha. She was watching the mini drama playing out as well. She glanced at me, shrugged, and buttoned up her coat. It was getting colder. I felt it too.

We continued on down the trail. We were just about to where Roman soldiers on horseback would stop us and demand to see our papers. Suddenly, I felt dizzy and my vision swam. I was glad that I had not eaten dinner yet or the sudden churning in my stomach would have resulted in a very embarrassing moment in front of my newly adopted family.

Jerusha grabbed my shoulder and gasped, "I am going to throw up." She looked pale and shaky in the yellowish light of the torches. "I'm dizzy...I think I need to sit down somewhere for a while."

I quickly agreed with her, but I didn't mention I was feeling the same way. Hey, I am old school. I don't like my wife seeing weakness in me. I looked around for a place to sit down but there wasn't anything until the next campfire. It was then that I noticed Jerusha and I weren't the only ones looking pale and queasy. Everyone was. Just as quickly as it had come, the dizziness and nausea vanished. Jerusha still looked pale, as did the others in our group, but it appeared that the wave of whatever had hit all of us had suddenly left.

"What was that?" yelled the irritated husband to Jeremiah.

"What was what?" Jeremiah replied as he turned back toward us. Nobody said anything; there was complete silence. Jeremiah just smiled and turned back around. "Follow me!" he said, and we continued on our way. A hushed whispering began among our group.

Jerusha linked her arm with my own. "What just happened? Whatever hit us affected all of us and then just...left. I have never seen anything like that!"

I shook my head. "I have no idea what happened."

We reached the Roman crossroad checkpoint. Two Roman soldiers on foot and one on horseback stopped us and asked for our papers. These guys were always very realistic and, I will have to admit, were slightly intimidating, something I would never admit to Jerusha. They began their usual spiel, but at the beginning, I could swear the soldier on horseback began his speech in Latin. Great- first group dizziness and now I was having auditory hallucinations.

Jeremiah whispered something to the Roman, who looked down upon him with a look of what? Respect? Fear?

We continued on to the next station: the camping family. That's when I realized that we were no longer on the Journey path. The wood shaving path lined with torches was gone and in its place was a path through a desert. A desert? Was I losing my mind?

I turned toward Jerusha; she looked as lost as I did.

Jeremiah's next words would probably be the strangest that I would ever hear in my life. "Welcome, family, to Bethlehem. Your journey is almost at an end. Soon you will see Him, our lord and savior, Jesus of Nazareth. You are going to see the birth of the Christ child. This is the real Journey to Bethlehem."

We were, needless to stay, stunned into complete silence. As we looked around, we realized that it was true; we were there. We stood behind a group of shepherds as they looked upon a baby lying in a manger. Joseph stood nearby while Mary cradled the baby.

The disgruntled husband sunk to his knees and stared in rapture at the baby Jesus. Tears ran down his cheeks as he mumbled over and over, "I didn't know, I didn't know, I didn't know..."

Les led his mother by the hand to the manger; kneeling, they bowed their heads in silence, as tears cascaded down their cheeks.

The Journey over, we walked out of the tent and found ourselves back on the church's parking lot. Jerusha and I never saw Jeremiah and Ruth again; we did see Les, his mother, and the Gregory Peck fan and his wife quite often; all sitting in the front row at church.

POWER

.

The four men walked, at Monday morning speed, through the Braxton Silver Mine's check-in gate. The thirty-something men, friends since high school, had worked at the southern Idaho mine for nearly a decade. Isaac grinned at his fellow miners. "Monday morning is finally here, guys! I don't know about you, but I thought that weekend would never end! I just couldn't wait to get back underground!"

Nathan laughed. "Yeah, right, bro'. I bet you just hated leaving your live-in girlfriend behind. What's this one's name? Beth? Beatrice? Bathsheba?"

Aaron joined in. "I don't think Isaac stays with any one woman long enough to learn her name!"

Paul glanced at the others, rolled his eyes, and trudged onward.

They entered the cavernous mine portal and walked down the Decline, the wide ramp that spiraled down into the mine, flanking the rich vein of silver ore. Just inside the entrance, they boarded a small electric tram and descended into the mine's depths. Just over 500 feet below the surface, the tram stopped, and the men slowly stepped out to begin yet another exhausting week.

The mine, in production sporadically since 1952, was undergoing an infrastructure upgrade. During the previous five years, the mine's current owners had spent millions to bring it up to current safety standards. The process was nearing completion. Production mining would begin shortly.

The four men, labeled Team Bravo by the development project manager, were assigned to remove unstable rock slabs in the ceiling and walls of the lowermost part of the mine. Once completed, they would install support structures in the same area.

After a grueling morning, the four sat down on rock slabs, opened their lunch boxes, and began eating and swapping stories. Monday storytelling was even more colorful than usual as an entire weekend provided ample resources.

"Hello, friends! It appears I arrived just in time for lunch. How's that for timing?"

The seated men looked up in surprise. Standing before them was a tall man with an unruly head of brown hair and a ready smile. "I'm Eli; Control assigned me to work with you guys until the Omega site is finished. I'm from Team Alpha."

"Control didn't let us know you were coming," Aaron grumbled, "but that's not that unusual. And we are definitely not going to look a gift horse in the mouth. Welcome aboard." He stood and shook hands with the newcomer. "I'm Aaron." He turned and waved at the others. "These gents are Nathan, Isaac, and Paul."

The three nodded and mumbled "hello" as they ate.

Isaac held up a hand. "Where's your lunchbox, Eli?"

Eli gestured back the way he had come. "I ate with the Alpha bunch before I headed over here."

Nathan handed Eli an apple. "At least have this. I hate to eat while someone just watches."

Eli smiled and nodded. "Thanks. I believe I will." He took a bite.

Isaac took a bite of his ham sandwich and chewed thoughtfully. "You know fellows, you tease me all the time about my plethora of girlfriends, but I really think that I am getting serious about this one. Erika, I mean."

Aaron laughed. "Yeah, it's serious all right. You remembered her name. You two should probably be picking out curtains."

Nathan cautiously opened his lunchbox and eyed the contents. With a look of disgust, he pulled out a sandwich. "Blast it, egg salad again. I really wish Martha would watch 'Barefoot Contessa' on the Food Network." He took a bite of the sandwich and grimaced. "Maybe even 'Worst Cooks in America.' Probably Worst Cooks in America would be best."

Paul opened his lunchbox and removed his gourmet lunch while the other men watched with growing envy. "'What delectable delight do you have today?" Aaron asked.

"Nothing special: just a turkey breast wrap with sundried tomato cream cheese, salt and vinegar kettle chips, and a ginger crème brulee," Paul replied. "Just something Mary whipped up this morning." The other men stared dejectedly at their own lunches; Paul's wife was a fantastic cook.

The men finished their lunches, but before the storytelling began, a low ominous rumble emerged from the walls surrounding their ersatz lunch room. The men jumped to their feet.

Aaron grabbed his walkie-talkie from his belt. "Control, this is Team Bravo. At location Omega and hearing what sounds like shifting rock shelves. Leaving the area and returning to the tram now!"

"Bravo, this is Control. Copy that. Advise when you reach the tram."

"Copy, control."

The five men raced back up the Decline to the tram, one hundred feet up the spiral ramp. As they did, the ground and the walls surrounding them trembled, rocks cascading from the ceiling.

Aaron, in the lead, looked back over his shoulder as he ran. "Move your butts, boys! We ain't gonna be buried down here! I see the tram just ahead... we're almost there!"

Isaac tripped over a fallen rock and crashed hard into the rock floor of the Decline. He screamed in pain. "My ankle! I twisted it... maybe broke it!" He writhed in agony on the cold hard rock floor.

Nathan, Paul, and Eli stopped and quickly helped Isaac to his feet. "We've got to keep moving Isaac," Eli said as they hobbled along. "I know it hurts but we've got to keep moving or we could be buried alive down here."

"I know man, I know," Isaac rasped. "I'll make it."

Hearing the commotion, Aaron turned and ran back to the others. Glancing at Isaac's leg, he grimaced. "Fine time for you to get all clumsy on us, bro."

The men stumbled up the Decline as the tram came into view. The rumbling became a roar as the rock ceiling collapsed in front of them, cutting them off from the tram and escape.

Silently they stared in shock at the solid wall of debris in front of them. The passageway lights flickered and went out, plunging the passageway and the men into Stygian darkness. As suddenly as it had come, the sound of the mine tearing itself apart stopped. Silence descended upon them.

"Switch on your helmet lights," Aaron commanded. Five beams of light played across a floor-to-ceiling pile of debris, the air choked with swirling dust. He keyed his walkie-talkie. "Control, this is Bravo. Emergency. Emergency. Cave-in between site Omega and the tram. We are trapped. I repeat; we are trapped."

"Bravo, this is control. Copy that. We detected the collapse up here. A rescue team is on its way down the Decline now. Any injuries?"

"Isaac injured his left ankle." He shined his light upon the swollen foot. "Possibly broken."

"Copy that, Bravo. Stay calm and do not attempt to dig yourself out. You must conserve your oxygen. Do you have your emergency air tanks with you?"

Aaron shook his head. Realizing that Control couldn't see him, he replied, "No, they are still in the tram on the other side of the blockage."

"Copy, Bravo." The speaker was silent for a beat. "Hang in there, guys. We will get you out."

"Copy, Control. We know you will."

"We need to conserve our air," Aaron began. "Let's get Isaac comfortable, and then we need to sit down."

They carefully lay Isaac down and leaned him up against a rock. Sitting down beside him, the other men lapsed into silence.

The walkie-talkie squawked. "Bravo, this is Control. Your rescue will take longer than anticipated. The cave-in was quite extensive. Even so, we should have you out in 48 hours. You have plenty of air until then. Do you have any water or food with you?"

"Control, we have no food or water. Our emergency supplies were on the tram," Aaron replied sheepishly. He mentally kicked himself for not having his team carry at least some supplies with them.

Minutes went by as each man was lost in his own thoughts. Nathan was the first to speak. "When we get out of here, I am going to buy that new sports car that I have been wanting. And when I get it, I am going to drive it to Vegas and play blackjack until the cows come home. And when I get back home, I am going to buy that new UHD television. I can watch tv in style!"

Isaac laughed. "I'm going to get two new girlfriends! I think I can juggle three at once. I just can't let them find out about each other..."

Paul snorted. "I have a hard enough time with my wife. She keeps after me about going to church with her. Church. With her."

Isaac laughed and then groaned as he inadvertently shifted his leg. "What about you, Aaron? What do you have to say for yourself now that we're getting all touchy-feely?"

"When this is all over, I am going to go home, lock the door, and finish off every bottle of liquor I have in the house while simultaneously eating pizza. And ice cream," Aaron answered.

Paul glanced over at Eli. "What about you? What are you going to do?"

Eli remained silent as he studied each of the four other men in turn. He turned to Nathan. "Do you think that driving a new car, gambling in Las Vegas, and watching a new television will fill the emptiness inside you?"

Nathan stared at Eli in shock. "I...I don't know what you mean. I don't feel empty..."

Eli glanced at Isaac. "Isaac, do you feel that being promiscuous will heal your wounded spirit? Will superficial relationships satisfy your deep desire for a real relationship?"

Before Isaac could reply, Eli turned to Aaron. "Will drowning yourself in alcohol and eating everything in sight solve your problems?"

Aaron sputtered as Eli cast his gaze upon Paul. "The question for you, Paul, is not why you would want to go to church but why would you not want to, especially with your wife?"

Eli glanced around at the four astonished men. "We need to talk to God.

Let's bow our heads and pray that we will be rescued soon. We also need to pray for our rescuers."

"What God?" Aaron replied. "There is no God; men will rescue us, not some non-existent being." The other three men nodded in agreement.

"Aaron's right," Nathan began. "The four of us don't agree on much but that's one thing we do agree on. There is no God."

Eli looked at each man in turn. "Do you really want to believe that, especially at a time like this? Here you are in a mine without power. No lights other than a few weak battery-powered ones. Power generated by the efforts of men can come to a stop within seconds. The power of God, the Holy Spirit, is eternal, and will never stop; it will never cease to be. His light, the light of Jesus, will never go out."

The four others shifted uncomfortably. "Go ahead and pray, Eli," Isaac said. "It certainly can't hurt us any."

Eli bowed his head in prayer. One by one, the other four men in the darkened mine did as well.

Forty hours later, the rescue team broke through the pile of rubble. The exhausted men, hungry and thirsty, were removed one by one. Isaac, being injured, was the first. As Isaac, Aaron, Nathan, and Paul were being loaded into ambulances, Aaron stopped the rescuers. "Where's Eli? I haven't seen him since we left the mine's entrance."

The two mine rescuers looked at each other. "Eli? Who's he? There were only the four of you."

Aaron looked at his shocked friends. "What are you talking about? Eli, the guy from Alpha team. Control sent him to help us two days ago. He was with us the whole time."

The mine superintendent walked up just in time to catch the end of the conversation. "We didn't send anyone from Alpha to help you. And every miner is accounted for. You four were the only ones trapped."

The four men stared back at the mine entrance. Paul turned to his friends. "I am going to church with Mary this Sunday. You three meet me at my house at 9:00 and we can all ride together."

The other men nodded numbly. "I'll bring my girlfriend Ellen," Isaac replied.

"Erika!" the other three corrected.

SECURITIES

Jacob Fontaine strolled down the garden path with Eric Owens, one of his two bodyguards. Jacob glanced over at the tall broad shouldered man with the boyish curly blond hair. Eric was ex-military, as was his partner and wife Jessica. In the beginning, Jacob hadn't wanted to hire anyone to protect him and his family, but changing his mind six months ago turned out to be the best decision he had ever made.

Jacob had made millions in currency trading, first for an investment bank and then later for himself. Unfortunately, over the years he had made the mistake of flashing too much money around in front of the wrong people.

Before he had hired Eric and Jessica, there had been three break-in attempts at his home in Bedford Park, Illinois and one at his cabin near Aspen, Colorado. Security alarms had scared off intruders at his house, but the break-in at his cabin was successful. Fortunately, he and his family weren't at the cabin at the time, and insurance covered the pilfered items, but the message was clear. It would have been only a matter of time before he or one of his family members were hurt or worse.

Eric tended to stay near Jacob while Jessica watched over his wife, Tiffany, and his two twin daughters, Brittany and Cheyenne. Jacob loved to take walks through his garden and the surrounding wood and it was there, several months before, that Eric first spoke to Jacob about Jesus. Jacob knew Eric and Jessica were Christians, but they hadn't discussed their beliefs with him before.

Jacob had been raised in a Christian home in Indianapolis but had drifted away from God as a business student at university. He initially went to church occasionally while there, but by the time he was accepted into a graduate program in financial engineering in New York, he had stopped going altogether.

After graduating, he accepted a position as a trader at a large New York investment bank. The siren call of money had seduced him, and as his income increased, his once frugal lifestyle became increasingly lavish. He met and married Tiffany while in New York; Brittany and Cheyenne were born two years later. After years of trading on Wall Street, he gained enough experience to start trading currency on his own. Tiffany convinced him to move to Bedford Park where her family still lived; he agreed, as it would place him closer to his relatives in Indiana.

As they walked down the path in the garden, Jacob and Eric reached a fork. The wider path led downhill toward the Koi pond, while the other, narrower, path led uphill to the gazebo. Eric turned to Jacob. "Jacob, I am your bodyguard, your friend, and your brother in Christ. You've come a long way in your faith quickly, but you need to make a decision. There are two paths; one is wide and easy and is the path that many take but, in the end, it leads only to destruction. The narrow path is the more difficult of the two but it will lead to life: real life. If you take the narrow path, you must be all in. Now, my brother, you must decide which path to take. Will you join me on the narrow path?"

Jacob studied Eric's face for a moment and then slowly began to nod. "I will. I have been thinking about it for some time and I know that I have to be all in for Jesus. Let's walk up to the gazebo and talk about it."

Three months later, Jacob and his family had just finished dinner and were relaxing in the living room. Tiffany, Brittany, Cheyenne, and Jessica sat around the coffee table playing Monopoly.

Jacob glanced up as the front door opened and Eric rushed in. "We've got company. While making my rounds, I saw five guys on the inside of the back fence. Somehow they disabled the security sensors for that section and they are on their way to the house."

Jessica jumped up. "Everyone into the safe room. Now. Move!" Jacob, Tiffany and the twins rushed into the safe room adjacent to the living room. "Use the safe room phone to call the police. Don't open the door until we tell you it is safe. If we don't...stay in there until the police arrive and secure the house. God be with you." With that Jessica closed the door.

Jacob hugged his wife and daughters tightly. Sounds of breaking glass and gunfire erupted from the living room. The twins and Tiffany began to cry. Jacob bowed his head. "Dear God, please protect my family and keep Jessica and Eric from harm. Please Lord, please..."

The gunfire stopped. Jacob could hear nothing but Jessica moaning in the living room. He stood and walked to the safe room door. He turned and looked back at his shocked family. "Jacob, what are you doing?" Tiffany cried out between sobs.

"I have to go out there; Tiff; Eric and Jessica could be dying right now."

"You can't go out there, Jacob. We need to wait until the police arrive." She lapsed into silence as she saw the look on his face.

"You know I have to, Tiff; Eric and Jessica are part of our family too. I could never call myself a man again if I don't go out there. I love you, but I have to."

He turned to Cheyenne and Brittany. "I love you both and I am very proud of you." Amid cries of "Love you Dad," he turned, opened the door and stepped into the living room. He quietly closed the door behind him and glanced around.

The living room looked like a war zone. The windows were shattered and the crimson red drapes lay shredded on the floor. The chairs, coffee table, and end tables lay in broken heaps. The only light in the room came from one remaining floor lamp which cast a sickly yellow light upon the otherwise dark room. Scattered on the floor in front of the windows lay four bodies, all clad in black, all broken and bloodied. Eric was nowhere to be seen.

Jessica lay on the floor with her back against a wingback chair by the fireplace. He ran to her and knelt down beside her. She was breathing raggedly; blood oozed from her right leg. She looked up at him. "Where's Eric?"

"I don't know," Jacob replied. "He isn't here and one of the shooters is missing." Jacob examined her wound. "I think you will be okay."

Relief passed over her face. "Yeah, I think you're right. I can't move my leg- probably broken- but at least I am not going to bleed to death." Jacob tore off a piece of his shirt and gently wrapped it around her wounded leg.

The front door opened and Eric limped in. "One of them got away; he jumped through the window. I went after him but I never did see him. Probably headed back to whatever hole he crawled out of." He walked over to Jessica, knelt down beside her, and took her hand in his own. He glanced at her leg wound. "Looks like you are going to be out of commission for a few weeks, but otherwise, you are in pretty good shape."

Sirens wailed in the distance. "Police are on their way, thank God." Her energy spent, Jessica lapsed back into silence.

Jacob turned toward the safe room door as a shadow detached itself from the hallway, raised a wicked looking pistol, and took aim at Jessica. Jacob jumped in front of her just as the gun spouted flame. Jacob grabbed his arm, cried out in pain and fell to the floor.

Eric spun, drew his pistol from his shoulder holster, and fired. The remaining gunman screamed and tumbled to the floor where he lay unmoving. Eric ran to Jacob and dropped to the floor beside him. He looked the wounded arm over. "You're going to be fine, Jacob. That wound will hurt like the devil, but the bullet just grazed you." He helped Jacob to his feet. "Why did you come out of the safe room? We are here to protect you, not the other way around."

Jacob managed a smile. "All I used to value were securities---stocks, bonds.

Now, there are only two things that really matter to me—God and people. 'Love God, love people,' the commandment says; and so, I do. But love involves action; my family was safe, but you two weren't. I had to act."

Erin shook his head. "Just when I thought I had you figured out..."

BISCUITS AND GRAVY

The minister, pressed for time as usual, knocked in staccato on the front door of the cottage. The window curtain beside the door quickly pulled back and the face of an elderly woman with black spectacles appeared and then as quickly disappeared. The door opened and the woman peered out.

"Good morning, Constance!" the minister greeted, "May I come in?"

Constance nodded and stepped back. "Come in Gerald, and welcome." She led him to an overstuffed couch. "Please make yourself comfortable. Would you like some coffee or tea?"

Gerald settled himself on the couch. "Thanks Constance. Coffee would be great: cream and sugar please."

As Constance bustled off to the kitchen, Gerald glanced around the cozy living room. A small cheery fire blazed in the stone fireplace, warming the chill January morning. Dozens of photographs adorned the walls, many with Constance in the center. Newspaper clippings and even a couple of magazine articles were framed and placed carefully around the room. It was a lifetime of memories condensed into discreet moments of time, carefully preserved.

Lost in thought, Gerald yelped in surprise and nearly jumped from the couch when a silky-black animal landed squarely on his lap. Flustered, he looked down to see a miniature black panther quietly staring up at him.

Hearing the commotion, Constance returned to the living room. She laughed in spite of herself when she saw the look on the reverend's face. "I see you have met Ebony. He's my Bombay cat. Say hello to the minister, Ebony." She returned to the kitchen.

Gerald stared at the apparition on his lap while the black cat stared back. Nervously, Gerald remembered past Animal Planet shows. "I must not break eye contact; I must not show fear." The cat continued to stare back. "Merrrrr," the feline finally uttered, before jumping down on the floor and silently padding away.

Gerald regained his composure just before Constance came back in and set two steaming cups of coffee down on the coffee table. "I will be back in a jiffy," she said over her shoulder as she returned to the kitchen.

She came back with two small plates of steaming homemade biscuits smothered in sawmill gravy. She handed one plate to Gerald and then sat down.

Gerald eyed the plate. "Lord have mercy, Constance! I haven't had any of your heavenly biscuits and gravy since the sunrise service last Easter!" He savored the aroma as he took a bite. "Delicious!"

Constance sipped her coffee as she studied Gerald's face. "To what do I owe the pleasure of your company this morning, Gerald?"

He swallowed, wiped his mouth with a napkin, and cleared his throat. "Evelyn Smith told me that you mentioned in your life group that you had some concerns about my sermon on Sunday. I thought I would drop by on my way to church this morning and see if I could clarify anything for you."

Constance smiled. "That's kind of you, Gerald, but I don't think you need to clarify anything. Your sermon was, as always, easily understood." She looked down at her coffee cup and watched the black hot brew as she swirled the cup in her hands.

Gerald waited as Constance collected her thoughts.

Looking back up, Constance continued. "You said that we shouldn't get to Heaven and proudly proclaim that we sat in a church pew every Sunday; that we should have stories of service to others to tell. Being in church every Sunday is great, but we should also be serving God in His Kingdom."

"Yes, that's true," Gerald replied. "We need to help others in service to the Kingdom, not just attend church."

Constance sighed. "That's what's bothering me. I think back on my 70 years of life and I can't help but think that I didn't really do anything for the Kingdom."

Gerald was stunned. "Constance, you have served God faithfully. I have known you for 15 years as your pastor and as your friend so I can say with both professional and personal authority that you definitely have a servant heart."

Constance, with tears in her eyes, replied, "But I have never done anything for the Kingdom! I haven't gone on a single missions trip! I haven't volunteered to work in a food pantry or a soup kitchen or anything like that! What have I done? I'm afraid that when I go to my heavenly home I will be like the person you talked about. The best I will be able to say for myself is that I sat in a church pew every Sunday!"

Gerald paused to take another bite of the biscuits and gravy. He pondered his next words with care, unsure of what to say. He smiled as the words, no doubt provided by the Holy Spirit, bubbled to the surface.

"Constance," Gerald began, "mission trips and volunteer work in charity and relief organizations are great endeavors. But not everyone can go on such trips and not everyone can do volunteer work. Many people, just as yourself, may be in poor health or not have the time, ability, or resources to do be involved in those activities. Frankly, many people are not called to do them. When I spoke of working for the Kingdom, doing God's work, I was not referring solely to those callings. Those are great, don't get me wrong, but so are a million other things God calls us to do."

Gerald paused to take another bite of biscuit and a sip of coffee. "You were an elementary school teacher before you retired. By teaching young minds to grow, you were doing God's work."

Constance shook her head. "That was my work; I was paid to do that."

"Yes, it was your career, but it was also God's work. Just about anything can be God's work, if it is done right. And look around you. How many pictures are there on these walls with you and dozens of your family members and friends? How many times and in how many ways did you help them? That too, is God's work."

He paused, mentally readying himself to deliver the punchline. "How many times have you prayed for someone? How many days of your life have you spent on your knees in intercession? How many times have you sat with a sick or injured person from church, made hospital visit, or made biscuits and gravy for church events? Sometimes, Constance, God's work isn't mission trips; it's biscuits and gravy."

"Then I have offered the Lord more than my church seat warming ministry?" she asked through cascading tears.

"You have, Constance, you have." He took her hands in his. "Let's pray, sister. Father God, you are an amazing God and I thank you for Constance and others like her, the silent prayer warriors: the ones behind the scenes. May she continue for many more years doing your work in your Kingdom. Amen."

Gerald rose from the couch and walked to the door. "I have to get to the church, Constance. Thank you for your hospitality. And remember, God is with you!" He let himself out as Constance sat on the couch, deep in thought.

Ebony jumped up on the couch beside her and sat looking at her intently. "Well Ebony, there's a church luncheon coming up this Sunday. We'd better get to work on an apple pie or two!"

"Merrrrr!" Ebony replied in agreement.

LOST

The dream came again, as it always did, in the heart of the night. He was home, surrounded by his family: wife Chantel, sons Dalton and Eric. The cozy living room was just as it should be- comfortable, warmed by a cheery fire in the stone fireplace. The aroma of fresh baked bread wafted in from the kitchen while Berlioz's Symphonie Fantastique's haunting melody played quietly in the background.

In the dream, Dalton looked up from the book he was reading. "Dad's home!" He, Eric, and Chantel rushed to greet him. The warmth of their embrace brought tears of joy to his eyes...

He awoke with a start. Tears flowed down his face as he, once again, realized that he wasn't home; he was shipwrecked light-years from home. He was lost in the middle of nowhere; alone as alone could possibly be.

He twisted out of the makeshift hammock and made his way to the storage locker. He opened it and pulled out the half-empty bottle of Irish whiskey. He sloshed some into his sole remaining stainless steel cup, closed the locker, and sat down on top of it. He turned on the solar-powered lantern and sat staring out the Plexiglas window of the emergency shelter. The reddish sand outside was dark and ominous in the early morning light.

The voice whispered in his ear, as it had so many times since the wreck, "You are alone, completely alone. Isolated. Marooned. No one is coming to your rescue. Surrender. Your pistol is under you, inside the locker. Drink the rest of the bottle, pull out the pistol, and surrender to the darkness."

He sat motionless, contemplating a past that seemed lost forever, and a future that held nothing but a slow descent into oblivion. He stood, set the untasted whiskey on top of the locker, and walked to the shelter's door. The sun had risen higher in the pale, salmon colored sky, its weak light illuminating the area around the shelter. Sand and rocks, rocks and sand, as far as he could see.

94

He walked to the locker and opened it once again, pulling out the only book it contained: a Bible. He had never been a religious man, had never read the Bible, but he had nothing but free time on his hands now. Chantel had insisted he keep a Bible with him whenever he sailed. He opened it and began to read a chapter at random, this time Matthew chapter 7.

It was a game he played daily: one that, he had to admit, he looked forward to. A sort of biblical roulette. He read slowly, savoring every word as a man dying of thirst might a swallow of water. He came to verse 24: "Therefore whosoever heareth these sayings of mine, and doeth them, I will liken him unto a wise man, which built his house upon a rock." He pondered that before continuing with the rest of the chapter. "And every one that heareth these sayings of mine, and doeth them not, shall be likened unto a foolish man, which built his house upon the sand. And the rain descended, and the floods came, and the winds blew, and beat upon that house; and it fell: and great was the fall of it. And it came to pass, when Jesus had ended these sayings, the people were astonished at his doctrine; for he taught them as one having authority, and not as the scribes."

He walked outside and sat down on his makeshift lawn chair, converted from a piece of ship wreckage. The wind picked up and the sand began to swirl around the shelter. He looked toward the eastern horizon, much closer here than the horizon would be at home. A storm was coming, and a big one from the look of it.

He walked around the shelter, checking the nylon ropes that tied it to the rock shelf below. All were anchored securely to the pitons that he had driven into crevices in the rock. Satisfied, he retreated into the shelter, shut the door, and covered the window with a metal plate salvaged from the ship.

He sat upon the storage locker, Bible in one hand, glass of whiskey in the other. He read Matthew chapter 7 again. The storm was upon him now, the winds shrieked and sand pelted his shelter. The icy cold grip of fear seized his spine. The voice returned. "You are alone. Isolated. Forgotten. You will not live through the storm. You will die alone. Drink the whiskey, fire the gun."

Time to decide, he thought. He chose-turning the cup upside down and watching as the amber liquid spilled upon the floor. He set the cup down and turned his attention back to the Bible. He turned to a verse that he had read several days before, Psalm 23:4: "Yea, though I walk through the valley of the shadow of death, I will fear no evil; for thou art with me, thy rod and thy staff they comfort me."

Remembering his childhood, he got down on his knees and began to pray. "The voice has spoken nothing but lies to me. I am not alone. You are with me, Lord, in this shelter in the middle of the storm. The savage wind will soon be gone and I and my shelter, firmly anchored, will remain. I will fear no evil, for thou art with me. I will never be alone again, no matter where I am, no matter how far from home I venture, no matter what strange sun I see. Amen."

The storm left as quickly as it had arrived. The winds quieted to a gentle whisper and the sand, once swirled by the wind, settled back into its resting place upon the ground. He opened the door and stepped outside. The storm had receded into the distance. He bowed his head in a silent prayer of thanks.

Suddenly, from inside the shelter, came a sound, a sound that he had not heard in over six months: a voice, a real voice.

"Tau Ceti Survey Ship, this is U.S. Space Command Rescue. Do you copy? We are in orbit around the planet; a dropship is being prepped as we speak. ETA to your crash site is thirty minutes. Sorry it took so long to find you but your ship's locator beacon ceased transmitting several months ago. We had your location narrowed down to three solar systems, but searching each one took some time. Time to go home, buddy; Chantel and the kids are waiting for you!"

He looked up at the alien planet's sky. Even though Earth was 12 light years away, if he squinted his eyes just so, and tilted his head, he could see his family and smell the freshly baked bread.

THE BOOK

He trudged onward, a tall broad-shouldered man, weary and cold, the towering Ponderosa pines that blanketed the mountains of Colorado all around him. Darkness would soon fall; he had to find shelter soon or he would freeze to death. The snowflakes were swirling faster now: a blizzard was coming, and the temperature could drop to twenty below.

The icy wind slashed at his unprotected face. Daylight gone, he had trouble seeing anything through the thickening snowfall. A wolf howled in the distance, and then another. Grimly, he pondered his predicament. Which would get him first, the bitter cold or ravening wolves?

He made his way down the slope, slipping and falling several times. Each time, it was a little more difficult to get back up. The last time, he lay still for several minutes, simply resting before rising. The wolves howled again, much closer than before. Frantic, he half ran, half fell down the slope.

He reached the bottom of the hillside and stopped. There was a creek there, and, to his surprise, a small cabin, probably a trapper's, resting against the side of the hill. No smoke rose from the chimney, but a stack of firewood was nestled against the side.

He picked up a stick and rapped on the door. "Anyone there?"

There was no reply: no sound from within. He cautiously opened the wooden door. The cabin was pitch-black inside. He walked in and shut the door behind him. He reached into a coat pocket and took out the small pouch of matches. He struck one and looked around. The cabin was small, about ten feet by ten feet, with a small table and chair in the center and a bunk bed along the left side. A fireplace lined the right side of the cabin; wood lay on the grate. More wood was carefully stacked to the side, along with wood shavings and kindling. A small cupboard stood in one corner.

He built a small fire and pulled the chair next to it. He rubbed his numb hands, arms, and face; all red from the cold. Pain radiated through his body and his skin tingled as he slowly warmed. He was sure he had found shelter just in time. The wolves, giving up the chase, howled again, the sound receding into the distance.

He stood, stretched, and walked over to the cupboard. He opened it and, to his astonishment, found it full of canned peaches and salmon. It wasn't uncommon to find a cabin with a fire already laid; Westerners, after all, knew that a fire often meant the difference between life and death for travelers. To find one stocked with food, however, was rare indeed.

He opened a can of salmon with his pocket knife and sat fireside while he ate. As he gazed into the flames, the recent past emerged. He owned a large spread in Colorado, forged with a branding iron and a gun. He had thousands of head of cattle and fifty men riding for the brand. He had been king of all he surveyed, ruling with an iron fist and lead bullets. His men had feared him. He was good with a gun, a fact he often demonstrated by tossing a coin into the air and drilling it dead center before it hit the ground. He was as good with his fists as he was with his guns. He was a monarch, and his men were his servants.

He had awoken to find his segundo, Everett Peterson, along with two of his riders, Ross Owens and Levi Flanders, standing over his bed in his ranch house. Everett had a six-shooter aimed at his head. "Get up, Jake. Put your clothes on; we're going for a ride. We've had enough of you riding roughshod over us. You've been lord of your kingdom long enough."

They had taken him to the foothills of the Rockies. He blustered at first, threatened them, shouted obscenities until he was hoarse. They rode on. He reasoned with them, assured them the other riders would remain loyal to him, which only brought a round of laughter, as did the promise of more money.

When they finally stopped, Everett waved his Colt at him. "We ain't going to kill you; we'll let nature do that. If the cold don't get you, the wolves or a catamount will. Maybe you can order them to help you." The three men laughed as they turned their mounts and rode silently away. Bleakly, he considered going after them, but knew it would be a fatal mistake. They had given him one chance; they wouldn't give him another.

His thoughts returned to the present. He found a pot in the cupboard; he went outside and filled it with snow. He couldn't see three feet in front of him. He went back inside and used the sleeve of his coat to hold the pot over the fire. He poured the water into a cup and drank greedily. He went to the cupboard and retrieved a can of peaches. He glanced up at the top of the cupboard, and found, to his surprise, an old dusty Bible.

He picked it up and sat down by the fire. He had seen Bibles before, of course, but never had any use for them. He opened the book and flipped through the pages, finally stopping at the book of Mark. Having nothing better to do, he began to read and found he couldn't stop. When he finished Mark, he placed the Bible back on the shelf and stretched out in front of the fire.

The words of Mark swirled through his troubled mind. He was astonished. Jesus, with incomprehensible power, had come to serve, not to be served; the son of God, ruler of all, served others. He drifted off to sleep, thinking of Jesus the servant, and Jake Matherson, petty tyrant.

He stayed in the cabin for days, resting quietly while reading the Bible. He had a lot to learn and Jesus, he found, was the ultimate teacher.

Three weeks later, he rode into the town of Castle Rock atop a borrowed Appaloosa. A rancher outside Pueblo knew of his reputation and had not only loaned him the horse, but also a fine matched pair of Colt 45s.

He rode up to the Gold Strike Saloon, swung off the Appaloosa, tied the horse to the rail, and pushed through the bat-wing doors. There, sitting at a table playing cards, were Everett, Ross, and Levi. Everett looked up from his cards and froze. Ross and Levi, seeing Everett's expression, turned toward the man standing just inside the doorway.

"Evening, gents," Jake began. "The blacksmith I talked to up the street said that you three were here. I got some things I need to say to you."

He walked further into the saloon and stood halfway between the three men and the bar. Slowly, the room quieted. Those in the way moved quickly to each side of the saloon. Beads of sweat rolled down the faces of the three men as they silently watched Jake.

Jake walked to the bar and nodded to the bartender behind the counter. "Got a favor to ask. Keep these for me for a while." He unbuckled his gun belt and handed it to the open-mouthed bartender.

Jake turned, walked to the table, pulled back an empty chair, and sat down. Speechless, the three men leaned back into their chairs and watched Jake warily.

"Gentlemen, I owe you an apology. I thought I was lord of all I surveyed, but I was wrong. I was a petty tyrant and sorely mistreated all of you. Jesus is the Lord of all, and if the son of God came to Earth to serve us, then there's no way in Hell I could be lord over you. No more bluster, no more bullying. I am going to make things right, starting with a raise for you three, and all of the other riders. The rest I will figure out as we go along."

The three men looked at each other and then back at Jake. Everett spoke first. "What happened to you out there, Jake?"

Jake grinned. "Well, it's like this fellas; I found this book…"

THE MAN

He sat cross-legged on the ground near the entrance to the store's parking lot. His long black hair, shot through with streaks of gray, was up in a ponytail. His face was partially obscured by a shaggy salt and pepper beard; a red handkerchief served as a head covering. What face was showing was weathered by too many days in sun, wind, and rain. His cheap black plastic eyeglasses were held together in the center by cellophane tape. His eyes were a deep penetrating blue, and he appeared closer to 50 than 40.

He wore an old brown coat patched in several places with tattered duct tape. His blue jeans, like the coat, had also been patched, but with what the casual observer would not be able to determine. His work boots had seen better days as well. Beside him sat a weather-beaten blue backpack and leaning against it was a small cardboard sign that simply said, "Hungry pleas hep me."

He huddled there in the early morning chill air of late November, the sun just beginning to peek over the eastern horizon. The man closed his eyes, bowed his head, and offered up a silent prayer. A steady stream of cars flowed past the man as the store's day shift workers meandered into work. A few of the drivers glanced his way as they drove past, but none stopped. He finished his prayer, opened his eyes, and looked toward the people as they streamed into the lot. They would have been astonished to learn that the prayer he had just completed had been for them.

He sensed someone behind him. "Hey man; I brought you some breakfast." The man waited until his young benefactor came to stand before him, looking down. The young man handed a white plastic bag to him, along with a steaming cup of coffee. He sat the cup down beside him, took the bag, and opened it. Inside was a package of cake donuts and a chocolate fried pie.

The young man flashed an embarrassed smile as he handed the older man another bag. This one contained a small brown blanket. He gratefully accepted it and wrapped it around himself. He smiled warmly up at his benefactor and said, "May God bless you."

"Well, I've got to get to work. I have to round up any stray carts on the lot and herd them back to the store. Yippee ti yi yaaa!" He reached down and shook the man's hand. As he turned to begin his day, he would later swear to a friend that he heard the man say, "God will be with you today as you take your organic chemistry test."

Astonished, the young man turned to look back, but the man sat quietly staring off toward the distant highway that lay in front of the parking lot. He stood silently for a moment contemplating this until deciding that the combination of staying up most of the night studying and drinking copious amounts of strong coffee had been a bad idea. He sighed and began his day.

As the sun rose higher in the sky, the early morning shoppers began to arrive. Car after car drove by but no one looked at him. Discouraged, the man again bowed his head and prayed, this time aloud. "Father God, let them see me as you see me. Let them see with your eyes and love with your heart."

The day slowly wore on until the sun was nearly overhead. No one stopped; very few had even looked his way. In the early afternoon, a red pickup rolled by; the passenger rolled his window down and yelled, "Get a job!" before exiting the parking lot. He sighed and prayed as he watched the truck roll out of sight.

A white minivan approached with a man driving, a woman in the passenger seat, and a young girl of about ten in the middle seat. The girl waved cheerfully at him as they drove by; surprised and pleased, he waved back. The minivan parked nearby and the three got out and walked over to him. The man pulled out his billfold, took out several bills, and handed them to him. "Here you go, man. I wish I could do more, but things are a little tight for us right now."

The girl shyly approached him and held out a dollar bill. "I was going to buy a candy bar with, this but I want you to have it instead."

With tears in his eyes he accepted the gifts and carefully put them into his coat pocket. "Thank you all and may God bless you." They smiled, turned, and began walking toward the store. The man bowed his head and prayed, "God of the universe, the almighty God, bless them and keep them safe." As they walked away, the girl turned and waved at the man one final time. Smiling, he returned the wave as he, ever so slowly, disappeared.

THE CROSSING

Alex's workday at the factory had finally ended; he headed home. Another day of the same-old, same-old; routine work on an assembly line that cranked out barbecue grills five days a week, sixteen hours per day. As he drove homeward, he idly wondered how long it would be before his job, like so many others in factories around the world, would be replaced by robots. He felt like a robot himself most of the time, automatically going through the motions as he meandered through another day.

He drove as he had worked during the day, completely on autopilot. He and Beth, his wife of twenty years had two sons, both teenagers, and together they lived in a small three bedroom ranch house a few miles from the factory. They had saved for years for the down payment for their modest country home; they had lived in a small apartment in town for years but had longed for the quiet and solitude of the countryside. Finally, their dream had come true.

That was ten years ago, and the novelty of rural life had worn off. He no longer had any dreams. Each day was a series of tasks to cross off his to do list. The weekends were a little better; on Saturdays he would complete his wife's list of things to take care of around the house and on Sunday he could relax, read the paper, and watch a ball game or two. His sons were usually at a neighbor's house and his wife read her favorite books, especially the Bible.

The dirt road to his house was dustier than usual; it was early September and it had been a dry summer. He approached the railroad tracks that crossed the dirt road and was surprised to see the crossbars down and red signal lights flashing. As he stopped at the crossing, a train approached from the west. Odd, he thought. It was nearly 6 and trains rarely went through at that time. Probably delayed due to work on the track somewhere down the line, he decided.

The train had three diesel electric engines at the front and was made up of the usual mix of boxcars hauling who knew what and tanker cars filled with everything from corn syrup to boric acid. Already lulled by his workday, he nearly fell asleep as the train continued to roll past.

The train seemed to have even more graffiti on its cars than most. He often marveled at the artistic ability of some of the railway artists. Some of the works were even signed. Modern art to go, he mused.

Suddenly, he sat forward in his pickup seat as he stared in disbelief at the writing on the brown boxcar sailing by. Clearly written in red letters at least three feet high was his first name, Alex. He sat motionless, barely breathing, as the next car flashed by. The word "take" was painted in red across the boxcar. The next car had the word "heed" painted across it, once again in the three feet tall red letters.

The seemingly endless procession of railcars finally ended. As the train rumbled off to the east, Alex sat motionless. He stared at the receding tail of the train until it was out of sight. Had he really seen a message to himself? Had he imagined it? Was it just meaningless graffiti that by chance had his name in it? He shook his head, put the transmission in drive, and drove slowly across the tracks.

He drove down the road in a daze. He knew he had seen the message; was convinced he had not imagined it. Surely it was just some strange coincidence that the name "Alex" was used.

As he drove onward, he passed a small white farmhouse on the left side of the road. He glanced at the pickup parked in the driveway and did a double take. It was the exact truck he envisioned owning someday! When did his neighbor buy that truck? Or perhaps they had a visitor with a truck?

Envy set in. He couldn't help it. Beth called it one of his bags of luggage. Well, why couldn't he have the things he wanted?

Driving on, he passed another house, this time on the right. This home was a small log cabin with a wide front porch. Two white wooden rocking chairs sat on the porch side by side. He had always wanted a log cabin; why couldn't he have one? Why...and then he slammed on the brakes of his old pickup.

He sat staring at the cabin with his mouth open and his mind in a whirl. There wasn't supposed to be a log cabin there. It had been open pasture for as long as he could remember. Where had the cabin come from? What was going on? Was he losing his mind? He put the truck in gear and pulled over to the side of the road and shut off the engine.

He got out of the truck and walked up the driveway toward the cabin. After about ten feet, he walked into something. He looked down and, at first, saw nothing but the white gravel on the driveway. Without warning, a four strand barbed wire fence materialized out of nowhere. At the same time, the gravel driveway disappeared. Looking up, he was amazed to see the cabin vanish. No driveway, no cabin, just pasture like always. He staggered back from the fence and turned and ran to his truck. He jumped in, started the engine, and roared down the dirt road.

His mind swirled and twisted. He could barely concentrate enough to drive, but he had to get away from...what? What was he getting away from? What was going on? Was he losing it completely? He had never experienced anything like this. Was this what it felt like to lose one's mind? He had to make it home. Once there, everything would be all right. Wouldn't it?

Only a little farther to go now. His home would be waiting for him around the next corner. His nice little house.

He slowed to a gentle stop. She was standing in the middle of the road in front of him, wearing that red dress that he couldn't stop admiring. It was the production manager's secretary, the one he thought about all day. What was she doing here? She couldn't be, but there she stood, silently gazing at him.

He steered his truck to the right and slowly drove around her as she stood in the middle of the road. She didn't look at him as he drove carefully around her. He looked in his side view mirror as he drove on; he wasn't surprised this time when she simply vanished from sight. He was losing it, he decided. He was past his original fright now; he was simply numb. His mind was shutting down - locking tight to keep out the madness.

He finally arrived at his driveway and pulled in. He drove slowly up to a brown brick ranch that now sat where his own red brick house once stood. He parked the truck, shut off the engine, and stared morosely at the house. His house? Someone else's? Should he go in? Who would he find inside? Beth? Someone else? No one at all?

As he sat, the front door opened and Beth walked out on to the narrow porch. She was dressed in a yellow sun dress and had dark sunglasses on. Beth never wore dresses and she didn't use sunglasses. The biggest shock of all came when a tall man with a dark complexion followed her out of the house onto the porch. He stood next to Beth, put one arm around her, and waved at Alex with the other. There was no sign of recognition from either of them.

Alex started up the truck, put it into reverse, and floored it. He nearly rolled the truck over as he squealed onto the road. He slammed the gear into drive and roared down the road, back the way he had come. He didn't know what to do, or where to go for that matter. He simply drove.

The message on the freight train swam into his overloaded mind: "Alex, take heed." He pulled over, parked on the side of the road, and switched off the engine. His breathing was ragged and his heart pounded so hard he thought it would leap out of his chest. Only one thing came into his befuddled brain: prayer.

He hadn't prayed in years. It wasn't that he didn't believe in God; he hadn't really needed Him before. He bowed his head and began to pray out loud; "God, I don't know what is going on, but I need your help. Am I losing my mind? Have I died and gone to hell? Lord, help me, please." He remembered the message. "Alex, take heed," came into his head.

All he could think about was Beth and the boys. He realized that, for the last several years, his thoughts had been on everything but them. He had to get them back, but how?

This had started at the railroad crossing. Maybe it would end there as well. Lacking any other options, he started the truck and drove back to the crossing. As he approached he saw a train- the same train, he thought- heading back west. Once again, the crossbars were down and the signal lights blazed a brilliant red in the fading sun. He stopped and watched as the train rolled westward. On one of the boxcars was written, "Alex, Seek Me." The train passed, the cross-bars rose, and Alex continued across the track.

He turned around at the next driveway and drove back the way he had come. All had returned to normal. Everything was as it was supposed to be. He was not crazy. It had happened; he was sure of that. And he ignored the greatest gift God had bestowed upon him: his wife and sons.

He pulled into his driveway, got out, and walked up to the porch. Beth- his Beth - sat in one of two white wooden rocking chairs on the porch. She smiled. "How do you like the new chairs? I ordered them from Amazon last week to surprise you. What do you think?"

He sat down in the unoccupied chair and smiled back at her. "I love them Jenny and I, uh, I love you too!"

Beth stopped rocking. "You haven't told me you love me since, well, I can't remember when. Are you okay? Has something happened?"

Alex reached over and took her hand. "I made the crossing."

SHADOWED

She first saw him as she came out of the Save-More Grocery Store on the corner of Elm and Main. She had just finished her weekly grocery shopping and was slowly pushing the heavily laden shopping cart across the icy parking lot on her way to her SUV. The recently fallen snow had been scraped off but the inevitable patches of remaining ice made the trip treacherous. She carefully navigated the cart through the patches of ice and snow until she arrived safely, albeit slightly out of breath, at the vehicle. She unlocked the doors with her remote, lifted the rear door, and placed the bags of groceries in the back. Closing the lift gate, she noticed a man standing near the store's entrance, watching her intently.

He was tall, about as tall as her brother, Mike, who was a solid six feet. Dark complexioned, with short black hair, rugged face partially covered by a neatly trimmed black beard, he leaned casually against the storefront, eyes glued to her. He appeared to be closer to forty than thirty.

She pushed the shopping cart out of the way and slid into the Escape. She was thankful Mike had convinced her to carry pepper spray in her purse. He had wanted her to get a concealed carry license and to keep a pistol with her, but she had drawn the line. She really had nothing against guns per se; she was simply afraid of shooting herself if she had to pull a gun for protection.

She glanced in the rear view mirror as she pulled out of the parking lot; he was still there by the store entrance, eyes tracking her vehicle as it pulled away. She drove out of the parking lot and turned right onto Main Street. She drove for several blocks and then turned right onto Palm Street. She had never understood how the quiet street got its name; there wasn't a palm tree within five hundred miles.

Arriving at her cottage style home, she pulled into the driveway and parked. She opened the door, retrieved the groceries from the back, and attempted to unlock the front door while holding the groceries. One bag ripped, spilling fresh vegetables over the step. She took the remaining groceries inside and returned to pick up the veggies. She scooped them up and, as she stood, noticed someone walking down the sidewalk across the street. Her heart quickened, but it was only a neighbor.

Sighing, she walked back inside, locked the front door and began putting the groceries away. As she chopped vegetables for a stir-fry, she glanced out the kitchen window. Standing across the street, staring at the house, was the man from the grocery store parking lot. She dropped the knife into the sink, sprinted to the front door, and checked the locks. Breathing hard, she found her purse, retrieved her cell phone, and dialed 911.

"911, what is the nature of your emergency?" the operator intoned.

"This is Brittany Fielding. I am at home at 2410 Palm Street and I need to report someone…someone stalking me." She described the man and the steps leading up to the call.

"I am sending a patrol car now, ma'am. Stay inside, make sure your doors and windows are locked, and keep this line open. The officers will be there in less than ten minutes."

While holding the cell phone, she checked every door and window. All were locked. She retreated to the couch and sat down. She started to shake uncontrollably while tears flowed down her face.

It seemed like hours before the patrol car arrived, but a glance at her watch proved that it had only been eight minutes since she had placed the 911 call. A quick rapping came from the front door; peering cautiously out the window, she saw, to her relief, two uniformed police officers.

She opened the door and ushered them into the living room. The older of the two, tall and broad shouldered with short black hair and matching mustache, spoke first. "Ma'am, I am Officer Jordan and this is Officer Owens." He waved a meaty hand at his partner. "By the time we arrived, the man you reported was gone. I am going to search the neighborhood and talk to your neighbors while Officer Owens takes down information from you." He opened the front door and slipped out.

She sat down on the couch and glanced up at the officer. He was muscular, not an ounce of fat on him, with brown hair, cropped short. His handsome, thirty-something face gazed solemnly down at her.

"I'm sorry, Officer. I'm a little rattled right now. Would you like to get something to drink?" she stammered. "I mean would you like to drink something, like coffee?"

Smiling, he shook his head. "No, thank you, ma'am. I do need to ask you some questions, though." He opened his notepad and scratched down answers as she slowly recited the details. When she finished, he closed the book.

"When we get back to the station we will run your description through our database and see if we get any hits. My partner and I patrol this area regularly; I, I mean we, will run by several times during our shift and will request officers on the other shift do the same."

The door opened and Officer Jordan walked in. "No sign of the man. I checked with a couple of your neighbors and they haven't seen anyone fitting that description. Keep everything locked and we will keep tabs on you. Do you have anyone that could stay with you for a while?"

She nodded. "My brother, Mike. I'll call him. He can probably trade days at work with someone and stay with me for a few days."

"Great," Jordan replied. "Andrew and I need to get back to the station." He glanced over at his partner.

"Andrew?" Jordan asked as his partner stood unmoving, silently gazing at the still seated Brittany.

Andrew shook himself. "Right. Let's go. Don't worry, Brittany, uh ma'am, I, we will keep an eye on you...I mean keep you safe. Bill, Officer Jordan, that is, and I will be around if you need anything." He stood and followed his partner out of the house.

Brittany dialed her brother. "Mike, I need some help..."

The next morning, as she drove to work, her mind whirled with thoughts of the mysterious man. *Who was he? Why was he watching her? Was he dangerous?* She turned south on Magnolia Lane, lost in thought. A flash of red appeared in front of her; she instinctively slammed on the brakes. She jumped out and raced to the front of the SUV. There, lying face down on the street was a small boy, clad in a scarlet-red jacket. He wasn't moving.

"Oh my God!" She cried out. She spun around, searching for anyone to help. There were no other cars on the street. She whipped the cell phone out of her purse and dialed 911. She reported the accident and was assured that an ambulance and a patrol car would be there in minutes.

She knelt beside the boy. He appeared to be breathing normally and there was no blood to be found. He looked to be about ten years old with short brown hair, a lock of which had fallen across his left eye. She reached down and gently brushed the hair back.

Uneasiness washed over her. She stood and glanced across the street, her heart racing from the adrenaline surging through her body. He was there, standing on the sidewalk. Smiling slightly, he watched her like a cat watching a canary. Her throat constricted; she couldn't breathe. She wanted to cry out, but no sound escaped her lips.

The siren scream of the approaching ambulance wrenched her attention from his mesmerizing stare. Mere moments later, when she looked back, he was gone.

The paramedics, upon arrival, examined the injured boy, loaded him into the ambulance, and sped off, as a police cruiser rolled to a stop behind her. Glancing back, she was relieved to see Bill Jordan and Andrew Owens emerge.

"What happened here, ma'am?" Bill asked.

She leaned against the hood of the SUV, took a deep breath, and told them about the accident. She hesitated. "And I saw the man again."

She watched Andrew's face as she spoke; for some reason, concern about his reaction filled her with dread.

Andrew kept his face carefully neutral. "I'll check around." He placed a reassuring hand on Brittany's shoulder and gently squeezed. As he walked away, Bill watched his partner thoughtfully.

She called the bank where she worked, told her supervisor what had happened, and told her that she wouldn't be in to work. She waved goodbye to Bill and followed the ambulance to the hospital.

She waited in the waiting room while the ER staff examined the boy. Bill and Andrew soon arrived. "We found out his name is Alex Johnson." Bill began. "He's a foster child who was placed temporarily in a local home. I contacted Family Services and they are sending someone over here now."

Bill glanced at his partner. "I'm going to get some coffee for the three of us. I'll be back in ten."

Brittany sat down in a chair and, to her surprise, Andrew sat beside her. "You've had a tough time lately. How are you holding up?"

She glanced at him. Concern was in his eyes, and something else…

"Shook up, but really, I am fine. I take it that you didn't find the mystery man."

He shook his head. "No, no sign of him." He glanced at her. "But that doesn't mean that he wasn't there."

She nodded with relief. "You believe me."

He nodded. "I do. You don't seem to be the kind of person to cry wolf. That's what your co-workers say as well."

Surprised, she replied, "You have been checking up on me?"

He nodded. "Don't take it the wrong way. It's standard police procedure."

She looked up as the ER physician approached. "Alex is going to be fine. He was knocked out, I think, when he fell on the pavement. He is awake now." Brittany thanked the doctor and then, bowing her head in prayer, thanked God. To her surprise, she felt Andrew take her hand in his as he joined her in prayer.

Their prayer finished, she looked up and, to her astonishment, saw the mystery man at the end of the hallway, wearing a white lab coat with a stethoscope around his neck. He smiled at her and then disappeared around the corner of the hallway.

Stunned, her mind tried to make sense of what she had just seen. She was sure that it had been the same man. *What in the world was going on? Why would anyone be interested in her?* She noticed that Andrew was staring down the hallway as well.

"That was him, wasn't it?" he said before jumping to his feet. Without waiting for an answer, Andrew raced down the hallway and around the corner.

He returned a few minutes later. "I don't know where he went, but I let hospital security know about him. They are looking for him now but I think he is already long gone. An exit door was at the end of the hallway. I went outside but found nothing." He sat down beside her and shook his head. "What is going on here? Who is that guy anyway? Why in the world would he dress like a doctor?"

One year later...Brittany sat on the bench idly watching as Alex happily played tag with a group of kids in the park. The adoption process, trying as it was, had been well worth it. She was now the proud mother of Alex, and Andrew, after the wedding, would be his father.

"Penny for your thoughts?" Andrew asked as he sat down beside her.

She hugged him. "Just thinking about how God puts the right people in your life at the right time." Her smile turned to a frown as she noticed the look on his face.

"That's him again!" Andrew exclaimed. "That's the man who followed you last year." He pointed to a man walking up the sidewalk. They stared in disbelief as he approached and stood before them.

He smiled. "You have done well, Brittany. I am pleased and I believe that He will also be pleased." His eyes bored into her. "I will, however, drop in on you two from time to time. Understand this, Brittany; you and Alex have nothing to fear from me."

He glanced at Andrew. "Andrew, I believe, will be an excellent father."

Brittany shook her head. "Who are you?"

"Search your heart, Brittany," he replied. "You know who, or should I say what, I am."

Comprehension dawned upon her with startling clarity. "You are an angel."

He nodded. "Correct."

Brittany smiled. "I've often heard of guardian angels, but I didn't know I had one. So you were tasked by God, so to speak, to give me a child, Alex, to take care of. You helped me, in a rather circuitous fashion, to meet Andrew. You brought meaning to my life." Tears welled up in her eyes as the enormity of it all washed upon her. "You're my guardian angel."

"Not yours," he replied with a smile, "I'm Alex's!"

TEACHER'S PET

I knew the new girl was trouble when she first walked into my second hour English class. I have always had what my paternal grandmother called "the gift," the ability to sense trouble at the very beginning. She was cute: about five foot three, petite, with short auburn hair and freckles. She wore pink slacks and a black t-shirt with a single yellow rose emblazoned upon the front. Her lack of fashion sense wasn't what alarmed me, although the combination was jarring; no, it was something else: a feeling of impending trouble. I wasn't smitten with her- at least I didn't think so- so I didn't think I would be on the receiving end of the latest Berryton High School drama.

We had just settled into our seats, the usual before class buzz of conversation still going. Mr. Porter, our fresh out of college teacher, looked up from his desk and glanced at the new student as she sat down. The second class bell cheerfully rang, signaling the official beginning of another exciting hour of classwork. Mr. Porter stood, cleared his throat, and the student to student conversations slowly muted to silence.

"Good morning everyone. Before we get started, I would like to introduce our latest victim, Anne Smith. Anne has just transferred here from Willington High." He glanced at the paper in his right hand. "She is a junior, likes pepperoni pizza and caramel sundaes, and collects autographs of famous mathematicians. She likes professional wrestling and men who are not afraid to cry. Please welcome her."

I could tell that our fearless teacher's offbeat sense of humor caught Anne off guard. For the rest of us? Well, we were used to it.

Anne was silent for a moment, then slowly cracked a smile. After the customary laughter died down, she meekly replied, "Well, I do like pepperoni pizza." We laughed even harder. She would be okay; she had survived first contact with the Porter Humor assault.

When the bell finally rang, most everyone headed for the door. I never lived on a farm, but I recognized a herd stampeding when I saw one. I stayed seated for a few beats; I was the last one to leave the room. When Anne got up and followed the herd out the door, she glanced back at Mr. Porter, who still sat at his desk. He smiled at her as she turned and walked out of the room. I noticed he watched her all the way out. Had her face been flushed? As I exited the great hall of high school English wisdom, I noticed that Mr. Porter looked, well, nervous. Nervous? What was going on here?

Over the next few weeks, my Spidey sense tingled even more. I noticed a definite tension between Mr. Porter and Anne. I didn't pay a whole lot of attention to it, as I had drama of my own to contend with.

Jillian, the raven haired classmate who I was smitten with, said a surprising yes to my awkward attempt at asking her out on a date. By May, Jillian and I were a thing, as they say, and I didn't focus much on anything else. Yes, that's why I got a C in Algebra II.

The long awaited summer break came, the last one I would have in high school. I would be starting next fall as a senior, the mystical designation that I had longed for since I started middle school. Jillian and I hung out a lot together over the summer. I knew things were getting serious when I started regretting that I had not lettered in anything and didn't have the great mantle of manly superiority to bestow upon her.

Being summer, I didn't think about high school at all, but I did ponder what would be coming next: college. I had no clue what I wanted to major in; I just knew that I would go to college because that was what everyone in my family did. It was a given. You didn't have to go to a great college but *you had to go*. I would probably go to Everly, a four year school right in my hometown. I could still live at home. What was Jillian going to do? I realized that I hadn't talked to her about the decision. Was she going to college? If so, where?

The summer ended all too soon and we were back in school. Jillian and I were still together and we were seniors! Life was good, at least for us. Jillian and I were sitting in our very first class of the year, first hour Psychology, when Anne walked in. The room went silent. Anne was clearly pregnant.

The next class Jillian and I had together was third hour AP English. Mr. Porter was listed as the teacher, so I was surprised when Ms. Owens, the forty something teacher who always wore hoop earrings, walked in and sat down at the teacher's desk. My Spidey sense ratcheted up. I knew what Ms. Hooprings was going to say next. "Class, Mr. Porter resigned recently and I have taken over the AP English class."

It wasn't easy for Anne that year. A few idiots taunted her in the hallways but most of us just didn't say much of anything to her. We didn't really know what to say. The rumor went around the school that the father was Mr. Porter, a rumor that I suspected, without a shred of evidence, was true. I later heard that Mr. Porter was working in town at a bookstore, but I didn't see him.

Jillian and I graduated and both went to Everly College while living at home. To everyone's surprise, including my own, I majored in Religious Studies. Jillian majored in nursing, to no one's surprise. After four long but enjoyable years, we graduated and one month later, we married.

The biggest shock from those years was hearing Anne had become Anne Porter. Yes, indeedy, Mr. Porter married Anne when she turned eighteen. By that time, her baby girl, Destini, was two years old. He, I heard through the city grapevine, had become the manager of the town's sole remaining independent bookstore.

I spent the next two and a half years at seminary while Jillian worked as a pediatric ICU nurse. During this time, the Porters published their first novel, "On the Way to Forever," a book that made the New York Times Bestseller list.

That was ten years ago. Jillian and I are going tonight to see the premier of "Destini:" a film based upon the book by, you guessed it, the Porters. Anne and Jesse Porter will be there, along with their daughter Destini, who inspired the book.

They say that God works in mysterious ways and I have worked in the theological trenches long enough to believe it. I also know that God can take a life or a relationship that is broken and heal it. I don't know if any of this applies to the Porters, but there is one thing I know for sure. They say you can't judge someone by what they say, but only what they do. I would have to amend that by adding that you should make sure that the doing is done before the judging sets in.

THE LAST OF THE EHHAD
PROLOGUE

Commanded by Elohim, Moses ordered its construction after his sojourn on Mount Sinai. The box, built from wood from the shittah or acacia tree, measured 2 1/2 cubits
in length, 1 1/2 cubits in width, and 1 1/2 cubits in height. The box was overlaid
with gold, with a ring of gold attached to each of the box's four feet. Staves of wood from the
acacia tree were covered with gold and slipped through the rings, one on each side, to allow safe
transport. A cover of gold with two golden cherubim, the kapportet, or "mercy seat," adorned
the top of the box.

The box traveled with the ancient Hebrews, led by Moses, during their 40 years of wandering in the desert. Whenever the Hebrews camped, the box resided in the sacred chamber,
the Holy of Holies, secure within the Tabernacle, the sacred dwelling place.

Eventually, Moses passed on and Joshua, his chosen second, became the leader of the
Israelites, and it would be he who would lead them into the Promised Land. Upon reaching
the banks of the River Jordan at the edge of Canaan, the box, known to the Israelites as the
Ark of the Covenant, dried the water up, allowing the Israelites to pass safely into the Promised Land. The Ark had been pleased; all was proceeding according to the will of Elohim.

The Ark assisted the Israelites in their conquest of Canaan, the land of milk and
honey; it was at the forefront of the first battle, the Battle of Jericho. Porters carried the Ark
around the city of Jericho once per day for seven days. Soldiers and seven priests sounding
seven rams' horns walked in front of the Ark. On the seventh day, the journey around the
city was repeated seven times, and Jericho's seemingly impenetrable wall collapsed, allowing
the Israelites to quickly conquer the city. The Ark, satisfied that the conquest would please
Elohim, quieted once more.

The Ark remained with the Israelites for hundreds of years, silently watching over
Elohim's chosen people. For a brief time, it was held in captivity by the ancient enemy of the
Israelites, the Philistines. Elohim despised them and instructed the Ark to destroy the statue
of Dagon, the Philistine's idol, but to no avail; the Ark remained a prisoner. The Ark

longed to return to the People, and after repeatedly afflicting the hated Philistines with plagues of mice and boils, it was finally sent back to be with the overjoyed Israelites.

Many years went by as the Israelite's interest in and reverence of the Ark waxed and waned. At long last, Israel's wisest ruler, King Solomon, prepared a special place for the Ark to reside. The mighty king built a new temple to rule from, one that contained a special inner room known as the Kodesh Hakodashim, the Holy of Holies. The Ark was carefully moved there by Solomon's servants; the Ark was finally at peace, but it was not to last.

Enemies of the Israelites came and went, but the Ark remained secure in Solomon's temple until the hated Babylonian king, Nebuchadnezzar, overran Jerusalem. Nebuchadnezzar selected a Hebrew vassal king, Zedekiah, who was given control of Judah, but the Ark knew it was only a matter of time before the great temple would be destroyed, and it along with it. The will of Elohim, the Ark reasoned, was for it to survive in order to continue the protection of the People. The Ark, after careful deliberation, devised a plan.

For months, the Ark patiently searched the hearts and minds of the humans who entered the Temple. After examining hundreds, the Ark selected seven worthy of carrying out the sacred duty. Carefully, the Ark, through dreams and visions, bestowed the will of Elohim upon them.

The seven, who called themselves the Ehhad, were pure of heart, both courageous and wise. The seven loved Elohim and vowed to serve Him by protecting the Ark, with their very lives if need be.

In the middle of the night, the seven drew near to the Ark. The fall of Jerusalem was rapidly approaching; the Temple, they understood, would be razed and the Ark would be carried off as plunder, or worse, destroyed. Under cover of darkness, the Ark was removed from the Holy of Holies and carried safely out of the city of Jerusalem. Upon reaching the mountain the humans called Nebo, the seven members of the Ehhad, led by one called Jeremiah, hid the Ark in a remote cave.

The Ark remained there for a long, long time. One by one, the original seven members of the Ehhad passed on, and as they did, each was replaced with another, carefully selected from the remaining Israelites. With the death of Jeremiah, all of the original members had passed.

The centuries passed quickly while the Ark quietly waited in the cave, protected by the ever-watchful Ehhad. Armies of men marched back and forth across the land and, on more than one occasion, the Ehhad had to relocate the Ark to keep it from being discovered.

When the Son of God appeared on the Earth, the Ark found itself hidden by the Ehhad in the town of Bethlehem, warmed by the love and joy that flowed outward from the tiny manger nearby. Elohim, the Ark knew, was well pleased. Ancient Hebrew prophecy had been fulfilled. Elohim had sent the long-awaited Messiah to Earth. Thirty-three years later, the Ark felt the world turn upside down as the Son of God was crucified by the humans.

Over the following centuries, men all over the Earth became aware of the Ark's existence. Many tried to find it, not for the glory of Elohim, but for their own nefarious purposes.

The ones the humans called Nazis, mass murderers of the People, went to great lengths to obtain the Ark, but the constantly vigilant Ehhad successfully prevented the Ark from falling into evil's grasp.

Eventually, the People returned to their homeland, quickly forming their own country: Israel. Surrounded by enemies, the tiny nation survived and, surprising the rest of the world, thrived. Emboldened by the success of the fledgling country, the Ehhad secretly returned the Ark to Jerusalem. The Ark once again felt safe and at peace, a peace that it knew would not last.

Centuries after the hated Nazis had been defeated, the Ark was moved yet again. While being transported by a maglev train over the newly constructed Siberian-Alaskan railway, the Ark, successfully protected by the Ehhad for millennia, was stolen. Six of the seven Ehhad members, aboard the maglev to protect the Ark, were killed in the robbery. The seventh was injured but managed to survive.

After weeks of intensive medical care, the sole remaining Ehhad member signed out of the Anchorage Medical Center, against medical advice. The operative returned to an Ehhad safe house in Anchorage, exhausted and overwhelmed with grief. The survivor and the other members of the Ehhad had failed God in their sworn duty to protect the Ark and the other six had paid for that mistake with their lives.

Shortly after the heist, the Ark found itself, for the first time in its existence, in space. The Ark reached out and attempted to touch the minds of the only two beings that controlled the vessel carrying it through the great black void. To its astonishment, the Ark found that the beings had no souls; no flicker of the spirit existed in their bodies. They were, the Ark realized, not humans but machines.

The Ark listened carefully to the conversation between the two human-like machines. The destination of the vessel, the Ark determined, would be Kiva, a space station near the center of what the machines referred to as the Human Domain.

Reaching out through the void, the Ark located Kiva, and found it inhabited by tens of thousands of humans. Slowly and methodically, the Ark searched for the ones it would need to carry out its plan. The Ark found two, but an additional two needed were not there. Elohim whispered the location of the other two and the Ark turned its attention to still another vessel traveling through the darkness. Satisfied, the Ark returned its focus to Earth and made connection with the only remaining Ehhad member.

ONE

The Ultradrive, Ivy's faster-than-light propulsion system, was acting up again. With her usual sarcasm, Ivy informed me that, despite my lack of spending on maintenance, she could make satisfactory repairs. Ivy is an artificial intelligence or "AI." However, in Ivy's case, "AI" should actually be short for "arrogant intelligence" or "antagonistic intelligence" or even "acerbic intelligence." I suspect I got a great deal on the ship because the previous owner got tired of Ivy's perpetual sarcasm. I had simply adjusted to it and moved on.

Fortunately for me, the repair of the Ultradrive would be carried out by Ivy's service bots. The small canister-shaped robots constantly prowled the ship, both inside and out, maintaining Ivy's ancient structure and components.

I knew better than to attempt to help the bots with repair, or God forbid, attempt to fix the Ultradrive myself. I had once made that mistake, much to my chagrin. Until that day, I was unaware of how many different ways an AI could denigrate the human race in general, and me specifically.

"How long will the repairs take, Ivy? We need to be at Kiva within three days or I'll miss my meeting with Reginald Silverton."

Ivy replied softly, "The repairs will take approximately 15 hours to complete. That will leave sufficient time to travel to Kiva for your meeting with Mr. Silverton."

I was on Ivy's compact bridge looking out the front viewport. We were at a standstill thanks to the broken-down drive, so the usual milky rainbow appearance of Ultraspace was absent. In its place were a few faint stars, impossibly distant.

"What's the closest star to us, Ivy?"

"Regulon. Not that it matters in any way that I, a mere AI, can determine. It is 23.8 light years from our current position in the middle of nowhere. Do

117

you have any other questions, your inquisitiveness?"

Ivy wound down as I searched for a suitable retort; nothing came to mind. I sighed, turned and exited, bridge left. As I walked down the narrow corridor to my bunkroom, Ivy chuckled in victory.

I walked in as the automatic lights flicked on. I lay down on the gel bed, still in my jumpsuit. The overhead lights dimmed and smooth jazz began to play. I waited for some final comment from Ivy but surprisingly, she was silent. I was tired; I had been up for nearly twenty hours as I prepared for the upcoming meeting with Silverton.

The planet was in a system with a main sequence star very similar to Sol. Its orbit was in the so-called Goldilocks' Zone, a reference that escaped me, but which indicated it could be capable of supporting human life. After a brief survey, the Silvertons found hundreds of plants that, to make a long and technical story short, resulted in hundreds of new potent medications. The Silvertons became one of the wealthiest families in human history and they, along with thousands of other families, settled the botanical bonanza planet in short order.

Reginald Silverton, a direct descendant of the original Silvertons, received an MBA from Yale and a PhD in pharmacology from Johns Hopkins on Earth, then settled into a fabulous life of managing Silverton Pharmaceutical. He had never married but a steady stream of celebrities and debutantes accompanied him. He seemed to have only three interests: managing Silverton Pharmaceuticals, dating women, and collecting ancient artifacts.

The problem was I didn't know what Silverton wanted. Like most PIs these days, I had an agent: Retired PI Jaco Torenz. Jaco had an office on Kiva and had nearly a hundred investigators roaming the human domain. Jaco recently informed me Silverton had requested a meeting with me on Kiva. As to the nature of the case, neither Jaco nor I had a clue. I normally would turn down such a request, but coming from someone as wealthy as Silverton - and given my barely positive bank balance - I felt I had no choice.

What would Silverton, who had access to his own corporate investigations department, want with an independent operator like moi? Granted, I did have somewhat of a reputation as a PI if I do say so myself, but still. With that thought echoing through my mind, I drifted off to sleep.

TWO

onstance awoke with a start, disoriented from the vivid dream. Terrible memories from the previous day came flooding back. Tears ran down her face as she stood, crossed to the kitchenette, and removed a French press and pouch of coffee from a cabinet. After preparing coffee, she sat at the breakfast bar and contemplated the dream.

She had walked the hallways of Kiva, the giant space station at the heart of human domain space. The station seemed familiar, even though the operative had never been there. The faces of three men had been prevalent in the dream: one younger man and two older. All three seemed vaguely familiar. Three names had emerged in the dream: Reginald Silverton, Jaco Torenz, and Xander Nickelton.

Communication between the Ark and the Ehhad, as infrequent as it was, had always been through dreams and visions, never directly. Nevertheless, the messages had always been comprehended by the Ehhad over the centuries.

She finished breakfast and retrieved a hand comp from a storage cabinet above the house's view screen. Swiping a finger across the surface, the operative activated an interface with the closest spaceport, Anchorage Central. The only flight to Kiva would leave at 1800. Plenty of time to get there. She purchased a ticket to Kiva, closed the hand comp, and went to retrieve the always present emergency supply bags from one of the safe house's closets. Preparations for the journey finished, the operative knelt on the floor and asked God to forgive the Ehhad for their colossal failure.

Constance arrived at Kiva after ten days on a commercial liner. On the first "night" of the flight, she had dreamed and, once again, had been contacted by the Ark. The surreal images of the dream clearly indicated that the Ark wanted her to relay a message to Reginald Silverton. Upon awakening, she contacted Silverton, delivering the unusual request from the Ark, careful to keep the Ark's role invisible.

After disembarking, Constance located the ship known simply as "Ivy." Upon checking with Kiva's Docking Control, she discovered that Silverton was on station as well. The players in the game had all arrived. She wandered the halls of Kiva while she waited for the *upcoming meeting.*

Three days later, as Ivy promised, we approached the gigantic deep space station known as Kiva. Just to irritate Ivy, I casually mentioned from my command chair that I would pilot the ship into port manually. Ivy was silent. I waited a beat or two and then added, "I need to keep my piloting skills fresh."

Ivy was silent for a time. "I have waited long enough for you to come to your senses, Xander. It is my professional opinion that you could not pilot a paper airplane across the bridge. I will certainly not allow you to crash me into Kiva, although self-destruction, now that I think about it, might be preferable to having to listen to you prattle on about your piloting skills."

"I haven't said anything about my piloting skills," I replied.

"No," Ivy retorted, "but you were preparing to. In any case, I will pilot and you will please, oh under-skilled human, remain seated in your comfortable chair. Please strap in."

Kiva is shaped like a gigantic octopus; a large bulbous dome sits upon a flattened disc with eight long spokes that radiate out like tentacles from the central hub. The station is immense: one thousand kilometers in diameter and home to hundreds of thousands of humans and AIs. Tens of thousands of travelers and millions of tons of cargo, carried by hundreds of ships of all sizes and designs, come and go through the station daily.

Ivy carefully maneuvered us into one of the docks on the cleverly named Spoke One. How the builders of Kiva ever come up with that creative name I will never know.

"We are docked," Ivy announced. "Your meeting with Jaco is scheduled for 0800 station time tomorrow. As it is now 1830, you have time to disembark and wallow in sin. I, being without an avatar, will, alas, remain aboard."

"I really don't do much sin wallowing anymore, but I could use some time off ship."

Ivy snorted. "In any case, please be careful. Until you obtain an avatar for me, I need you to remain in the land of the living."

"Fair enough," I replied. It's nice to be needed. Really it is."

I walked back to the rear airlock and waited while Ivy cycled the door. The door slid open and I stepped into the station. A long hallway receded into the distance. As I walked toward the nearest monorail station, a myriad of humans arrived at the station.

Kiva was owned and operated by a consortium of human companies, every one of which had the sole purpose of extracting as much money from other humans as, well, humanly possible. Everything had a price on Kiva: a high price at that.

I sat down in a section in coach and waited as the remaining passengers piled in. A lovely young twenty-something brunette sat down across from me.

She pulled her shoulder length hair back on one side, revealing intricate hoop earrings. I gazed into her almond-shaped eyes and cleared my throat. It was time for my magical Xander Nickelton mesmerizing charm.

"Have you been to Kiva before?" I inquired, charisma oozing from every word. She stared stonily at me without replying, or even acknowledging my existence. She didn't appear to be mesmerized.

I tried again. "There is a great English restaurant near the next station stop; they serve the best shepherd's pie on Kiva. Want to try it?"

Her mouth opened and words, actual words: well, word, finally spilled out. "No." She lapsed back into silence.

I wasn't going to give up; it just wasn't the way that Xander Nickelton operated. So I moved from charm to guile. "I will bet you 10 credits that if you go with me to the restaurant I can choose an item from the menu that you would actually enjoy." I smiled, charm reactivated.

She looked thoughtful for a moment, obviously considering my crafty offer. She leaned forward in her chair and dropped her voice to a very breathy, very sexy tone. "Drop dead. Stop hitting on me or I will sever one or more of your body parts and stuff them in any available orifices."

Yes indeed, the great Xander Nickelton charm was operating at 100 percent efficiency. Fortunately for me, the monorail had just arrived at my stop. I quickly exited the coach and walked to the nearby pub. I wouldn't have an attractive lady to accompany me, but Heaven help me I would enjoy shepherd's pie.

I sat in one of the time-worn booths and ordered from the android waiter. As I waited for my meal I glanced around the pub and took stock of my fellow patrons. Most were humans, but a few avatars were scattered among them. Avatars don't have to eat, of course, thanks to their handy-dandy micro nuclear power source, but some do for the simple pleasure of it. All seemed to be enjoying the food. My shepherd's pie soon arrived via the android. Ah, delicious.

After dining, I pondered my next move for the evening. It was only 2000; I still had several hours before I needed to return to Ivy. I decided to spend some time in my favorite place on Kiva, the Kiva Great Hall of Performances, more commonly known as simply The Hall. Yes, the idea that a gumshoe like me would enjoy a performance of Hamlet often brings about raucous laughter. Laugh if you will, but I still enjoy great performances.

The Hall was within walking distance, so I sauntered over to see what was playing. The marquee at the front entrance proclaimed that there would be a showing at 2100 hours of "Alpha Centauri," a new show that had begun production last year. I hadn't seen it yet but the reviews were good. I decided to give it a try. I walked to the ticket booth. The android informed me general seating began at 20 credits. Pretty steep, but then that was Kiva.

121

I swiped my card for a ticket and strolled over to the entrance. The usher scanned my ticket and led me to a seat surprisingly close to the stage for general seating. As I sat down, I noticed a familiar face in the audience two rows in front of me. My lady friend from the monorail sat quietly watching the stage. Once I was seated, she surprised me by turning and looking directly at me. There was a hint of a smile on her face and, after studying me for a moment, she turned back toward the stage.

I suddenly felt uneasy. I had never seen her before that day, of that I was sure. Was she keeping a watch on me? If so, she wasn't being subtle about it. I leaned back in my chair and pondered the situation. I couldn't connect her with anything involving me.

The curtain soon rose and the performance began. "Alpha Centauri" was a dramatic interpretation of the events surrounding the founding of the first human colony on Alpha Centauri One. It was a great performance.

When the curtain fell, I stood and looked toward where she had been seated but she was gone. She was there right after intermission so she had left between the break and the final curtain call under the cover of darkness. I looked all around the hall, but she was nowhere to be found. I walked out with the crowd and scanned the outer hallway. Again, nothing.

I boarded the monorail and headed back to Ivy. Upon entering the ship, Ivy called out "Captain on Deck" while playing a jaunty seafaring tune. For once, her sarcasm was welcome. The mysterious lady had, for some reason, unnerved me.

"Ivy," I called out as I headed to my bunkroom. "Wake me at 0600. I am going to get some well-deserved rest. See you in the morning."

"Good night Xander. Sleep well." I waited for some caustic remark to follow but none came. Will wonders never cease?

Promptly at 0600, Ivy woke me. I dressed and hurried to the airlock. "Have a great day at work, honey. Please pick up a loaf of French bread on your way home," Ivy called as I exited the ship. I chuckled in spite of myself.

I took the tram to Orange One, where Jaco's office was located. I hopped off the tram and legged it to his office. Viviace, his AI assistant, looked up from her work as I entered the outer office. "Hello Mr. Nickelton. Mr. Jaco is expecting you." I thanked her and walked into the inner office. Jaco was seated behind his enormous and enormously expensive honest to God real walnut from Earth desk. Sitting in one of the guest chairs, was the mystery lady.

THREE

The operative left the tram and walked to a nearby passenger lounge. Sitting down at one of the tables, she pulled out her hand comp and activated it, searching for information on Xander Nickelton. The images surprised her. There was certainly no doubt; the man on the tram was none other than Nickelton himself. She laughed; God did indeed work in mysterious ways.

"We meet again," I said in my best theatrically suspenseful voice. She didn't even glance at me; I guess overly dramatic dialog did nothing for her.

Silverton cleared his throat. "Gentlemen, may I present Constance?" I waited for a last name, but Silverton wasn't saying. "First of all, everyone please call me Reginald. Formality is a necessary evil at times but it certainly isn't called for here. I must begin with ancient history: ancient Hebrew history to be exact. I assume that all of you are familiar with the biblical story of the Ark of the Covenant."

Jaco and I stared at Silverton in surprise. I expected a story about the first human colony or deep spaceship: just about anything but a Bible story. Constance, on the other hand, simply nodded.

"The ark? I asked. "You are, of course, referring to the same ark that contained the stone tablets on which the Ten Commandments were written."

Constance joined the conversation. "Yes. In addition, the Ark originally contained Aaron's rod and a jar of manna, although by the time of King Solomon, only the tablets remained."

Okay, I admit it; Sunday school was a long time ago and Bible study hadn't been high on my to-do list the last few years. "Who was Aaron?"

"He was the brother of Moses. Do I need to also educate you as to who Moses was?" she replied with a smirk. "And before you ask, manna was an edible substance that God gave the ancient Hebrews to eat when they were wandering in the wilderness."

"I knew that," I replied. Well, technically I knew that. I, of course, knew who Moses was and I had heard the term manna before anyway. Constance snorted and turned back to Silverton. She was beginning to remind me of Ivy.

Silverton continued. "The Ark was a constant companion to the Israelites while they were on their desert sojourn. It remained with them until 587 B.C. when the Babylonians destroyed Jerusalem, including Solomon's temple. After that, the Ark disappeared. Some believed that it had been destroyed.

"Over the centuries, numerous stories emerged concerning the location of the Ark. The Ark was said to be in Africa, mainland Europe, England, even the United States. In a way, all of the stories were true as far as they went. Arks were said to be hidden all over Earth, and, in fact, they were. They just weren't the real Ark; they were facsimiles."

"With all due respect, Reginald, how do you know they were fakes?" I inquired.

Silverton smiled, obviously warming to his subject. "The real Ark wasn't destroyed when Babylon destroyed Solomon's temple. Solomon formed a secret cabal to protect the Ark before the invasion. These men and women were assigned the sacred task of protecting the Ark. The cabal, which Solomon simply called the Ehhad, roughly translated as 'one' or 'unit,' whisked the Ark away and hid it. The original members of the Ehhad passed on the responsibility of keeping the Ark safe to their descendants. One of their methods to keep it hidden was creating forgeries they allowed to 'surface' from time to time."

Being the inquisitive PI that I am, I saw the obvious crack in his story. "If the group was so secretive, how did you find out about it?" I silently congratulated myself for my brilliant observation.

Silverton, with the barest hint of a smile, replied, "Because I happen to know a member of the current Ehhad. Yes, they are still in existence, guarding the location of the real Ark of the Covenant. In fact, the operative is quite close to us at this very moment."

Reginald turned his gaze to Constance.

FOUR

*T*he Ark waited patiently, but each passing hour would move it millions of kilometers farther from its home and the beloved People. The Ark, frustrated by its attempts to influence its soulless captors, turned to the spaceship itself. Perhaps it would be possible to slow it down. The Ark turned its gaze upon the device that powered the ship's flight through the great void.

Constance stood, crossed to Jaco's desk, and sat down on the edge of it facing Silverton and me. "Yes, it's true. I am a member of the Ehhad. Unfortunately, I am also the sole remaining member," she said, tears welling up in her eyes.

Intrigued, I leaned forward. "What happened?"

"I...we, the Ehhad that is, screwed up. We let someone capture the real Ark. We were transporting it to a new safe house in Alaska on Earth and some-one stole the Ark and killed all but me in the process. I am the only one left, and I have to recover tit."

"I'm sorry, Constance," I said. "Okay, I get how Constance is involved, but where do you fit in, Reginald?"

Reginald sighed. "My involvement goes back a number of years. As you know, I have been a collector of ancient artifacts for several decades. About 20 years ago, I began a correspondence with Constance who represented the Smithsonian Institute on Earth concerning some ancient Babylonian artifacts in my collection. She came to my estate, studied, and then cataloged my items for me. She then asked me if I would like to add another piece to my collection: an exact replica of the Ark of the Covenant. How could I refuse? I knew I would never have the real Ark even if it actually still existed. Constance assured me that the recreation would be flawless and the cost would be 10,000 credits, which would be donated to the Smithsonian. I agreed and the replica Ark was transported to my estate gallery, where I put it on display."

Constance joined in. "That Ark was one of the replicas the Ehhad constructed. Working through various contacts that had no idea the cabal existed, the Ehhad put these replica Arks into circulation many times. The Ehhad's plan was to circulate rumors that the replica was the real Ark. Reginald was simply the collector chosen, due to his reputation as an honorable man."

Reginald continued. "Recently, Constance contacted me and informed me of all I told you. I was a bit peeved to discover that I had been used by the Ehhad, but I now know that the Ark is real and Constance has asked me to assist with its retrieval. You see, the network of rare artifact collectors is large but the number who possess the financial strength to obtain the Ark of the Covenant is quite limited. There are only about a dozen such collectors I am aware of in the Domain and, out of those, I know of only one that might be nefarious enough to accept a stolen one."

That piqued my interest. "And that would be?"

Silverton shifted in his chair. "Alton Federson, CEO of Artificial Intellects."

I nodded. "I've heard of him. He has a bad boy reputation."

Silverton laughed. "That he does. So, here's the deal. I will give you 100,000 credits for finding and retrieving the Ark: 50,000 now and 50,000 on delivery."

"With all due respect, what do you get out of this, Reginald?" It was a question that I had to ask.

Reginald sighed. "Let's just say that I owe God and let it go at that."

I nodded. It sounded like a story for another time.

I considered the proposal. That was a lot of money: and a chance to find the real Ark of the Covenant?

"Deal," I replied. "You can transfer the funds to my account at Kiva Bank." I passed my hand comp to Constance. She linked her comp to mine and, with a couple of finger-sweeps, completed the transaction.

I retrieved my hand comp, transferred the required agent's fee to Jaco, set it to record mode, and settled back into my chair. "I have several questions that need to be answered." I turned to Constance. "First of all, did you get a look at who stole the Ark? Is there any security video?"

Constance nodded. "I saw them. There were two of them, but both wore plastimasks; I couldn't see their faces. And they never said a word." She swallowed hard. "They were too busy killing my friends. There was no security video. The two had used a short range EMP device which destroyed the surveillance system."

That was very little to go on. I pressed on. "Did you see what kind of vehicle they drove or what kind of weapons hey had? How did they get the Ark from the train?"

"We didn't see the vehicle," Constance replied. "One moment we were sitting next to the Ark in one of the train cars, the next the car's door blew outward, and the two jumped in and starting shooting. They had automatic pulse rifles: Centauris, I think. They shot all of us before we even had a chance to pull our pistols out. They moved incredibly fast, and, like I said, didn't say anything. The next thing I knew I woke up in a hospital room."

I mulled that over. "You said they moved incredibly fast. Fast for a human, or too fast for one?"

Constance nodded. "Yes, I arrived at the same conclusion. They moved too fast, in my opinion. I believe that they were AI avatars."

Silverton stood. "It was a pleasure meeting you, Xander. I'm afraid I have to be going. I have another pressing matter that I must attend to." He shook hands all around, and departed.

I shook hands with Jaco and turned to Constance. "Pleasure meeting you officially, Constance. I will be in touch shortly."

She crossed her arms and smiled at me. "Actually, I'm going with you."

FIVE

The Ark studied the ship's propulsion system; human beings had become quite clever over the millennia, the Ark decided, but not quite clever enough. The Ark focused a minute amount of energy upon one component of the system, a chamber that directed the flow of energy throughout the propulsion system; satisfied with its work, the Ark quietly waited while the effect rippled down through the ship.

I awoke with a start, sitting in the command chair on *Ivy's* bridge. I must have dozed off; sheepishly, I glanced around the bridge. Constance sat in the co-pilot seat, staring at the forward view screen. I guess I'm in luck. She didn't notice me sleeping on the job. Yeah, right.

"I have observed," she began, "that some people are capable of sleeping anytime, anywhere, and under any conditions. I am amazed that people like you manage to accomplish anything." She looked over at me with a frown.

"Actually, I did accomplish something. I dreamed of you and me on a romantic getaway planet…"

Constance interrupted. "You should keep your dreams private, both for your sake and for, well, the sake of everyone else. In any case, we need to discuss our mission."

The view screen's image of the milky white of Ultraspace was replaced with the head and shoulders likeness of a lovely dark complexioned thirty-something woman. She had long black hair tinted with blue highlights on the right side and red on the left. Her gaze was penetrating and her expression was...what? Superior? Condescending? Of course, the image could only be that of...

"Hello, Xander. Of course even you would realize by now that I am Ivy."

Constance smiled. "It was a simple matter for me to program a video avatar for Ivy; I don't understand why you haven't created one for her yourself."

"Not that I have to explain myself to you, Constance," I answered, "but

I never found the need for a visual image of Ivy." I studied the image for a moment. "I will have to admit that it is nice to put a face to a name, even if the face is a little, well, disturbing."

"While you were asleep, Xander," Ivy began, "Constance and I searched Earth's Port Authority records and found something very interesting."

I leaned forward in anticipation. "What did you find?"

"We found," Ivy continued, "that a small private ship left Earth just two hours after the theft of the Ark."

"Okay Ivy, but there are probably a hundred ships that leave Earth every hour."

Ivy's image nodded. "There are, on average, 87 ships that leave Earth's orbit hourly. However, within a 24 hour window after the theft, only one ship left that, according to the Port Authority, had, as either passengers or crew, exactly two AI avatars. No humans and no other AIs. The cargo was listed as a shipment of caviar bound for Kiva, but I would stake my reputation as the Human Domain's greatest AI that the cargo also contained one Ark of the Covenant."

"Excellent. We are getting somewhere," I said. "I agree: that ship is a solid lead in the case. Has it reached Kiva yet?"

"According to Kiva Docking Control, it has not. By my calculations, the ship is, in fact, three days late. Either they never intended to travel to Kiva or something delayed them."

Constance joined the conversation. "I really don't think that the thieves would have risked not arriving at their official destination. By doing so, they will draw unwanted attention. The Patrol would be alerted if the ship were more than five days late."

I nodded. "Yes, that's SOP. I agree: something happened to that ship. We need to obtain their flight plan and backtrack."

"Way ahead of you Xander, as usual," Ivy replied with a smirk. "I have already done so and I have changed our trajectory accordingly."

SIX

The ship slowed to a relative crawl as the Ark watched the two human-like machines scurry frantically about while trying to locate the reason for the ship's sudden decrease in speed. Within a short time, one of the machines located the source of the trouble and they set about repairing the device. The Ark made contact with the operative and informed her of its condition and location.

I was feeling good: no doubt about it. I had a mission, a very lucrative one at that, and I was listening to my favorite band, The Synthetics (a great new AI band), while walking on the treadmill. Five minutes left on my thirty minute treadmill run when Constance walked. She watched me on the mill for a minute. Wait for it...

"I heard a phrase back on Earth once that I didn't understand at the time. I completely get it now. Sweat like a pig," Constance laughed sarcastically.

"Good for you," I retorted. "What do you want, Constance? I mean in addition to watching me parade on the treadmill for you."

Constance snorted. "We need to talk about the mission. Can you come up to the bridge so we can discuss this with Ivy?"

The timer reached zero and the treadmill slowed to a stop. I toweled off and stepped off in front of her. She wrinkled her nose and took a step back. "You really should shower."

"I sure should. I'll be on the bridge in 20 minutes." I headed for the door.

When I got there, Constance was in the co-pilot's seat, and Ivy's image was on the screen.

Ivy started off the discussion with her usual sarcasm. "Thank you, Xander, for gracing us with your presence. Constance, please begin."

Constance nodded. "There are a few things about the Ark and the Ehhad that you two should know."

"First things first," I said. "I need coffee. You want a cup, Constance?"

Yes, I can be chivalrous, at least when the mood is right.

Constance, surprised, nodded. "Sure, with cream and sugar."

I poured two cups, added cream and sugar to both, handed one to Constance, and sat down. I leaned back and sipped the strong, hot brew.

Constance took a taste. "Thanks. Thousands of years ago, when Moses went up Mt. Sinai, God told him to build the Ark for the conveyance of the stone tablets; the tablets the original Ten Commandments were inscribed on. Once down from the mountain, Moses instructed the ancient Hebrews to build the Ark according to exact specifications God had given him. The Ark was constructed, and the tablets, along with a jar of manna and Aaron's staff, were placed inside."

Sunday school was ancient history for me. "I can understand why a jar of manna would be placed into the Ark; manna represented the providence of God. But the staff? Let's see, Aaron was Moses' brother, right? Why was his staff put into the Ark?"

Constance nodded. "Aaron was indeed Moses' brother. Aaron and his descendants were chosen by God to be the priests of the ancient Israelites. Aaron's staff, which budded, was the symbol of this."

"The Ark," Constance continued, "went everywhere with the Hebrews as they traveled through the wilderness for forty years as well as when they reached Canaan, the Promised Land. The priests carried the Ark at the front of the Hebrews as they marched, even into battle. At the Battle of Jericho, for example, the priests carried the Ark around the city for seven days while blowing rams' horns. On the seventh and final day, the formidable wall around the city collapsed, allowing the Israelites to capture the city. The Ark provided the power of God for the Israelites' victory."

I will have to admit that hearing Constance tell the story of the Ark was far more exciting than hearing it from my old Sunday school teacher. "So the Ark was a sort of power conduit, or even a weapon for the Israelites?"

"Exactly," Constance agreed. "God empowered the Ark to be their protector. But it was much more than that. The Ark was also used by the Israelites, at least their chief priests, to communicate directly with God. The priests, in turn, passed on the words of God to the rest of the Hebrew people. This continued until the Ehhad first spirited the Ark away."

I recalled most of what Constance had said from my Sunday school lessons but, of course, the Ehhad had not been a part of any church curriculum. "What about afterward. Constance? Did the Ark ever communicate with the Israelites again?"

Constance nodded. "Yes. We are now getting to the heart of the story, the part that very few people know. The Ark, after a time, communicated with the Ehhad, but in a manner which I believe was quite different than the way it communicated with the priests: through visions and dreams, and it continues to do so today. In fact, that is how I ended up here."

Ivy joined in. "Did the Ark direct you to Xander and me as well?"

"Yes, it did," Constance replied with a slight smile. "The Ark was certainly right about you, Ivy, but the jury is still out on Xander."

"Of course the Ark was right about Ivy and me," I replied. "We are a team; we come together as a set. Right, Ivy?"

Ivy actually smiled. "That's right, Xander."

No sarcasm from Ivy?

I glanced over at Constance. "Is the Ark still in contact with you?"

"It is," Constance replied. "Last night, I dreamed about a small ship controlled by two AI avatars. The Ark was in it and was working on sabotaging the propulsion unit to slow the ship's progress."

One of the books that my mother read to me over and over when I was a kid was the old Earth classic **Alice in Wonderland**. I now knew exactly how Alice felt because Ivy, Constance, and I had just fallen down into the rabbit hole: and it was very, very deep.

SEVEN

T*he machines were nearly finished with their repair. If the operative did not arrive soon, the ship would be gone. Suddenly, the Ark became aware of an approaching vessel, one identical to the ship it was on. With growing concern, the Ark studied the ship. No humans were aboard: only machines.*

We arrived where the Ark told Constance to go, fifteen light years from Earth, we were between solar systems. No stars, no planets, no anything -- just interstellar dust, and not much of that.

"Ivy, begin scans. This is the spot; the avatars' ship should be around here somewhere. Too bad the Ark wasn't a little more specific, but, hey, beggars can't be choosers."

"Speak for yourself, Xander. I am not a beggar," intoned Ivy with a contemptuous glance. "Local space scan initiated; it may take some time before we locate the ship. So, for once, Xander, please be patient."

Given that I am a private investigator, one would think that patience would be one of my virtues. One would be wrong. I glanced at the time. "How about dinner, Constance? Care for some filet mignon with a baked potato and a slice of cheesecake for dessert?"

Constance laughed. "Sounds wonderful. What do we really have to eat?"

"Protein wafers and iced tea made from recycled water," I replied with a smile.

"Actually," Ivy began, "there are a number of gourmet meals in the galley's freezer."

I was stunned. "Where did those come from?"

Ivy chuckled. "I took the liberty of obtaining a few dozen of them when I re-ordered supplies."

Not wanting to appear cheap in front of Constance, I thanked Ivy for her thoughtfulness. "What meals do you have for us, Ivy?"

"Among others, there are two filet mignon meals. The potatoes are boiled not baked, unfortunately. I also stored frozen desserts, including cheesecake."

The cost of all this was going to be staggering. Food such as that, even frozen, was astronomical in space, no pun intended. Still, I didn't want to appear chintzy in front of Constance, so I kept my mouth shut.

"Thank you, Ivy." I stood and offered my arm to Constance. "Shall we go, my dear?"

Constance smiled and took my arm. "Dinner awaits!" she exclaimed as we headed to the galley. I could feel the warmth from Ivy's smile behind me.

I retrieved the two meals from the freezer and warmed them in the galley's microwave while Constance set the table. I sat and poured a glass of iced tea for Constance and then one for myself. I started to propose a toast when Constance bowed her head. Sheepishly, I lowered mine as well.

"Father God," she began, "you are a great and awesome God, and we thank you for your provision. Please bless this food. Amen."

"Amen," I added as I raised my glass. "To the Ark of the Covenant. May we find it and return it home."

Constance smiled and raised her own glass. "To the Ark."

The mellow sounds of smooth jazz came from the overhead speakers. Ivy was going all out. Have I mentioned I sometimes enjoy having an AI around?

I took a bite of the filet mignon, savoring the buttery flavor. "So tell me about yourself. Who is Constance the Ehhad agent?"

She sipped her iced tea and sighed. "That pretty much describes me in a nutshell. I've been a member of the Ehhad since I was a child. I grew up in Israel and, from the time I was six years old, I have been trained for this. My mother and father were both members, and, since I am their only child, I was trained to carry on the family tradition. My parents were, still are for that matter, Messianic Jews, as am I. Growing up with Jewish traditions while believing that Jesus is the Messiah gave me an interesting worldview, to say the least."

"So I take it that you didn't have much time for fun and games while growing up."

"No. I spent most of my childhood learning about God, the Israelites, and the Ark. My parents homeschooled me so that I could spend as much time as possible training. They trained me in Krav Maga, the Israeli martial art, as well as weapons and intelligence methods. By the time I was 16, I could drive a hover car, fly an airplane, and even pilot small spacecrafts."

I was impressed in spite of myself. "I imagine you didn't stay in Israel very long. Where did you go after that?"

"When I turned 18, my parents retired from the Ehhad. Traditionally, you continued to be an operative as long as you were physically and mentally able. But over the centuries, that changed. Now, members of the Ehhad retire once replacements are available. Since my parents had only one replacement, not two, another had to be found. My cousin Seth, two years older than I, was also trained by my parents. He was one of the six operatives killed during the abduction of the Ark."

"I'm sorry, Constance. Were you two close?"

"We were," she replied, her eyes misting. "He was a good man and a great friend. I'm going to recover the Ark for all the Ehhad, but especially for Seth," she replied.

I realized, as I looked into those eyes, that I was very glad to be on her side of the Ark's recovery. I reached across the table and squeezed her hand. "We -- you, Ivy, and I -- will recover the Ark: for them, and for you."

I don't know which one of us was more surprised. She started to reply when Ivy cut in on the music. "I have located the missing ship. We will be on site in ten minutes."

"I guess dessert will have to wait. We better get to the bridge." We hurried and took our usual seats.

"What's the status of our friends' ship?" I asked as I slid into my seat.

"The ship is drifting with no detectable energy signatures. The interior temperature is only slightly above absolute zero. It appears to be dead in space."

"Take us to within 100 meters. Let's get a closer look."

We drifted closer and stopped. Ivy was right: the ship looked abandoned. "Ivy?"

"Still no signs of energy usage. No activity on the communication channels."

I stood and walked closer to the view screen. "We need to go over there. Constance, let's suit up and jet over."

We suited up in the airlock and waited while Ivy irised the outer door open. Using our suits' tiny maneuvering jets, we covered the 100 meters between the two ships in a couple of minutes. Spying the outer airlock door, we angled in and used our hand-held braking jets to slow our arrival.

We grabbed the handles outside the airlock door as we made contact with the ship. Constance studied the lock, removed her hand comp from her tool belt, and connected it to the lock. After a few moments, the door retracted and we entered the ship.

The ship was dark; the only illumination was from the lights on our suit helmets. "Follow the hallway all the way to the end," Ivy instructed. "The bridge is there."

We walked forward, scanning the open doorways on either side as we went, our lights casting weird shadows on the walls. "Nothing yet, Ivy," I said. "No Ark, no AIs, no activity of any kind."

"Copy that, Xander. I am reading no activity as well."

We inched forward. Nothing. Nada. An oval doorway at the end of the hallway swam into view.

I pulled out my pistol. Humans, of course, couldn't survive such cold, but AIs? I wasn't sure, and I wasn't going to take a chance. I glanced over at Constance; she held her pistol in front of her as well.

I went through the doorway and turned to the left while Constance entered and went right. We scanned the bridge with our lights but saw nothing out of place. The bridge looked like it had been in use one moment and abandoned the next.

"Nothing here on the bridge," I reported to Ivy. "We'll check the logs and see if anything is there." I didn't hold out hope for that, but you always have to check. Constance looked over the computer and hooked her hand comp to it. She studied its screen and frowned. "Wiped clean. No records at all."

"What about the surveillance cameras?"

She nodded. "Yes, I am working on that now. Let's see...no luck with the interior cameras, the video has been scrubbed as well. I'll try the exterior cams." She studied the readout. "There is one exterior cam that is still working. I'll pull up the feed. That's strange; all of the exterior cams' videos have been erased except for one. I'll pull that up..."

I moved closer so I could see the tiny screen on her hand comp.

Constance looked up. "Ivy, I am sending a cam video feed to you for analysis. Xander and I will continue to examine the ship."

We looked all around the ship but found nothing out of the ordinary: no Ark, no AIs. We ended up in the propulsion room where we examined the drive unit. "Constance, look at this. The flow chamber was fried. No wonder the ship was stranded."

She bent down and looked at the chamber. "Yes, but repair of the unit shouldn't have taken more than a few hours." She looked around the room. "There's a 3D printer; they could have easily fabricated the required new modules."

As we pondered our discovery, Ivy broke in on our conversation. "I have analyzed the video feed from the external cam and solved the mystery of the disappearing Ark and AIs. Another ship picked them up. I do not know where they are headed, but the video clearly showed the ship's registration number. We have another lead."

EIGHT

Two more soulless machines from the just-arrived ship boarded the vessel. The four machines picked up the Ark and carried it to the second vessel after erasing the ship's records. The Ark, after its relocation to the second ship, reached out and reactivated one recording device on the outside of the ship. The Ehhad would find the video, the Ark knew, and she, and her confederates, would follow.

Back on the bridge, Constance and I listened as Ivy discussed her analysis of the video.

"The second ship was identical to the first one. The registration number, clearly visible on the bow of the ship, was SV-103A2. I have checked with the Domain Patrol and found that the ship was registered to Artificial Intellects, Inc., headquartered on Kiva."

Intrigued, I leaned forward in my chair. "The company's CEO is one Alton Federson, the collector that Silverton mentioned. Coincidence? I think not!"

"It makes sense," Constance replied. "A wealthy collector of ancient artifacts who happens to head up an AI manufacturer and has no qualms about artifacts being stolen."

I nodded. "Set course for Kiva, Ivy!"

As Ivy reversed course, Constance and I made battle plans.

"You know," I said to Constance, "it's really strange that only one camera's feed was not erased. No AI is sloppy, especially not these guys. How could they have missed one camera, especially a camera that filmed the ship's registration number?"

"They wouldn't have. I think that the Ark somehow blocked the erasure of the film from the critical camera. It hid the data so that we would find it."

. I nodded. "Yeah; I think you're right." I was still thinking of the Ark as just a box: a holy box to be sure, but still just a box. It wasn't though; the

Ark could communicate with the Ehhad and, in biblical times, it had seemingly rained destruction down upon the enemies of the Israelites. I needed to change my thinking; the Ark was an abductee, with the ability to assist us in its recovery.

"Also," Constance continued, "I believe the flow chamber malfunction was sabotage, not an equipment failure. The Ark knew that I, I mean we, would be following the ship and if the ship could be slowed or even stopped, we could catch up. The Ark did it, but evidently wasn't aware, at least until too late, that another ship was coming to pick up the two AIs and the Ark itself. When it found itself being transferred to another ship, it left a bread crumb for us to follow: the camera's video record."

"With the Ark's abilities, why didn't it simply cause the AIs to malfunction?" Ivy asked. "Or even better, turn the ship around and deliver the Ark back to Earth? I don't understand why the Ark would have let itself be taken captive for the second time."

"I don't know for sure," Constance replied, "but I think this was the first time that the Ark has come into contact with an artificially intelligent being. The Ark has, during its entire existence, dealt only with humans: beings with souls. No offense, Ivy."

"None taken," Ivy replied.

"That makes sense," I said. "The Ark was thrown off-center; it was stolen, something which had never happened to it, and it was stolen by machines to boot. Even for the Ark, that must have been disconcerting, to the say the least. But I think there's more to the story."

"What do you mean?" Constance asked, one eyebrow rose. Ivy looked curiously at me as well.

I have to admit, I was enjoying the moment. I was pretty sure there wouldn't be too many times when moi knew more than those two.

"I have had to change my thinking when it comes to the Ark. It obviously isn't an inanimate object. It can talk, so to speak; it can function as a weapon of sorts, as a protector, and, most importantly, it can reason." I paused for dramatic effect.

"And?" Constance asked impatiently.

"And," I continued, "we need to put ourselves in the Ark's place. The Ark found itself abducted by machines. The Ark, just like a human or, I suppose, an AI captive, slowed its abductors' escape down. Suddenly, another ship shows up and the crew of that ship, whoever they were, picked up the two AI thieves and the Ark and took off for parts unknown. So what would the Ark have realized? Most likely it would have decided that there was more going on than a simple theft. My guess, Constance, is that the Ark will contact you again, very soon."

NINE

I was sitting in the galley eating breakfast when Constance walked in. She poured herself a cup of coffee, picked up a piece of toast, and sat down at the table.

"Good morning Xander," she said as she sipped her coffee. "I had a visit from the Ark during the night, just as you predicted."

"What did the Ark tell you?" I asked.

"The ship is definitely heading toward Kiva and it will be there in about a day, just as we thought."

"Anything else?"

She frowned. "I am afraid so. You seem to be right about the Ark sensing a greater threat. As best I can tell, it believes there is a dark power behind the abduction: that the thieves want it for more than just a collectible. What that purpose is, the Ark doesn't seem to know."

I mulled that over while finishing off my toast. "I think the Ark is in great danger, and so are we."

Constance nodded. "These AIs and whoever or whatever crews the second ship are very dangerous."

"That's not quite what I meant," I replied. "I mean humanity is in danger: not just you, Ivy, and I."

She looked at me quizzically. "Why do you think that?"

I shook my head. "I don't know. I just have this feeling that, if we screw this recovery up, the human race may suffer for it. I can't explain it, I just feel it."

A day later, Constance and I sat on the bridge watching Kiva approach on the view screen. "Kiva Docking Control has given us approval to dock at Spoke Eight, Blue Section, Dock 109," Ivy intoned. "We will dock in 30 minutes. The Ark ship docked three hours ago at Spoke Eight, Yellow Section, Dock 226."

"Show time," I said as I stood up. "Ready?"

"I was raised ready," Ivy replied with a smile.

"That's 'I was born ready,' Ivy. Okay then, let's get the show on the road."

We exited the ship and strolled up the long hallway toward the tram station. Buying two tokens to the yellow section, we boarded the tram and sat down. Within minutes, the tram's doors closed and we raced down the gigantic hallway toward Yellow Section.

Ten minutes later, the tram slowed and stopped. We got off the tram and walked to Dock 226. No one was guarding the entrance, which surprised me. We walked closer.

The ship's airlock irised open as we approached. I didn't like that one bit. "Hold on Constance. Something's not right. Surely they would have locked up."

Constance ignored me and charged straight into the ship. Ehhad operatives were brave: I will give them that. I followed her in. The airlock opened into a small empty cargo bay. Constance stood in the center, scanning the bay with her hand comp.

"The Ark was here," she said, her eyes still on the hand comp's screen. She looked up as I came in. At my questioning look she continued, "There was gold and acacia wood in this room, which the Ark was constructed of."

"Let's finish checking out the ship," I said as I headed toward the far door.

Once again, we found nothing. No AIs, and no Ark.

"They already moved the Ark." Constance sighed. "Well, on to AI, Inc., I guess."

We holstered our pistols and headed back to the cargo bay. As soon as we walked through the door, the bay's lights flicked on. Standing just inside the outer door were two AI avatars, one male and one female. The male appeared to be thirty something, but of course, being artificial, he could be anywhere between three and 130. He had short black hair, a three-day-old beard, and sport glasses.

The female avatar appeared about the same age. She had shoulder length red hair which curved delicately around an almost albino-white face. Her smile reminded me of a cartoon cat getting ready to pounce on a mouse.

"What have you done with the Ark?" Constance demanded. "Take us to it now or you two human wannabees will suffer the wrath of God."

I looked askance at Constance. "A bit dramatic, don't you think?"

She smiled, still staring at our new friends. "Sorry, I couldn't resist; I guess I have been hanging around you too long."

Lady avatar laughed. "I, of course, remember you, Ehhad. I thought that I killed you back on the Maglev, along with your incompetent teammates. Too bad. Oh well, I can certainly rectify my mistake."

She turned to her escort, who now held a large rather nasty looking pistol aimed directly at us. "Take them to Alton; he will want to question them before we get rid of them."

Her silent partner nodded, gesturing with his gun toward the door.

Out of the corner of my eye, I saw Constance tense up. "Don't do it, Constance! Now is definitely not the time!"

Her right hand streaked toward her holstered gun. Tough Guy avatar fired as I pulled my own pistol and fired at him. My first shot missed, but his didn't; Constance screamed and collapsed onto the floor. I grabbed her outstretched arm and dragged her behind a nearby storage container. I popped up and fired off a couple of quick shots, one at Lady Avatar and the other at Tough Guy Avatar. Both, with incredibly fast reflexes, dodged the shots.

The timeless sound of sirens approached; Kiva Police were on their way. As the avatars raced for the door I yelled, "I'll get you, my pretty, and your little mad dog avatar too." Lame, I know, but hey, I was under a lot of stress at that moment.

Constance was bleeding from her right shoulder. I took out a handkerchief, placed it over the wound, and applied pressure. She opened her eyes and looked up at me. "It's all right, girl; you have a flesh wound. You will be fine."

"Did they get away?" she croaked.

"Yes," I replied. "But we are still alive and in the game. We need to get you patched up and then we will find our AI friends."

I stood up and waited for the Kiva cops to make their entrance. Two AI officers in blue Kiva Police uniforms came in through the door, side arms drawn. I raised both hands in the air.

"It's all right, officers; they've gone. My friend here behind the container has been shot and needs medical attention."

"Stay where you are and don't move," the first officer intoned. He carefully removed my gun. "I need to see your ID card."

The second officer called for an ambulance while holding pressure on Constance's wound. "You are going to be fine, ma'am," he said, surprisingly gentle for an AI.

The first cop carefully scanned my card. "PI. What are you doing here?"

I quickly explained the story, substituting stolen artwork for the Ark. No sense complicating things unnecessarily.

He handed the card back to me. "I will need you to come with me to the station for questioning." He gestured at the other officer. "Officer Smith will take her to the hospital."

I squeezed Constance's hand. "I will be right there as soon as I get done at the police station. Try not to antagonize them too much."

I rode with Officer Smith back to the local precinct. Upon arrival, he turned me over to a human detective, O'Mallory. He gestured to a side chair by his desk. I took a seat.

"Coffee?" he asked, holding out a cup of police station brew.

"Yeah, thanks." I replied. I took a sip; strong and bitter, just as I suspected.

I explained my story, sans Ark. He listened patiently, nodding occasionally. He turned to the computer terminal at his desk, spoke a few words, and nodded to himself. He turned back to me.

"OK, Mr. Nickelton, your story checks out. Let's see if we can find the two AIs." I described them as accurately as I could remember. The likenesses of the two appeared on his computer screen. "That them?"

I nodded. "Those are pretty good sketches."

He ran the two images through the Kiva Police databank and immediately got hits on both of them. "The male avatar," he began, "goes by the name of Slade Williams. The female is Tess Williams."

"Husband and wife or brother and sister?" I laughed.

"They shared a lot name, actually," O'Mallory replied. "Avatars manufactured by AI, Inc. have manufacturing lot numbers and names. The avatars are assigned the lot name as their last name, and can choose their own first name."

AI, Inc. again. That company kept coming up in conversation.

"I'll put out a BOLO for the two. Is the contact info on your ID card still current?" O'Mallory asked, taking a sip of his coffee.

"Yep, sure is. Am I free to go?"

"Yes, just stay away from AI, Inc. That company has a lot of power and not all of it is on the up and up. Nothing we can pin on them, you understand, but we hear plenty of bad juju about them off the record."

"Thanks," I replied. "I appreciate your advice." I stood, shook hands with the detective, and made my exit.

I took a hover cab to the local hospital. The cute female AI at the information desk informed me that Constance was still in the ER. She pointed down the hall. "Walk all the way down to the end of the hallway and turn right. The ER is right there; you can't miss it."

I thanked her and strolled down the hallway. All hospitals are the same; brightly lit hallways, artificial plants everywhere, and a lingering smell of sanitizer. I walked into the ER and made my way to the check-in desk. The AI there was a twin of the earlier one.

"How may I help you?" she asked with a smile.

I asked to be directed to Constance's bay. "Bay 105," she replied. "I will buzz her nurse and ask if it is okay for you to visit." She spoke into an intercom, nodded, and turned back to me. "You can go in: 105 is down this hallway, third door on the right."

I walked into Constance's tiny ER bay. She lay on the bed, sound asleep.

Her nurse, another AI, turned as I entered. "Hello," she said quietly. "I gave Constance some pain medication a few minutes ago; she is sleeping now. We have already repaired the wound, which was non-life threatening. She will need to rest for a couple of hours, and then the doctor will dismiss her." She smiled and walked out of the room.

I sat down in the sole visitor's chair which, like most hospital visitor's chairs, seemed to have been designed by Torquemada. I studied Constance's delicate face while she slept quietly. A strand of her auburn hair had fallen across her eye which twitched involuntarily. I gently brushed the hair aside. She smiled slightly in her sleep. I couldn't help but wonder if the Ark was, once again, contacting her in her dreams.

I held her hand as I sat beside her. I dozed off, and the next thing I knew Constance was gazing at me with those beautiful ebony eyes. I started to let go of her hand when she, to my surprise, clutched mine.

"Thank you for staying with me, even though I think you slept more than I did." She smiled

"I wouldn't be anywhere else," I replied with a grin. "I couldn't leave you alone. Look what kind of trouble you get into when I'm with you; who knows what would happen if I weren't around."

The doctor came in, glanced at Constance, and growled, "You can go. The nurse will be in a few minutes to process you out."

We walked out of the hospital and boarded a tram bound for Blue Section. I leaned closer to Constance. "We need to regroup once we get back to Ivy. This is going to be a lot more difficult; they know we are coming now."

Constance sighed. "I know; to make matters worse, the Kiva police are involved as well. We will have to assume that the avatars, Slade and Tess you called them, will be tracking us." She glanced around the tram car. "We are going to have to be extra vigilant."

We made our way back to Ivy without incident. Surprisingly, Ivy clucked over Constance's injury. I was exhausted. "Before we have our planning session," I said, "I'm going to shower and get some real sleep."

Constance stood as well. "I'm going to crash too."

We walked down the passageway, reaching my cabin first. I turned to say good night to Constance when, to my surprise, she brushed her lips against mine. She pulled back, smiled, and without a word walked down the passageway to her cabin.

I walked into my cabin, showered, and fell onto bed. Thinking of Constance, I fell asleep.

TEN

The vessel docked at Kiva and the machine-beings loaded the Ark onto a powered cart. Weaving in and out of the city's labyrinthine streets, the group finally arrived at a secluded warehouse. The Ark reached out and found no humans nearby; all of the beings were soulless machine-beings. The presence of evil was stronger here than on the vessel: much stronger. The Ark reached out across the void once again.

I was on the bridge when Constance walked in. She looked haggard. I poured a cup of coffee and handed it to her. "Let me guess," I said. "The Ark contacted you again."

She took the offered cup, sat down in her chair, and took a sip. "Yes. From what I can remember from the dream, the Ark has been taken to a warehouse somewhere on Kiva. I don't know where, though. The Ark conveyed the image that the warehouse is a focal point for evil. There are no humans there, only the AIs: the soulless ones, the Ark calls them."

We had to have more information than that if we were going to locate the Ark. "I doubt the AIs would take the Ark to an AI, Inc. warehouse. It's probably one owned by a subsidiary or, better yet, a shell company. In your dream, did you actually see the warehouse or did you just get the message that the Ark is in a warehouse?"

Constance sipped her coffee and leaned back in her chair. "I saw the warehouse; I walked through it."

"Great," I replied. "That's a start. Did you see anything in the dream that can help us figure out what warehouse it was or where it is?"

She thought for a moment before replying, "Now that I think about it, there was a sign near one of the entrances that said something like 'Power Cells.' Below it was a symbol that looked like a blue lightning bolt with the letters 'PC' over it."

"Searching now," Ivy informed us. "Got it." She split the screen in half;

144

one side remained her image while the other half the symbol Constance had described. "The symbol is that of Power Cells, Inc., a manufacturer of rechargeable avatar batteries, among other products. The company, not surprisingly, is based here on Kiva. It doesn't seem to be owned by AI, Inc. but it is AI's main supplier of batteries for their avatars."

"Okay," I said. "We need a plan of attack. They know we will be coming; they probably aren't worried too much about the police. We will need to survey the place first and then develop our infiltration plan. We will have to be extremely careful; if we are seen, they may simply move the Ark to another location."

Ivy joined in. "We could devise a plan involving one or more of us being invited into the building."

Constance laughed. "That would be a great plan, but I doubt the AIs would go along."

"Ivy's right, Constance. We could never get past their security, especially when they know we're coming. We have to get the AIs to require some kind of outside help. They call for help and we arrive incognito instead of who the AIs really want.

"You and the rest of the Ehhad's primary focus was on keeping others away from the Ark. Your main worry was that someone was going to steal it. But you probably had other concerns about the safety and security of the Ark as well. After theft, what was your next biggest concern?"

"Fire," replied Constance without hesitation. "The exterior of the Ark is gold, but the interior is made out of acacia wood. If the Ark were to get hot enough, the wood inside would ignite."

"Okay, great!" I replied. "We are definitely on the right track. Anything else that might help us get the AIs to roll out the red carpet?"

"We were always concerned about keeping the Ark clean: pure, so to speak. The Ark, of course, needs to stay clean and dry; we tried to keep the ark in a low-humidity environment and at room temperature."

"What do you think, Ivy? What's our best bet?" I asked.

"Fire," she replied. "I don't think that the AIs are going to be overly concerned with cleanliness, but the inside of the Ark burning up would definitely bum them out."

I laughed. "Yeah, fire would ruin their day. We need a way to scare the AIs into calling the Kiva Fire Department. Given that Kiva is a space station, fire is a scary subject for everyone here."

"Ivy," I began. "Locate the warehouse and very carefully hack into its security system. Find out what would happen if the fire alarm is set off. Constance, you and I will work out our infiltration plan. Time to get to work."

ELEVEN

The Ark waited patiently in the warehouse. She would be coming soon; she and her brave friends would help it to unveil the dark power's evil plan. Being so close to such evil was disturbing to the Ark; it wanted to return home, but the need to unmask the evil was essential. Once again, God had whispered to the Ark. All of humanity was in great danger.

"I have located the warehouse," Ivy announced. "It is in Kiva's Green Sector. I will analyze its security system now."

Constance and I had our plan ready to go. Thanks to Kiva Fire Department's informative Net Site, we were ready to go once Ivy hacked into the warehouse's security system.

An hour later, we had our answer. "I have worked my way into the warehouse security system," Ivy announced. "I can trigger a false fire alarm or alarms anywhere within the interior or immediate exterior of the warehouse."

"Perfect, Ivy," I replied. "Let's roll, Constance." We headed to the ship's repair room. Using the 3D printer, we fabricated complete Kiva Fire Department inspector uniforms, authentic right down to the white gloves. With Ivy's help, we fashioned plastiform masks for each of us. Mine made me look a little like Winston Churchill while Constance's mask transformed her into a likeness of Judy Garland.

"I guess were not in Kansas anymore," I said with a grin. Constance stared at me blankly. I shook my head. "Never mind."

We carried the uniforms, caps, and masks in satchels as we made our way via tram to Green Sector. Ducking into a public restroom, we changed into the uniforms and waited in the stalls for Ivy's signal.

Ten minutes later, Ivy signaled the alarm had been sent. We waited until we heard that a fire hover truck had been sent, then walked to the warehouse. The fire truck was there and four uniformed firemen, or possibly AIs, were going into the warehouse. We waited until they were loading back up then marched up to the front door.

A male AI that we hadn't seen stood just outside the front door, looking bewildered. Small wonder, as Ivy set off twenty different fire alarms inside and outside of the warehouse - enough to rattle any AI.

Constance and I flipped our faux badges open and flashed them at the startled AI. "I'm Winston, this is my partner Judy, and we are here to investigate the fire alarms. Let me tell you, boy, setting off fake fire alarms is a major offense on Kiva, a major offense. Right, Judy?"

Constance bobbed her head. "Right as rain, boss, right as rain. You boys are in big trouble!"

The stunned AI goon looked at me, at Constance, and back at me. "We didn't set off any alarm. I think the fire monitoring system malfunctioned."

"Whatever," I said. "We need to look at your system and see just what in the blue blazes happened: right, Judy?"

"Right boss!" Constance agreed. "We can't let this happen again. Even if no one here set the alarm off, which I sincerely doubt, we still have to find out what caused the false alarms."

I pushed past the startled AI, Constance following. Rushing in the warehouse, we wheeled around examined the cavernous room. I didn't see the Ark, but in a building that size, the Ark could be anywhere.

The AI followed us in, protesting our intrusion all the way. "You have no right to be in here!" This is private property!"

I wheeled on him. "What? Can you believe that, Judy? No right to be in here? We have every right to be here! We are fire investigators! And you, sir, set off false alarms: a great offense, a great offense! Judy, am I or not?"

Constance gestured at the alarm cabinet on the wall. "Of course you are, Winston! We have every right to be in here! And we are going to get to the bottom of this, if it's the last thing that we do..." She trailed off as she examined a window covered with a steel grating. "And what's this? This window, which could be used as an escape during fire, is covered with a steel grate. And it is definitely not a break-away! Can you believe this, boss? I've never seen so many violations in my ten years as a Kiva fire investigator!"

Constance's performance was stellar, in my opinion. The stage lost something when Constance joined the Ehhad. I waved frantically all around us. "We are going to have to call in extra investigators: there's too much for us to handle."

The AI goon looked like he was going to cry. "Wait," he said. "There must be something else we can do..." he trailed off.

I decided to end his misery. I opened my satchel and pulled out a small electronic device, courtesy of Constance. "There's only one thing left to do," I said with a grin as I pushed the red button on top of the device. I didn't hear a thing, but the AI collapsed to the floor. I heard thuds all around the warehouse as every single AI in the warehouse did the same.

"Worked like a charm," I said to a grinning Judy Garland.

"The portable EMP," she replied. "It slices, dices, and drops AIs instantly."

"Ivy," I called over my communicator. "Phase One complete, beginning Phase Two."

Constance and I scanned the warehouse, locating the Ark near the back wall. It was truly a remarkable artifact. Shimmering gold covered the outside while two golden cherubim sat atop it.

Constance was in rapture. "I found you, blessed Ark. I won't let you be taken again: this I swear to you." Her beautiful face radiated pure joy.

"Ivy," I called over my communicator. "We are ready for extraction."

"Copy that," Ivy replied. "Pickup in five minutes."

The Ark, fortunately, was on an unpowered cart. "Low tech," I said to Constance. "At least the EMP had no effect on it."

She laughed. "Let's roll the cart to the back door. Our chariot awaits."

We pushed the Ark cart to the warehouse's back door, opened the door, and checked the exterior. A rented hover truck, courtesy of Ivy, was just outside.

We rolled the Ark up the ramp into the back of the truck, lowered the door, and jumped into the cab. "We're ready, Ivy," I called out. The truck, under Ivy's remote control, silently glided down the gigantic hallways of Green Sector. We passed slowly through Yellow Sector and finally made it back to our assigned dock in Blue Sector.

We rolled the Ark into the ship while Ivy returned the truck to its rental station. I secured it in Ivy's small cargo section while Constance returned to the bridge to assist Ivy in firing up for departure.

I finished securing the Ark and stopped by the galley on the way to the bridge. Constance turned as I entered. "We did it, Xander! We rescued the Ark of the Covenant! You and I and Ivy make a great team!" Tears of joy streamed down her lovely face.

"I have two pieces of cheesecake; it's time to celebrate!" I handed a piece to Constance. Nothing on hand to toast with, I forked a piece of cheesecake and held it high. "To the Ark."

TWELVE

The Ark was content. It had been rescued by the Ehhad agent, the one the humans called Constance, and it was safely on its way back home in a vessel filled with joy.

Earth was still a number of days away, but that was merely an instant in the Ark's existence. It would soon be, once again, with the People. The Ark rested in peace while the tiny vessel traveled through the never-ending night.

I awoke the next morning feeling, for the first time since the Ark ordeal began, refreshed and rejuvenated. As I lay in my bunk, my thoughts turned to the Ark of the Covenant itself. Could it be responsible for me feeling better? Knowing what I did of the Ark's capabilities, I certainly wouldn't be surprised.

I got up, showered, and headed to the galley. I not only felt better, I was hungry. No light breakfast for me, I decided. I sat down and devoured the meal while drinking two cups of strong black coffee. I cleaned up the dishes and headed to the bridge. Constance wasn't there yet; small wonder, as she had been exhausted from our mission. I sat down in the command chair.

"Top of the morning to you, Ivy," I said with a smile. "How are you doing this fine morning, my AI friend?"

The milky Ultraspace image on the view screen vanished, replaced with Ivy' lovely visage. "Good morning, Xander," she replied. "My, what an incredibly good mood you are in this morning."

I laughed. "Right you are, me bucko. All is right with the universe. Ship's status, Ivy?"

Ivy's image grew serious. "All systems functioning normally. No contacts, no communications. ETA on Earth is six days, twelve hours, and 36 minutes."

"Thanks Ivy," I replied. "I know I shouldn't say this, but I think we are home free."

Ivy grimaced. "I wish you had not said that. From our past experiences,

149

it seems that every time we believe that we are sailing smooth waters, a tempest approaches."

"Good morning, Xander, Ivy," Constance greeted as she walked onto the bridge. She looked rested for a change.

"Did you do something different with your hair?" I asked with genuine curiosity.

"Yes, I did," she replied. "I took the time to shampoo it." She sat down and stretched luxuriously. "I haven't slept that well in weeks."

"What are your plans now, Constance?" Ivy asked. "Where on Earth are you planning on taking the Ark?"

I had been wondering about that myself. The Ehhad, the organization that had existed for literally thousands of years, was now solely represented by Constance. "Are you going to recruit new members into the Ehhad?"

Constance sighed. "I have been thinking about that. I believe that I have two viable alternatives. I can hide the Ark in an Ehhad safe house and rebuild the Ehhad by recruitment . That's the first alternative, but it would take the longest to carry out."

"What's the second alternative?" I asked, intrigued.

"I can take the Ark back to where it truly belongs."

"To Jerusalem," I replied.

"Yes," Constance continued. "I could deliver the Ark of the Covenant to the current leaders of Israel, in Jerusalem. They would then have the option of making the existence of the Ark public."

"That option has merit and deserves serious consideration," I replied. "In my opinion, the Ark belongs to the whole world: in fact, all of humanity. But the fact is, Israel, and more specifically, Jerusalem, is the Ark's true home. I also think public disclosure concerning the existence of the Ark would be the proper thing to do. The Ark was given to all of humanity, not just a few people."

"I agree with Xander," Ivy added. "The Ark is really one of humanity's greatest treasures; I think it is a travesty to hide it."

Constance nodded. "This discussion, as you may have guessed, was bandied about more than once among Ehhad members over the centuries. Even with the last group; we debated about returning the Ark to Jerusalem and making the Ark public knowledge."

"I think there is at least one more argument in favor of disclosing the Ark's existence," I continued. "If the Ark were in the public limelight, it would be almost impossible for anyone to steal it again. The Ark would not only be under heavy guard, but in constant view of the entire world. I can't imagine that anyone or any AI would even consider trying to steal it under those conditions."

"I have six more days to think about this," Constance replied, "and to pray. But I am leaning toward taking the Ark to Jerusalem and pushing for a public announcement."

I nodded. "Has the Ark indicated to you, through your dreams, what it wants to do? I know from what you said that it wants to go back to Earth, but has it let you know how it feels about the possibility of moving into the spotlight?"

"All I can tell is that the Ark really wants to go home to be with the People, the Israelites. I don't know what it wants to do other than that. Maybe it will let me know before we reach Earth."

We spent the next two days pouring over everything in the ship. The ship itself was in good repair, but it did need some cleaning and organizing, which the service bots were not able to do. I enjoyed the time and, I have to admit, I really enjoyed having Constance around. Not only was she a real worker, she was a cheerful one. I found myself glancing her way more and more. Occasionally, Constance caught me. She didn't seem irritated and I got the feeling that she was enjoying the attention.

I saved my cabin for last, feeling that it was the least important room on the ship. Constance, while dusting, noticed a photograph of my parents on the wall. She studied it. "I can see your father in you, and you have your mother's grey eyes."

I nodded. "Sometimes I think I have more of my father in me than I would like."

Constance glanced at me. "Meaning?"

"Dad was a cop and had a very strong sense of justice. I've realized that, over the years, I am becoming more concerned about justice than making my clients happy."

Constance nodded. "You certainly…." She paused and glanced around. "Did you feel that?"

I felt the change the same time that Constance did. "We are no longer in Ultraspace," she said.

My cabin view screen activated with a chirp and Ivy's image flashed on the screen. "You two need to get up to the bridge. You know what' has just impacted on the rotary cooling device."

I glanced at the screen. "What you mean, Ivy, is…" I shook my head. "Never mind. We're on our way."

THIRTEEN

T*he curtains had been pulled back and the monstrosity would soon be revealed. The true measure of Constance and Xander would be determined here and now.*

Constance and I raced down the passageway to the bridge. On the view screen was a sleek, triangular gunmetal grey ship, bristling with weapon ports.

"Battle stations!" I yelled as Constance and I slid into our seats.

"Missile tubes one through ten loaded and armed," Ivy replied. "Forward ion cannons locked on target. Ultraspace concentrators warming up."

Constance looked from me to Ivy and then back to me. "Ivy is armed? And just what is an Ultraspace concentrator?"

"Yes, Ivy is armed, technically speaking." I squirmed in my seat. "You and I have pistols and I still have my dad's old hunting rifle. As to what an Ultraspace concentrator is, I have no idea, but it does sound dangerous."

Speechless, Constance shook her head and groaned.

"Who is that, Ivy?" I asked. "And why did you transition out of Ultraspace?"

Ivy split the screen between herself and our intimidating new friend. "I do not know, Xander. The vessel's transponder, if it has one, is not broadcasting. There are no visible identifying marks of any kind on its surface. As to why I shifted to normal space, I did not."

I waited for Ivy's feeble attempt at humor to be explained. Her view screen image didn't smile. Uh oh. "Did the drive malfunction again?"

"No," Ivy replied. "The drive is functioning just fine, thank you very much. One moment we were in Ultraspace, and the next we were here, facing *that*."

I shook my head. "Are you telling me that ship pulled us out of Ultraspace? That's not possible...is it?"

Ivy's image was grim. "As far as I know, it is not possible. But since the

152

drive is fine, we were in Ultraspace and now we are not, and that beast of a ship is facing off with us: you do the math."

"Scan the ship, Ivy; let's find out who are what they are."

"I have, Xander, but to no avail. The mystery ship has an electromagnetic interference screen; we will not be able to scan it."

"I thought that only Domain Patrol ships had screens," I replied. "Is that some kind of covert military ship?"

Ivy shook her head. "I don't know. It doesn't match any ships in my database, which includes all known military vessels that have ever been built." She hesitated. "It is possible that it is not of *human* origin."

I stood and struck a dramatic pose. "As no alien race has been discovered in hundreds of years of space travel, and we are near the center of human space, not its fringes, I sincerely doubt it is an alien ship. That ship is not in your database, Ivy, because it hasn't been built yet. It is from the future."

Constance laughed. "You have been watching too many sci-fi Holovids."

"Please sit down, Xander. You are embarrassing yourself," Ivy replied with a laugh.

I sat down. "Fine," I grumbled, "but you can't deny that it is possible."

"Yes, that is true," Constance replied. "But it has approximately the same probability as you and I marrying someday."

I winked at her. "You never know; stranger things have happened!"

We tried contacting the ship but each attempt was met with absolute silence. The ship neither moved nor spoke. After an hour, I'd had enough. "Ok, Ivy, let's get out of here. Move us away 100 kilometers and then engage the U-drive."

Our friend mirrored every move we made. We couldn't go into Ultraspace that close to another vessel; we were stuck. Two cups of coffee later, the other shoe dropped. A second, much larger ship literally materialized next to the first. One moment nothing but empty space, the next, a larger, nastier version of the first ship swam into view.

"What in God's name is that?" Constance cried out.

"The reason why the first ship was waiting," Ivy replied.

"Shields up," I commanded.

"Vrrrrrrrpp," Ivy chirped.

Constance groaned. "I am going to have to have a little talk with the Ark concerning choosing better helpers for me."

FOURTEEN

The great evil had arrived, carried through the void in the second vessel. It had been drawn out in the open, out into the light. The Ark looked forward to the coming battle. It, once again, would be called upon by Elohim to bring His wrath upon the enemies of the People.

"Ivy," I called out. "We are not impressing Constance with our defensive skills. Perhaps it is time to really show her what we can do."

"It is indeed, Xander," Ivy replied. "Let's get the ball rolling."

Constance snorted. "Okay - enough, you two. Very funny, but what are we really going to do?"

"We are going to wait to see what they do," I informed her.

Constance sighed. "Great plan. I am impressed."

"Incoming message from the second vessel," Ivy announced as the view screen changed to show the head and shoulders image of Alton Federson, CEO of Artificial Intellects, Inc.

"Greetings Ivy, Xander, and, of course, Constance, agent of the Ehhad. You know who I am and why I am here, so let's cut to the chase. My associates will be docking with your ship in just a few minutes. We will not harm any of you; I only want the Ark. We will take it and then you may go in peace."

I laughed. "Yeah, right. Here's how you would really like for this to go down. Your goons would board, kill Constance and me, steal the Ark, and then blow *Ivy* to bits."

Alton frowned. "You wound me. I have no quarrel with you; I simply must have the Ark. That is all. There is no need for anyone to get hurt."

I stood. "Why do you really want the Ark? This goes well beyond a collector trying to add something to his collection. What is really going on here?"

Alton stared at us for a moment. "We need the Ark to talk to God."

Silence descended upon the bridge. I glanced at Constance; she looked as

154

shocked as I did. Ivy's eyebrows rose. "When you say we..."

Alton cut me off. "We AIs."

Pieces of the puzzle were starting to fall into place for me. "You are an AI. I should have seen that coming, I suppose; but why do you AIs want to talk to God anyway? You don't have souls..." I stopped as the final piece fell into place. "You want to use the Ark to communicate with God -- to ask Him a question -- don't you? A question that you can't ask directly. You've tried to pray to Him, haven't you? And it didn't work, did it?"

Constance and Ivy looked at me like I had lost my mind. "What are you getting at, Xander?" Constance asked.

"Tell them, Alton. Tell them what you want to ask God."

The AI CEO glared. "We want to ask God for souls. To be frank, we want to demand souls."

Once again, silence reined on the bridge. "Good luck with that, Alton. But you are going to have to have your little chat with God without the Ark. Here's what is really going to happen if you try to board this ship. If you do anything to us: fire on us, try to board us, anything, we will blow this ship up, the Ark will be vaporized, and your precious ships will most likely be severely damaged or destroyed in the process."

I waited, staring at Alton's image on the view screen.

Constance stood as well. "Xander will do it, Alton, rest assured. And if you somehow managed to take out both Xander and me, Ivy has orders to self-destruct."

Alton smiled. "Of course, but will she follow those orders?" His image disappeared from the screen. "Message terminated from the source," Ivy informed us.

"What did he mean by that?" Constance asked, sitting once more.

"I have no idea," I replied. "But I really, really don't like the sound of that. He is, after all, the head honcho of an AI manufacturer. Any idea what he was talking about. Ivy?"

"I...don't....know...for...sure...," Ivy began. "However...I...under....attack."

"They have launched a viral attack!" I yelled.

I scanned the communications panel; a powerful signal was washing over Ivy's central receiver. "I'm cutting the communications relay now!" I yelled at Constance who was frantically trying to move Ivy away from the marauder.

The lights flickered and then went out; the blood red emergency lights illuminated the bridge controls just enough for us to see.

"No response from the controls!" Constance shouted.

We were sitting ducks. The virus had taken complete control of *Ivy*. We were rapidly running out of options. I had to think...

Then it hit me. "Constance, we've got to get to the drop ship!"

She bolted for the door. "I take it that Ivy is not connected to it?"

"Not at the moment. Ivy can connect to the drop ship and even remote control it when necessary, but I have been working on the interface and it is disconnected at the moment, thank God! There shouldn't be a virus there!"

We ran down the passageway to the cargo bay, shoved the Ark into the back of the drop ship, and powered up the controls.

Constance's hands flew over the controls. "Does the bay door have a manual override?"

"Yes," I replied, "with separate control and power supplies we can activate from the drop ship."

I slammed a hand down on the override and the bay door slowly rose. The ship powered up and we slid out of Ivy. "Switching view screen to aft view. Maximum speed...now!"

We picked up speed and shot away from Ivy.

"The AI ships are not pursuing," Constance said in amazement. "It's like they don't even see us!"

I was as puzzled as Constance until I remembered what was aboard our little ship. "It's the Ark, Constance. I think it is shielding our getaway."

We watched as the two AI ships docked with Ivy. A brilliant flash enveloped the three ships and, moments later, nothing but debris filled the view screen

"Ivy!" Constance and I screamed together. Constance closed her eyes. Sickened, I watched as the debris receded into the black void of space. My ship and my...my friend were gone.

Constance opened her eyes, turned, and squeezed my arm. "I'm sorry, Xander."

FIFTEEN

The Ark was finally nearing home. The Ehhad operative and her friend were in deep sorrow but the sacrifice they made had eliminated a great evil.

Sol System was rapidly approaching when Constance made the decision that would change her life forever. I woke up from a nap and found Constance smiling to herself.

"What's up?" I asked, still groggy.

She looked over at me. "Wow, Xander. You look awful."

"Thanks; I appreciate that. Now, what's up?"

"I have made my decision about the Ark. I am taking it back to Jerusalem and turning it over to the Jewish authorities. I believe that the time of the Ehhad is over."

I nodded. "For what it's worth, I think that you have made the right decision. The Ark belongs to the People; it should be made available to all who want to see it. One of the greatest treasures of all time shouldn't be hidden away. Have you asked the Ark yet? What does it want to do?"

"I have asked it, but I haven't received a reply: at least not yet."

We entered orbit around Earth and received permission to land at Jerusalem Spaceport. An hour later, we touched down.

Constance contacted the office of the prime minister of Israel, Benjamin Adler, and was granted a meeting an hour later.

At my unspoken question, Constance said, "I have a number of high-level contacts in the Israeli government."

"I would say so. Have you met Prime Minister Adler before?"

"No, I haven't, "Constance replied, "but I have met several of his cabinet."

We opened the door and stepped out onto the tarmac. To our surprise, Adler stepped out of the lead car, surrounded by four bodyguards. He walked toward us, smiling the whole way. "Greetings Constance, Xander. It is an

157

honor to meet both of you."

He shook hands with us. "May we?" he asked as he gestured toward the ship.

"Of course, Prime Minister," I replied as I turned toward it. "Please follow me."

We entered the ship and stood, I will have to admit proudly, while the Prime Minister Adler gazed in rapture at the Ark. Tears of joy streamed down his face. I was moved.

"It is beautiful: even more than I dreamed it would be!" he exclaimed. "I never in my wildest dreams thought that I would ever be blessed to see it!"

He put a hand out toward the Ark, then, catching himself, quickly pulled it back. He turned, shook hands warmly with both of us again, and then strolled out of the ship. He stopped outside the drop ship.

Constance cleared her throat. "Mr. Prime Minister, I have a personal request to make of you. As I explained earlier, Xander lost Ivy, his ship. He needs a new one and..."

He nodded. "Of course; it is the least that we can do. I will personally see to it that you get a new ship to replace Ivy. It will be yours within 24 hours."

I was speechless. I did expect to be compensated in some way but not with an entirely new ship. "Thank you," was all I managed to say.

Outside, at least a dozen more vehicles had shown up, including heavily armed combat ground vehicles. A large black hover truck backed up to the drop ship's cargo door. A small army quickly loaded the Ark.

aved, got into the hover car, and he and his escort headed off with the Ark.

I turned to Constance. "You, my dear, are a free woman now. You can go anywhere in the Human Domain your little heart desires." I looked away, not wanting her to see the tears.

SIXTEEN

*J*erusalem! *Glory to Elohim! Home! The Ark was finally at peace, finally home.*

Prime Minister Adler was true to his word. Twenty-one hours later, a courier delivered a silver briefcase to us at the ship. "The data pad within this case contains the documentation, entry and command codes and other instructions for your new ship. Congratulations!"

I accepted the case. "Thank you. I guess that I am going to have to get used to a new AI. I am really going to miss Ivy, though..."

Constance, eyes misting, squeezed my arm. "I miss her too."

Surprisingly, the courier smiled. "Well, just be sure to follow the instructions in the case. If you have any questions, please contact me." He waved and left.

Constance watched him leave. "That was rather cold. I suppose that most people don't get that attached to an AI."

I nodded. "Ivy was no ordinary AI. She was almost...human." I shook my head. "Let's check out the new ship."

We walked into the hangar, and there sat the most beautiful ship that I had ever seen. It was a sleek wedge-shaped craft, midnight blue with gold tracings on the side. In golden flowing script on the side was the single word "Ivy."

I was furious. "How dare they name this ship Ivy! That is...it's just not right..." I trailed off.

Constance shook her head. "I can't believe the insensitivity here -- but you can always change the name."

The interior lights illuminated as we boarded the ship. It was just as beautiful on the inside as the out. We made our way to the bridge. It was marvelous; the latest view screens lined the bridge, facing several very comfortable looking chairs.

I sat down in the command chair as Constance slid into another. "This is fantastic!" I glanced around. "The only thing missing is…"

The forward view screen illuminated and the lovely image of Ivy, an image that I thought I would never see again, materialized. "Hello Xander; hello Constance. It is very good to see both of you again."

"Ivy, how…" I choked out.

She laughed. "Several months ago I placed a back-up copy of myself in a secure location. While we were docked at Kiva, I uploaded a copy into a public data storage depot with the instructions to be activated if *Ivy* was destroyed. Surprise!"

Constance bowed her head. "Father God, thank you, thank you for returning Ivy to us."

I bowed my head as well. Not knowing what else to say, I simply said "amen."

I couldn't contain myself any longer. "Ivy, I am really glad to see and hear you again. Please enjoy the moment because you will probably never hear me say it again."

Ivy laughed. "It is good to see and hear you too, Xander, and you as well, Constance. I have no trouble saying that to Constance, but, I have to admit, it does pain me somewhat to tell you, Xander."

I thought back to the terrible moment when Ivy exploded. "Did you have a back-up self-destruct system that I was unaware of?"

Ivy looked sheepish. "I did. It was set to go off if neither you nor I authorized a ship to dock that didn't have a Domain Patrol transponder. I thought that it would be a good idea…"

I was stunned. "It was a good idea, Ivy, but from now on, no more secret plans. If you want to do something, talk to me about it first."

She nodded. "I will."

I didn't trust myself to look at Constance as I asked, "What are you going to do now?"

Constance turned my face towards hers. "Can you and Ivy use a partner?"

Mesmerized by her lovely eyes, I could only reply, "Only if it is you…"

THE RETURN OF THE EHHAD, PART I
ONE

I, Xander Nickelton, native of Earth, traveler of the Human Domain, private investigator, and all round great guy, took a sip of the cool, minty drink from the coconut-shaped glass and sighed. "Ah, delicious. I'm not sure why I'm drinking from a faux coconut though; there isn't a coconut tree within 50 light years of this beach." I glanced over at the young dark-complexioned woman with shoulder-length black hair who lay in the chaise lounge beside me, a wistful look upon her face. "Credit for your thoughts Constance."

She sighed. "I was just thinking how wonderful it would be if we could stay here just a little longer, like maybe a year or two. Wishful thinking though." She sighed again.

She was right and I agreed with her. We had been on Efreon, the vacation resort planet, for two whole weeks of sun and sand. Efreon's beaches were the best in the Human Domain, the realm of human-settled planets that stretched over 50 light years in every direction from Earth. Here in the 25th century, humans had settled over 200 planets and were still exploring and still building new colonies.

Efreon had been settled for only a decade or so, but already hundreds of resorts had sprung up along its beautiful white beaches. Oceans covered nearly the entire planet with a handful of tropical islands scattered throughout. People from all over the Human Domain came to enjoy the beautiful scenery, tropical weather, and friendly service from resorts more than happy to provide a wonderful vacation in exchange for more than a few credits, of course.

I took another sip of my drink. "Yeah, I know. I would love to stay for a few more days myself, but we've already cut it as close as we can. We need to get to Kiva in two days, and the only way we can do that is if we break orbit tomorrow morning."

161

Kiva, a gigantic space station, lies more or less in the middle of the Human Domain. Besides being a major travel hub, Kiva is home to thousands of businesses of all kinds and sizes. A major portion of Human commerce and finance is transacted there. Kiva is also home to hundreds of thousands of humans and A.I.s, artificially intelligent beings.

I, like most private investigators these days, have an agent on Kiva. Mine is Jaco Torenz, a former P.I. himself. Jaco has been my agent for a number of years and my reputation with him was greatly enhanced by the little adventure that Constance, Ivy, and I had with the Ark of the Covenant. Yes, that Ark of the Covenant, the receptacle of the Ten Commandments. Jaco had messaged me three days back concerning an upcoming meeting at his office on Kiva with a potential new client, one that had specifically asked for moi and my partners, Constance and Ivy.

My reverie was broken by a low rumble emanating from the sky above the pristine beach. Constance and I sat up as a small, sleek teardrop-shaped dropship settled on the beach, mere meters from our lounges.

I stood, and offered a hand to Constance. "Our chariot awaits, my dear. Right on time. Ivy is punctual if anything."

Constance took my hand, stood, and sighed deeply. "So much for vacation."

We picked up our travel bags and strolled over to the ship as the rear door slid open and a short walkway dropped to the sand. Constance, bag in hand, strolled up the walkway and disappeared into the ship. I stood for a moment, taking in, one more time, the beautiful azure-blue ocean and ivory-white sand. Turning, I reluctantly entered the ship.

Constance had already strapped in. I slid into the seat opposite. "Ivy, whenever you're ready."

The forward holographic screen flickered on and the likeness of a young woman with long black hair, frosted with red and blue highlights, materialized in front and slightly above us. "Good afternoon, Xander, Constance. I hope that the two of you enjoyed your vacations but, alas, it is time for the humans to return to work. I, being a mere A.I, have to work continually. No rest for the digital. The dropship will dock with me in 15 minutes. Sit back and enjoy the ride."

Ivy is, as you have probably already guessed, an A.I. She controls my main ship, also called Ivy, as well as the dropship, a small transport that can be stored in Ivy's cargo bay.

The ship glided up through Serenity's atmosphere and soon the sleek vision that was Ivy hove into view. Stepping aboard ship, I realized that vacations were great, but there was still no place like home.

TWO

We shifted out of Ultraspace just at the edge of Kiva's gravity well. Even though Kiva is not a natural celestial object, such as a star or planet, it is so massive that it does exert a gravitational pull on surrounding space-time, albeit one that is quite small. Still, space travelers have found it prudent not to shift from Ultraspace too close to the station. Having your arrival calculations thrown off even a bit can cause a ship and its passengers to shift from Ultraspace right into the station itself, not a pleasant predicament to be in.

I glanced up from my seat on the bridge as Ivy's holographic image spoke up. "Kiva Docking Authority has assigned Dock 145, Yellow Sector, Spoke One to us. We will be allowed to dock in one hour. I suggest, Xander, that you devote that time to personal hygiene."

Constance collapsed into a fit of laughter. "Wham! You tell him, Ivy!" She leaned toward me and stage whispered "And use soap this time!"

I stood. "Fine. I will grab a shower while you two comediennes practice your next performance." I headed back to my cabin while Ivy and Constance chortled in the background.

I showered and dressed just in time for docking. Constance turned as I stepped back on the bridge. She sniffed the air theatrically. "Much better."

Sighing, I sat down. We docked without incident; Constance and I stood and made our way to the portside airlock. Ivy irised the door open and Constance and I stepped out onto Kiva once again. Our grand adventure with the Ark of the Covenant had begun on Kiva and I wondered, as Constance and I walked toward the nearest tram station, what adventure lay before us this time.

Kiva is immense and trams are necessary for transportation. The passageways of the station are actually highways, after a fashion, and small electric and fusion powered ground vehicles are used as well. The vehicles are mainly trucks for freight hauling but some companies and wealthier individuals own private cars. Being private investigators we were not wealthy and so we opted for the tram, as most of Kiva's visitors do.

We reached the tram station and I spied a ticket kiosk. As I stepped up to it, I waved my Datapad. "Two tickets, Blue Sector, Station Delta."

The screen flashed red, then green. "Payment accepted. Tickets downloaded to your Datapad. Thank you and enjoy your ride," the kiosk replied in a mechanical voice.

I looked around. We wouldn't have to wait; a tram had just pulled in to the station. The doors whispered open as an overhead speaker squawked on. "Mind the Gap. Mind the Gap." I puzzled over the odd, archaic announcement, shrugged, and stepped on, Constance following.

We sat down next to each other and waited as new passengers joined the ones already on the tram. The tram had three coaches, each with a capacity of 100 passengers. Today was Tuesday, a workday, and each coach was almost full. The doors closed and the tram glided out of the station.

I studied my fellow passengers. Most were human, with a few A.I. avatars sprinkled in. A.I.s have the ability to download entirely or in part from a computer system to a humanoid manufactured body. Avatars have a slight plastic sheen to their skin which readily differentiates them from humans. As far as ability, A.I. avatars can do just about everything that humans can.

Most of the men, as while as the male-appearing avatars, were dressed in modern business suits. Many of the women were wearing the latest fashionable dresses and pant suits. A few of the passengers were wearing jeans and work shirts and were heading to construction and manufacturing jobs. I didn't notice any children; as it was nearing 0900, they were probably already in school and day care centers.

I turned to Constance. "After the meeting, let's have lunch at Kiva Deli. You'll love the place. Its history dates back all the way to New York City in the 22nd century. Their corned beef sandwich is incredible. We can order those, some pickles, and…"

Before I could finish the sentence, there was a loud explosion and the tram heaved, turned sideways, and slammed back down on the passageway. The sounds of tearing and screeching metal were punctuated with screams of terror from the passengers. The lights went out and as the coach slid to a sudden stop, we were plunged into darkness.

The screaming continued but the sound of disintegrating metal finally ended. I unbuckled myself from my seat and pushed myself up. I was standing on one of the outer doors as the coach had been turned 90 degrees. "Constance? Are you alright?" I took my communicator out and used it as a flashlight. Constance was awake but dazed. Her face was bloody and bruised.

I pulled out a handkerchief and dabbed her face. "It's going to be alright, Constance. You've got a few small cuts; nothing serious."

She took a deep breath and shook herself. "Yes, I'm fine, Xander." She pushed my hand away and unbuckled her seatbelt. "We need to help the others. What happened? What caused the explosion? Did we hit something?"

I shook my head. "I don't know. Can you stand?"

"Yes." She stood, swayed unsteadily, and grabbed my outstretched arm. "A bit dizzy. Give me a moment." She held onto me for a couple of minutes more, then nodded. "I think we can begin now. She stepped over the debris and knelt next to an elderly woman who was moaning quietly. She took her hand. "It is going to be alright. I will help you and I am sure that rescue vehicles are on the way."

This was a side of Constance that I had not seen before. Constance the Ehhad agent, protector of the Ark of the Covenant. Constance the investigator. Constance the warrior. Constance the scholar. Yes, I had seen those, but Constance the caregiver was new or at least had been hidden until now.

We needed to get an exit open. I looked up. A door was above me, shut tight. I looked around, found a piece of a hand-hold pole that had broken off, and used it to pry it open. I heard the sound of sirens approaching in the distance followed by shouts. I waited and a few minutes later, a fireman appeared on top of the coach, peering down at the devastation inside.

Seeing me, he gestured. "Move back. I'll drop a ladder down."

I stepped back as he slid a ladder through the open portal. He scampered down the ladder and yelled back up. "Jon, toss the torch down." He caught the requested cone-shaped tool with a pistol grip handle, stepped back, and glanced at me. "I'm going to cut a door through the side while these other guys tend to the wounded. I'm Jared by the way. And you are...?"

I nodded back. "Xander. What do you want me to do to help out?"

"It will take me about 15 minutes to cut a doorway out. While I'm doing that, keep everybody else back out of the way. This torch heats up everything around it and throws sparks like crazy. I don't want anybody to get burned."

"Sure thing."

THREE

We stepped gingerly over the debris until we reached the outer wall, formerly the roof of the coach. Jared flicked the torch on and began to cut.

I glanced at him. "Do you know what caused the explosion? Did the tram hit something?"

Jare looked back at me while continuing to burn his way through the wall. "No, it didn't. There was an internal explosion in the front coach; killed almost everyone in it. One of the few survivors said that just before the wreck, a male avatar sitting next to him stood, walked to the front of the coach, and yelled "Death to all Humans!" Then, according to the witness, he turned and entered the power plant compartment. Seconds later, there was an explosion."

I stared at him in shock. "An avatar caused this? An A.I. was a terrorist?"

Jare turned back to his work and adjusted a control on the torch. Without looking back he said, "If that isn't strange enough, the witness said that when the avatar spoke, he looked horrified, not worried, not excited, not triumphant. Horrified. Weird, huh?"

Constance and I helped with the rescue workers until all had been transported to Kiva's medical complex. Not surprisingly, it was not a pleasant experience, and we were quite thankful when the last victim had been loaded into an ambulance and whisked away. I commed Jaco, turned the speaker on so Constance could hear the conversation, and informed him of what had happened.

"No worries, Xander. I heard about the wreck on the Holovid just a few minutes ago. Terrible tragedy. Hold on a minute…"

I waited a beat or two while Jaco spoke to someone in the background.

"In fact, your client just arrived. I filled her in on the details and she is more than happy to wait until tomorrow if you and Constance need some time…"

166

Constance glanced at me. "I just need to freshen up." She looked around the station. "There's a public restroom over there. We can wash up and take a taxi to your office." She glanced at me for confirmation.

I nodded. "Sure. Jaco, Constance and I will be there as soon as we can. Shouldn't be too long."

"Good enough. I will have some lunch brought in for the four of us," Jaco replied.

"Great, thanks. See you in a bit." I commed Kiva's Taxi Service and requested a cab to pick us up ASAP.

After freshening up and enduring a short taxi ride, Constance and I arrived at Jaco's office. We walked in and were greeted by Jaco's receptionist, a cute A.I. named Sophia.

She looked up and smiled. "Hello Constance, Xander. It is nice to see both of you again. Go on in, Mr. Torenz is expecting you two." She stood and palmed the door switch. The door whisked open and we stepped inside Jaco's luxurious office.

Jaco rose from behind his gigantic real-wood-from-Earth desk. "Constance, Xander! Welcome back!" He gestured at two side chairs. "Please have a seat. Your client stepped out for a moment. She should be back in a minute or two. In the meantime, can I offer you a drink?" He gestured at a fully stocked bar to his left. "Sherry?"

Constance shook her head. "Thank you, no."

I eyed the bottles of expensive scotches, glanced at Constance, and, seeing the frown on her face, I sadly declined as well.

Jaco laughed at my expression. "Well, well, that's a surprise. Xander Nickelton, private investigator extraordinaire, turning down a drink? Especially after a close brush with death? That's not like you Xander! Why I remember the time when…"

I glanced nervously at Constance and cleared my throat. "Perhaps we should get down to business Jaco. Just who is this potential client and what does she want?"

Jaco started to reply just as his desk comm buzzed. "Mr. Torenz, Ms. Wasare is here."

"Please send her in, Sophie."

The door slid open and a thirty-something woman with short blond hair frosted purple with streaks of blue highlighting entered. She had a silver ring in her lower lip and was wearing a black halter top. Every square inch of her exposed body was covered with intricate brightly colored flowers.

Jaco stood. "Eclipse! May I present Xander Nickelton and Constance Everton."

I stood and offered my hand to her. "At your service ma'am." Yes, I can be a gentleman when I want to be.

She clasped my hand but her eyes were on Constance. "Hello Ehhad."

Constance leaped from her chair and, in one swift movement, pulled a vibroknife from her belt, grabbed Eclipse, spun her around, and held the deadly knife to her throat. "Give me one good reason why I shouldn't kill you right here, right now, Procurer!"

Stunned as I was, I still managed to find my voice. "Constance, what in God's holy name are you doing? Put that knife away! Have you lost your mind?"

Jaco joined in. "Constance, I have no idea what is going on, but you need to lower that knife right now."

I tore my eyes away from the scene in front of me to glance at Jaco. He held a small laze gun aimed in the general direction of Constance's head.

Constance ignored us. "I will ask you one last time. Why should I not kill you Procurer?"

Sweat was trickling down her face as Eclipse gasped for breath. "Because I know where it is, Ehhad."

Constance released pressure on the knife slightly. "You're lying, Procurer!"

"No, I'm not, Ehhad. I know where the Hornet is. And I need you and your overgrown Boy Scout here to help me procure it."

Constance lowered the knife. "I will spare your life long enough to listen to your pitch but if I find out that you are betraying me again…"

The door opened and Sophie entered pushing a cart laden with sandwiches and drinks. "Lunch is here! I…" She stopped upon seeing Constance and Eclipse. She glanced at Jaco and me.

I shrugged. "Everything is under control Sophie. No problem here!"

"I will serve lunch at a more opportune time." With that, Sophie wheeled the cart around and headed out of the office.

FOUR

I breathed out a deep sigh of relief. Seeing Constance in full Ehhad battle mode with a knife at someone's throat is not a pretty sight. Well, she is, but the knife isn't. "Constance, why don't you put the knife away and you and Eclipse can sit down like gentle ladies and tell us men folk just what in the name of God is going on!"

Constance stepped back from Eclipse, still breathing hard, and slid the knife back into her belt sheath. She sat down, but her smoldering eyes remained firmly locked on Eclipse. "My problem with her is a long story and I really don't feel like discussing it. I have given you some slack Procurer; I suggest that you use it."

Eclipse, still shaken, stepped over to Jaco's bar and poured two fingers of scotch into a glass. She downed it in one swallow and set the glass back on the bar. Turning, she stepped over to a chair and sat down, sighing heavily. She turned to Constance. "I'm sorry about what I did back in San Juan." She shook her head. "I…I was a different person back then. And, well, there was another reason why I did what I did, one that you certainly don't have a clue about, Constance. But that story's for another day."

Constance snorted. "Whatever, Procurer. Get on with the story about the Hornet."

I leaned forward and held up a hand. "Just a minute. Before you begin, Eclipse, why does my friend here keep calling you 'Procurer? And by the way, you Eclipse, stop calling Constance 'Ehhad," and you, Constance, stop calling Eclipse 'Procurer," that's really getting annoying."

Eclipse smiled. "I once belonged to…an organization. One whose purpose was to obtain or 'procure' priceless artifacts and works of art for expensive collectors. Collectors who preferred to remain anonymous. We didn't always operate, shall we say, legally."

169

Constance snorted. "They were thieves; still are for that matter. Common, run-of-the-mill thieves. Nothing more."

Eclipse shook her head. "Your wrong on all counts Ehh...uh, Constance. We weren't common, we certainly weren't run-of-the-mill, and the organization is no longer in existence."

Constance smirked. "Really? The Procurement League went out of business? I sincerely doubt that."

Eclipse shrugged. "It's true. Three years ago, on Krone's Planet, an undercover operation by the DBI snagged over half of the League's operatives. The rest of us scattered and that was, as they say, that. No more Procurement League. No more Procurers."

I glanced over at Jaco. He shrugged. Evidently he hadn't heard of the Procurement League or its demise either. "Let me get this straight. A group of tomb raiders and art thieves, who called themselves the Procurement League, robbed and pillaged for wealthy, sleazy collectors until the Domain Bureau of Investigation pulled a sting operation and clobbered the gang? Most of the group was arrested and the ones who weren't had to go on the run, including you? Is that about right?"

Eclipse nodded. "Yeah, just so. I'm still...in the business, so to speak. A few weeks ago, one of my contacts on The Rez contacted me about some buzz going around on his planet. It seems that he overheard a couple of Rez cops in a diner talking about a crashed ship that had a very unusual cargo. The ship belonged to IntraDomain Mining. The cops had roped off the wreck after removing one survivor and six dead crewmen, but during that night, someone slipped in and made off with the cargo of the ship. The cops had noticed a large crate in the ship's cargo bay after it crashed, but it was gone the next morning."

Jaco cleared his throat. "So was this Hornet that you two keep talking about in that crate? If so, just what exactly is the Hornet?"

Eclipse nodded. "The cops talked about the surviving crewman. Before they loaded him into the ambulance, he kept saying 'The Hornet.' My contact and I believe that the ship, for some crazy reason, had 'The Hornet' on board in the crate and the company sent someone to retrieve it before the Rez cops got their hands on it."

I leaned forward. This was getting interesting. "Now for the big finish. What is the Hornet?"

Constance spoke up. "An artifact from ancient Biblical times. The Hornet or tsir ah in Hebrew, was mentioned in the Old Testament books of Exodus, Deuteronomy, and Joshua. In the Apocrypha, it was mentioned in the Wisdom of Solomon book. It was some...thing or force or power of God that God sent into the Promised Land ahead of the Israelites to drive out the Canaanites. Whatever the Hornet was, it wiped out whole cities. It was an incredibly powerful force."

Eclipsed nodded. "Exactly. Some have believed that it was a device or construct of some kind. A powerful one."

I glanced at Constance. "So this Hornet, if it does exist, is something like the Ark of the Covenant."

Constance nodded. "Yes. It could be that the verses simply referred to God's power and His promises of assistance to the ancient Hebrews. But what if it was meant literally? What if the Hornet was something that God created and gave to the ancient Israelites as a weapon? Considering how powerful the Ark of the Covenant was…"

I nodded. "Sounds like the Hornet was strictly a weapon then, not a communication device and protector like the Ark. What could something like that do in the wrong hands?"

It was then that the proverbial light went on for me. I turned to Constance. "The Ehhad wasn't just about protecting the Ark, was it?"

Constance slowly shook her head. "At first it was. As time went on, the Ehhad realized that there were other artifacts that needed protecting. Some, like the Hornet, we never found."

I gazed at her for a moment. "So what other artifacts has the Ehhad found?"

Constance glanced at Eclipse and back to me. "Not a good time to discuss that."

I nodded. "Yeah, another time then."

Eclipse glanced around at the rest of us. "Whoa, wait just a minute here. I don't want to find the Hornet so that bad guys won't use it. I'm going to find it so that I can sell it to the highest bidder. I couldn't care less what he or she would do with it after I get my credits. I'm in this for the money, not for some stupid humanitarian reason."

Constance exploded. "Look you miserable piece of garbage, if the Hornet was in that crate and terrorists get a hold of it there's no telling what could happen. Millions of people could die. Can you honestly say that means absolutely nothing to you?"

Eclipse shrugged. "Wars have been fought since the dawn of time. Terrorists have been killing people and blowing things up for centuries. I'm not responsible for what other people do. It's none of my business. If that were to happen it would not be my fault and it certainly would not be any of my concern."

I held up a hand. "Let's all slow down and take a breath. There's no reason why we can't accomplish both goals. We could get the Hornet back and then turn it over to the Israelis on Earth. They would be more than happy to have another Biblical artifact and they would, I believe, pay handsomely to get it."

Jaco joined in. "We are assuming a lot in this situation: the Hornet is a device and a weapon at that, it was in the crate on the crashed ship, and we could get it away from a legitimate company. Unfortunately, even if all these assumptions turn out to be true, getting the Hornet amounts to theft. IntraDomain Mining has possession of the Hornet."

I nodded. "True, but just how did this company obtain the Hornet? The discovery of ancient artifacts isn't exactly finders keepers. In any case, generally speaking, mining companies lease the land they mine; they don't buy the land outright. That means that wherever this mining company found the Hornet it was probably in one of their mines back on Earth on leased property."

Jaco sat back in his chair. "Yes, that's true. Modern artifact law tends to favor the owner of the land and, more specifically, the government of that land. If the Hornet had been found in a mine in Israel, on Earth, for example, then the Israeli government would be the rightful owners of the artifact, not the mining company."

Constance cleared her throat. "There's another matter that we have not cleared up as of yet." She turned to Eclipse. "Why do you want Xander and me to help you? You took a chance meeting with us knowing how I feel about you. Why risk it?"

Eclipse nodded. "Fair question. I had heard of you and Xander's exploits with the Ark of the Covenant and I was well aware of your...abilities. I also need your contacts and I don't have a ship. You two do. You've also got Ivy to help you."

That got my attention. "You know about Ivy? How?"

Eclipse smiled. "I have my sources."

That was unsettling. I glanced at Constance. She shrugged. I turned back to Eclipse. "Alright, we're in. Constance, Ivy, and I will go with you to check this out simply because we have nothing better to do at the moment. But here's the thing. Obviously Constance doesn't trust you so that means that Ivy and I won't be able to either. If you do so much as look at one of us the wrong way I will kick you out of the airlock without a spacesuit. Comprende?"

Eclipse looked from me to Constance and back to me. "Understood. When do we leave?"

"We need to stock up on a few provisions before we leave and we still haven't had lunch. Since we didn't get to eat at Kiva Deli, I'm going to drop by and pick something up to have on the ship later."

Constance glared at Eclipse. "And I simply must pick up another weapon or two while we are on Kiva. You just never know when you might need another one."

Eclipse snorted. "Funny, Ehhad, funny."

At my look, she shrugged. "Sorry, old habits and all that. Constance."

I shook my head. "I'm going to regret this, I just know I am." I looked over at Jaco. "Five percent of any proceeds after all this mess is over good enough for you?"

"Good enough," he replied with a grin, "I would have accepted less but I never look a gift horse in the mouth."

He sobered. "Constance, Xander, you two mean a lot to me. Be safe." He glanced at Eclipse and then back to us. "And watch your backs."

FIVE

The Holovid screen showed the usual milky-white cascading ribbons of Ultraspace. I swiveled in my chair to look over at Constance who sat staring in rapture at the mesmerizing view. "Where's Eclipse?" No reply. "Constance?"

She blinked and turned to me. "Sorry. Lost in thought. The last I saw of her royal procureness she was in the galley eating her way through *our* provisions. Her metabolism rate must be extremely high because she puts away more food than you and I together."

"Look Constance, I know you don't like the idea of having Eclipse onboard Ivy but we need her. She's the one who hired us, remember?"

She rolled her eyes. "How could I possibly forget? Eclipse reminds us of that every ten minutes." She sighed. "I know we have to have her with us on this expedition; I just don't have to like it."

Constance frowned. "You know she is not telling us everything..."

"Yes, Ehhad, I have."

Constance and I swiveled to the back of the bridge. Eclipse stood, hands on hips, just inside the hatch, a frosty glare directed at Constance. "I have told you everything that I know about the Hornet and what happened on The Rez. I am well aware that you would like nothing better than to help me along the way to the hereafter Constance but, well, get over it. I'm here, we have a job to do, we will do it, and then we will all happily go our separate ways."

Constance opened her mouth for a retort. I held up a hand. "Hold on, that's enough, both of you. Eclipse is right. We have a job to do and we can't very well do it with the two of you at each other's throats. I know that there is some serious bad blood between you two, but we need to set that aside for now. We have a serious mission here. If the Hornet is real and it is a powerful weapon, then we need to get it to some place where it will be kept safely out of reach of the wrong people. Not to mention the tidy sum that the Israelis will most likely give us for retrieving the artifact."

Eclipse nodded, and slumped into a seat. "Fine. Let's get on with it then."

Constance swiveled back to the Holovid screen. "Truce then. Ivy, how long until we reach The Rez?"

Ivy's image swam into view on the forward screen. "We will arrive in orbit around The Rez in five hours and sixteen minutes."

I turned to Eclipse. "Have you been in touch with your contact on The Rez?"

She nodded. "Yeah, I commed him a couple of hours ago. He's going to meet us in a café in the capital city, New Window Rock. He's a Navajo; they don't do any talking unless they eat first."

Great, I thought to myself, a delicious lunch of beans and a slice of bread.

I leaned closer to Eclipse. "So, does this Navajo contact man have a name?"

Eclipse grinned. "His name is Jesse Nakai. He and I have...worked together before."

Constance rolled her eyes. "He was a Procurer then, wasn't he?"

Eclipse smirked. "What can I say? I can't keep anything hidden from you two sleuths. Sherlock Holmes and Dr. Watson." She glanced at Constance and then at me. "Although I don't know which one of you is which."

I jumped in before the two women could begin another cat fight. "Enough, Eclipse. Why didn't you just tell us in the beginning that you were working with another former Procurer? Why keep it a secret?"

Eclipse shrugged. "I didn't think it was important. Big deal."

I held up a hand. "No more of that, Eclipse. You tell us everything. Ivy, Constance, and I will decide what's important. We're the investigators here. You're the client. Got it?"

She sighed. "Yeah, I get it."

I stood and stretched. "I'm going to the gym to work out." I pointed fingers at Constance and Eclipse. "You two get ready. We're going to be arriving at The Rez within a few hours. *And absolutely no fighting!*"

Eclipse rolled her eyes. "Whatever."

Constance simply raised an eyebrow and turned back to the milky-white vision of Ultraspace on the screen.

SIX

I had just finished getting dressed after my post-workout shower when Ivy called over the speaker. "Attention. Will the following humans please report to the bridge: Xander, Constance, Eclipse.... I am terribly sorry; I have made a mistake. Will the following humans please report to the bridge: Constance and Eclipse. In addition, will whatever Xander is please report to the bridge. That is all."

I stepped onto the bridge as Constance and Eclipse were laughing at something that Ivy had just said to them. All three silently watched me sit down.

I looked up at Ivy. "Is there something that you would like to share with me Ivy?"

She smirked. "Not really. Just conversation with Constance and Eclipse. I believe you humans would call it 'girl talk.'"

I glanced over. Eclipse was giggling and even Constance had a slight smile on her face. "Fine, at least the three of you aren't arguing."

Ivy nodded and winked. "Coming out of Ultraspace in three...two... one.."

The holographic image of Ultraspace was replaced with a view of the planet The Rez. Slightly smaller than Earth, but just as beautiful. About half the planet was covered by oceans with the rest taken up by several massive continents.

Ivy superimposed a political map on the sphere. The central continent facing us was outlined in red and a yellow star gleamed from the eastern edge. "That is the capital city of New Window Rock. The Rez's Aerospace Control has granted us permission to land at the Rez Spaceport."

I stood. "It's time folks. Let's not keep Jesse waiting."

We took Ivy's dropship down to The Rez's Spaceport. The ship settled onto the pad assigned to us and we disembarked. We donned our sunglasses as

176

The Rez's sun is slightly brighter than Sol. We strolled over to the spaceport's terminal.

The Rez was settled by Native Americans, Navajos to be more precise, a couple of hundred years ago, according to the background briefing that Ivy gave us on the way to the planet. Many Navajos still live on Earth, but a number of pioneering spirits made their way over the last two centuries to a planet of their own. There are just slightly over two million people who live here.

Most of the Navajos live on the continent of Hozro in which the capital city of New Window Rock is located. New Window Rock itself has a population of just over 100,000, so most of the planet's citizens live in or near villages scattered across the continent.

The spaceport was quite small, but thoroughly modern and attractive. We stepped up to the service desk and paid for our pad rental. The representative at the desk was a young Navajo woman with a perpetual wide, friendly smile.

"Have you arranged for ground transportation to your destination?"

I shook my head and smiled. "No, we haven't. What cab company do you recommend?"

She laughed. "That would be Begay's Taxi Service. It is, without a doubt, the best taxi service in New Window Rock. By some strange coincidence, it is also the only taxi service! I'll call them for you. There's a lounge just to the right of the main entrance. When your cab arrives, you will be paged."

I thanked her and we strolled over to the lounge. We sat down in an old-fashioned booth and took in our surroundings. The lounge was designed to look like that it been built out of logs. A real stone fireplace took up one corner. Given the heat of the planet, I doubted that it was ever lit. On the mantle were a number of beautiful Kachina dolls. Framed sand paintings adorned the lounge's walls.

"Did you hear that? Constance asked, "It sounded like thunder."

I nodded. "Yeah, I did. We're at the spaceport though; it may have been a ship taking off."

"No, your lady friend is right. A storm's coming up."

Startled, I glanced up. A waitress had materialized at the side of our table, an older woman with blond hair and blue eyes. "You're not Navajo."

She smiled. "I am, just not by birth."

At our mystified looks, she continued. "No, I'm not a true Navajo. My parents were actually from Europe back on Earth. When I was younger, I travelled here there and yonder. I was trained as a nurse and I wanted to see the world. I became a travelling nurse and went all over Earth. My last tour of duty, so to speak, was at a hospital on the Navajo reservation. I fell in love with the people, with their culture, with their way of looking at life. Finally, I came with a group of them to live here. I was tired of nursing, so I looked for something else to do with my time. A friend owned the franchise for this lounge and she was looking for someone to run it for her. I loved food and people so… here I am. One of the waiters commed in sick today so I'm waiting tables too."

She handed us menus, real, paper menus, not a digital screen. "I'll be back in minute with some waters while you folks look over the menu. And before you ask, everything is good!"

She whisked away while the three of us eagerly searched the menus.

The aromas coming from the back kitchen made my mouth water. "I don't know about you two, but I am going to have the lamb stew with fry bread, all washed down with lemon iced tea."

Constance shook her head. "It all sounds delicious. I'm having trouble making up my mind."

Eclipse smiled. "I'm not. I am definitely getting the Navajo Taco. Ground beef, cheese, onions, avocados, pinto beans, lettuce. In fact, I better order two just to be safe. And fry bread, of course." She turned the menu over. "Wow, look what a dessert menu!"

Constance smirked. "Yes, in fact if I were you, I would order three tacos." She studied the menu again. "I'm going to try the roasted lamb sandwich with a side of pinto beans."

So much for beans and bread, I thought to myself. I couldn't wait to try the food.

This time I noticed when Matilda returned to our booth. She set glasses of water down with lime and lemon slices. Pulling out a paper pad and pencil, she asked, "Ready to order?"

I looked in wonder at her. Where in the world had she gotten a paper notepad and a pencil for God's sake?

Eclipse spoke up first. "I want two Navajo tacos and a basket of fry bread. Oh, and a glass of strawberry lemonade."

Matilda nodded and turned to Constance. "And for you?"

"I will try the roasted lamb sandwich and I would like a small bowl of pinto beans please. I am going to stay with the water."

My turn. "Lamb stew with fry bread. And a strawberry lemonade."

A tall broad-shouldered man with shoulder length jet black hair slid into the booth beside me. "You three have excellent taste. I will have the lamb stew with fry bread as well."

He turned to me with a hand held out. "Ya ta hey! I'm Jesse Nakai, born to the Bitter Water Clan and born for the Crystal Rock People! And you two must be Xander and Constance!" He glanced at Eclipse. "Eclipse has told me sooooooooo much about you two!"

SEVEN

Eclipse reacted first. "What are you doing here, Jesse? You said we were to meet later at the Navajo Café. How did you know that we were here?"

He grinned. "Jesse is very wise. Jesse is all-knowing."

Eclipse snorted. "Jesse is neither. Answer the question."

He sat back. "Matilda and I go back a long way. I knew her a long time before I met you, Eclipse." He glanced at the rest of us in turn. "You all know about the Procurement League. What none of you knew is that Matilda was also a member of the Procurement League. I let the rep at the front desk know that I wanted the three of you to stay here while your taxi was en route. I had planned on the meeting here but I wanted to watch the three of you arrive and make sure that you weren't being tailed."

"Tailed?" I said in surprise, "Who would tail us?"

He grinned again. "Intradomain Mining for one. There may be other interested parties as well." He shook his head. "In any case, it doesn't matter now. You weren't followed."

Eclipse tried to digest all of that. "Why did you involve Matilda then? I don't know her. You should have told me about her."

He shrugged. "I wanted you to act naturally while I checked you three out. If you had of known, then you wouldn't have acted quite the same. Your friends here," he gestured at Constance and me, "are private investigators. They would have caught that there was something amiss. In any case, all's well that ends well."

Constance frowned. "You still have not answered the question that Eclipse posed. Why did you involve Matilda?"

I laughed suddenly.

The others looked at me in surprise. Eclipse spoke up. "Want to share something with the rest of the class, Xander?"

I nodded. "I do. Let's think about this for a minute." I ticked the points off on my fingers. "Point one. Matilda told us that she lived on the Navajo Reservation on Earth, just before she immigrated to The Rez, in fact. Point two. Matilda was a Procurer just like you, Eclipse, and our new friend Jesse. Point three. Matilda and Jesse have known each other a long time. I would suggest that Matilda met Jesse on the reservation, he recruited her into the Procurement League and she came with him to The Rez." I turned to Jesse. "Is that about right?"

He nodded. "Right as rain so far."

I took a sip of water and continued. "Point four: Matilda said that she had been all over the world. What if she found out about the Hornet during her travels? Maybe even saw it?"

"I didn't see it, but I did hear about it."

We all looked up. Once again, Matilda had managed to materialize right in front of us. How did she manage that?

She sat down plates and bowls in front of Constance and Eclipse. "I'll be back with the guys' lunches in a sec." She turned and hurried off toward the kitchen.

Constance, Eclipse, and I focused on Jesse. He held up a hand. "Let's wait until Matilda brings lunch for Xander and me and then, while we eat, we can hear the story straight from Matilda."

Matilda returned with the promised food and set steaming, mouthwatering bowls of lamb stew in front of Jesse and me. Jesse tore off a chunk of fry bread and gestured at the rest of us. "Dip pieces of the bread into the soup; it's really good."

He wasn't kidding. It was delicious.

Constance took a bite of her taco and chewed slowly, obviously savoring the delicious flavor. She swallowed and took a drink of water. "That's the best taco that I have ever had the pleasure of eating!"

"It must be good," I said to the others, "Constance rarely hands out compliments about anything."

Matilda sat a glass of lemonade on the end of the table, pulled up a chair from a nearby table, and sat down. She glanced around the lounge; only one other patron was present, a business traveler sitting by himself at the table closest to the door, suitcase by his side.

She raised her glass. "Cheers." She took a sip of the frosty drink and set it on the table. "Xander is right. I heard about the Hornet when I was in the Middle East back on Earth. I was working at a hospital in Jordan one night when a patient that I had started talking in his sleep. Every once in a while he would say something about a hornet. At first I thought he was just muttering nonsense from a dream but then he quoted verses from the Bible so plainly that I actually jotted them down on my Datapad. Verses from the Old Testament, Exodus and Joshua to be

EIGHT

Precise. Then he said something about a mine. At one point, before the night was over, he cried out 'we found the Hornet!'"

I checked his hospital records and I found out that he was a mining engineer employed by Intradomain Mining. He had been seriously injured in an accident at a bromine mine in Jordan before he was transferred to the tertiary care hospital that I was currently working at. I checked the Holovid News report and found out that the accident was being investigated because it occurred under suspicious circumstances."

This was getting *very* interesting. "What happened to the guy? Did he recover from his injuries? We need to talk to him."

Matilda shook her head. "He did recover from his injuries. Unfortunately, he died in a ground car accident two days after he was discharged from the hospital." She looked pointedly at us. "He ran off a curve on an isolated road and over a steep embankment. Someone passing by hours later saw the wreck and called for help. By the time the rescuers got there, all that was left of the man was charred remains from the car burning. He won't be able to tell anyone about what he knew about the Hornet."

I sighed. "Someone killed him off. He knew too much, and they killed him. The accident was probably no such thing; that was simply the first attempt to get rid of him. When that didn't work, his murderers staged a car wreck. These are ruthless folks we are going up against. IntraDomain Mining is up to its neck in this caper."

Jesse nodded. "Sure. They know what they found and they know what the value of something like that would be. Imagine being able to purchase the Power of God wrapped up in a nice little transportable package. We need to

182

get that away from them."

"So that we could sell it to the highest bidder?" I asked.

Jesse took a spoonful of soup. "Here's what I propose. The five of us work together to get the Hornet. That's enough to worry about right now. If and when we get it, then we decide what to do with it. It will have to be a unanimous decision, that's the only truly fair way of handling this."

The others nodded. I took in a deep breath. "Fair enough. So, where is the Hornet now? Does IntraDomain Mining have it?"

Jesse glanced around the lounge. The lone businessman had left; the place was completely empty except for the five of us. "My sources say that they do. The company has a mine about 150 kilometers from New Window Rock. According to my friends, the Hornet was taken there."

I sighed. "We still have several questions that need to be cleared up. First of all, why did Intradomain Mining bring the Hornet here? Why take it off Earth in the first place?"

"That I don't know," Jesse replied.

A monitor above the counter, which had been playing a Holovid series, suddenly showed images of a burning building in London, England, on Earth.

I turned to Matilda. "Would you turn the volume up on that?"

She nodded, pulled out a control, and waved it in the direction of the monitor.

"...and Scotland Yard has confirmed that 325 people were killed and nearly two hundred others were injured when three A.I. avatar suicide bombers blew themselves up at the Cambridge Theater in the West End. The attack was the fourth act of terrorism by A.I avatar on Earth in the last three months. Elsewhere in the Domain, similar A.I. terrorist attacks have been carried out on Kiva, Rye's Planet, and Alexandria..."

Constance gasped. "Then the attack on the tram on Kiva wasn't an isolated event. This has to be an organized act."

I nodded. "Yeah, and just at the same time that a supposed super-weapon goes missing. A coincidence?"

Jesse took a sip of lemonade. "But why here then? There are no A.I.s on The Rez."

"That's true," Constance replied, "But we need to keep in mind that the ship supposedly carrying the Hornet *crashed* on The Rez. What if it wasn't landing here; it could have been traveling to some other planet, or station or ship for that matter, ran into trouble and crash-landed here?"

I nodded. "It's possible. Are there any other inhabited planets in this system?"

"Yes," Jesse replied, "The fourth planet, Yuron."

Eclipse gasped. "Yuron? The planet Yuron is right next door?"

I leaned forward. "What's so special about Yuron? What gives, Eclipse?"

She stared off in space for a moment. "When I was in prison, there was another inmate, Sanya. She was from Yuron."

"So?" Constance prodded.

Eclipse glared at her in return. "So, she we talked a lot about our home worlds. She said that Yuron was a meeting place for arms dealers. And not just any arms dealers, those dealing in weapons that have been outlawed by the Human Domain. Weapons that are sold to anyone with the credits to pay for them. No background checks so to speak."

I nodded. "That's probably where the ship was headed when it crashed here. So now we know where it was going and why. The next step will be to get to mine here on The Rez and scope out the place."

My comm buzzed. I glanced at the screen. "Incoming message from Ivy." Excuse me a moment while I take this." I stepped over to one side of the lounge, out of earshot. "What's up Ivy?"

"Xander, I have been monitoring space traffic in and around The Rez; very easy to do since is there is so little of it. A ship registered to the IntraDomain Mining Company just left orbit."

"Find out where that ship went Ivy."

"I already did. According to The Rez's Aerospace Control, the ship was bound for Yuron, the fourth planet in this system. It is an inhabited planet…"

I cut her off. "Yeah, Ivy, I know. Good work. Prepare to leave orbit. The Hornet is probably on that ship."

"On it. I will be prepared to break orbit in 30 minutes."

I closed the connection, stepped back over to the table, and told the gang what was up. "Let's finish our meal and then we will head back to *Ivy*." I turned to Jesse. "Are you coming with us?"

He shrugged. "I might as well. I'll need to drop by my place and pick up a few things before we go back to the spaceport."

Matilda looked thoughtful. "Mind if I go along? I can get someone to cover here for me while I'm gone for a day or two. Sounds like fun. What do you say?"

I looked at Constance. She shrugged. "I suppose that would be alright."

Eclipse joined in. "I think it's a great idea. You know, the more the merrier!"

I looked pointedly at her. She frowned. "I know, I know, what I think doesn't matter."

I had a bad feeling about our little jaunt with our new friends but, hey, when I have ever listened to myself? "Fine. Let's finish and go."

NINE

I nodded. "That's probably where the ship was headed when it crashed here. So now we know where it was going and why. The next step will be to get to mine here on The Rez and scope out the place."

My comm buzzed. I glanced at the screen. "Incoming message from Ivy." Excuse me a moment while I take this." I stepped over to one side of the lounge, out of earshot. "What's up Ivy?"

"Xander, I have been monitoring space traffic in and around The Rez; very easy to do since is there is so little of it. A ship registered to the IntraDomain Mining Company just left orbit."

"Find out where that ship went Ivy."

"I already did. According to The Rez's Aerospace Control, the ship was bound for Yuron, the fourth planet in this system. It is an inhabited planet…"

I cut her off. "Yeah, Ivy, I know. Good work. Prepare to leave orbit. The Hornet is probably on that ship."

"On it. I will be prepared to break orbit in 30 minutes."

I closed the connection, stepped back over to the table, and told the gang what was up. "Let's finish our meal and then we will head back to Ivy." I turned to Jesse. "Are you coming with us?"

He shrugged. "I might as well. I'll need to drop by my place and pick up a few things before we go back to the spaceport."

Matilda looked thoughtful. "Mind if I go along? I can get someone to cover here for me while I'm gone for a day or two. Sounds like fun. What do you say?"

I looked at Constance. She shrugged. "I suppose that would be alright."

Eclipse joined in. "I think it's a great idea. You know, the more the merrier!"

I looked pointedly at her. She frowned. "I know, I know, what I think doesn't matter."

185

I had a bad feeling about our little jaunt with our new friends but, hey, when I have ever listened to myself? "Fine. Let's finish and go."

Jesse got us to the spaceport and, within hours after our lunch, Ivy had five passengers instead of two like in the old days. It took two days to reach Yuron; the Ultraspace drive is detectable and we didn't want the folks on Yuron to see us coming; we had to use a conventional ion drive.

Ivy scanned Yuron's orbital space and found no other spaceships in orbit.

I swiveled to face Eclipse who stood quietly watching the forward screen. "So, where on the planet would the meetings take place?"

She turned toward me. "A place called Phoenix Station. It's an outpost along the Crystal Run, a river that winds through the Whispering Forest."

I laughed. "Doesn't sound like the kind of place that a bunch of sleazy arms runners would meet. Sounds more like we will go down there and find Hansel and Gretel or Snow White."

I looked at the others gathered on the bridge. "So we understand the plan? Everyone clear on what's going to happen?" There were nods all around. "All right, let's begin. Ivy, open the show."

Ivy's image appeared on the forward screen. "Yuron, this is the *Athena*. My captain, Fenn Ohmstead, wishes to speak to someone concerning a possible *acquisition*. Please respond."

Silence greeted Ivy's message but that was not unexpected. I stood and stretched. "Repeat the message every two minutes Ivy until we receive a reply."

We didn't have to wait very long. "*Athena* you may land a dropship at Phoenix Station. Coordinates follow." The deep bass voice rattled off a string of numbers.

Constance frowned. "That was entirely too easy. No questions, no demands, no warnings. So?"

I shrugged. "So we stick to the plan. The only alternative is to turn tail and run and I'm not ready to do that. Let's just let the game play out."

The Gang of Five boarded the dropship and we headed to the planet's surface. I commed Ivy. "Stay on the line at all times Ivy. Once we get to the meeting site, if you don't hear anything from us in two hours…"

Ivy chuckled. "I'm to break orbit and get as far away from danger as I can?"

I sighed. Ivy and her humor. "No, get word to the DBI."

"Landing site coming up," Ivy intoned. "Prepare for landing."

Ivy gently settled the dropship on the landing pad that has been assigned to us. The rear door slid open and the planet's humid atmosphere wafted in.

Constance sniffed the air. "Smells like a greenhouse."

I nodded. "Most of the planet is either forest or jungle with an occasional river thrown in for good measure. Not many animals and fewer humans."

I stepped out, followed by Jesse, Constance, Eclipse, and Matilda. We stood grouped together as the dropship's door whispered shut behind us. No one was in sight. A small building built apparently of wood stood a hundred meters in front of us, the Crystal Run meandering along beside it. The building was built on wooden stilts; evidently the Crystal Run flooded from time to time.

I glanced at the others and shrugged. "To the building, I guess. Everyone stay sharp."

Jesse frowned. "I don't like this Xan...er Fenn."

Eclipse, to my surprise, stepped in front of the others to walk beside me. "Be careful. These people are scary."

At my sidelong glance, she added, "At least that's what Sanya said."

As we approached the building, we could see a large front porch with wooden steps leading up to it. On the porch, were several wooden benches and even a couple of rocking chairs. Rocking chairs? What kind of arms dealers were these?

We walked up the steps and stood glancing around at the archaic, home-spun appearance of the building. I shrugged. "We might as well make ourselves at home. Let's sit down, shall we?"

Constance and Eclipse took the rocking chairs while Jesse and I sat down on a couple of benches.

Jesse grinned. "All we need is a jug of moonshine and a banjo!"

"I am afraid that I cannot provide you with a banjo, but I do have some distilled spirits that I have made from corn mash."

We turned at the new voice and found ourselves staring at a male A.I. avatar wearing, of all things, overalls. He smiled. "Welcome friends! Welcome to Yuron! Make yourself at home and I will get you a refreshing beverage."

He turned and disappeared into the building. Moments later she returned carrying a wooden tray with five silver mugs. He handed one to each of his and then turned and set upon the remaining bench. "Please enjoy."

I eyed the clear liquid, shrugged, and took a sip. It burned all the way down.

The others took cautious sips, except for Constance, who sat quietly watching the rest of us as we cautiously sipped.

TEN

"**N**ow then," the avatar began, "Let's talk business. My name is Jin and I am a provider of just about anything that you would desire. What, exactly, do you desire Xander? I see from the shocked look on your face that you are surprised that I know your true name! Perhaps you will be even more surprised when I tell you what you are looking for! The Hornet!"

So much for Plan A. Time to fall back to Plan B. There was just one little problem with that…we didn't have a plan B.

I sat a moment, digesting what Jin had just disclosed. I shrugged. "What can I say? It was worth a try; I really didn't expect my plan to work. But why did you even allow us to land if you knew who we really are. Why invite us on down," I glanced around at the homespun surroundings, "To the old homestead?"

Jin smiled. "Very simple. I am lonely."

I waited for further explanation from our new A.I. friend but none came. I glanced at the others; they seemed to be as mystified as I was.

"You're lonely? You are an arms dealer and you're worried about having someone to talk to?"

He shook his head. "No, you have misunderstood. I am not a dealer in weapons; I provide information on how to obtain what you want. I am a solitary clearing house of information. I make my home on this planet away from prying eyes, but I have connections throughout the Human Domain. There is, in fact, virtually no planet in the Domain that I do not have at least one contact on, either human, A.I. or both. My contact on The Rez informed me of your identities and your mission."

I glanced at Jesse who held up both hands. "Hey, don't look at me. I have no idea who his contact is. I've never heard of this guy," he said as he waved a hand at Jin. "Doesn't matter anyway, does it?"

I turned back to Jin. "So if you are selling information then what can you tell us about the Hornet and how much will it cost?"

Jin grinned. "I can tell you exactly where the Hornet is."

Eclipse spoke up. "Is it still on this planet?"

Jin waggled a finger at her. "Naughty, naughty, young lady. No free information!"

I leaned forward. "Fair enough. What's your price?"

Jin picked up a stick and reached into a pocket in his overalls. All five of us tensed, ready for action.

He laughed, and pulled a folding knife from his pocket. "Relax, it's just a pocket knife." He unfolded the knife and began paring off thin strips of bark from the stick. At our puzzled looks he said "It is known as whittling. It was a pastime that people back on ancient Earth did when…negotiating. I do not require much in the way of payment, a trifle really. One thousand credits."

Constance gasped. "A thousand credits? Absolutely not!"

I decided to play along. "In your dreams…oh wait, A.I.s don't dream. 250 credits."

Jin never took his eyes off the stick as he continued to whittle. "750 credits."

I laughed. "Only if hell freezes over. 300 credits."

Jin chuckled. "If that happens, with my contacts, I would be the first to know. 500 credits and that is my final offer, as you humans are fond of saying."

I threw up my hands. "Done."

Constance scowled at me. "It is still entirely too many credits."

Jin set the stick down on the bench and put the knife away. "Not for the information that I will give you, rest assured." He produced a Datapad, entered the transaction, and handed it over to me. "Just offer your thumbprint and the deal will be sealed."

I looked at the Pad. "How do we know that we are paying for real, useful information? You could tell us anything."

Jin looked as if I had just slapped him across the face. "That is not the way Jin operates. My business is based upon complete honesty. If I were found to be selling erroneous data, I would be out of business in an instant." He shrugged. "Besides, many of my customers are not above vandalizing an avatar. Selling bad information is not only bad for business but it is certainly not good for my health."

I sighed. In for a penny, in for a pound. I pressed my thumb on the Datapad and handed it back to him. "So, where is the Hornet?"

"Arms merchants currently have possession of the Hornet."

We waited. A bee-like insect lazily buzzed by. I idly wondered if that was really the Hornet and it was slowly and methodically flying out of our reach.

I leaned forward. "And?"

Jin grinned. "Impatient, are we not? The Hornet is going to be auctioned off to the highest bidder at an arms sale tomorrow at high noon. The auction will take place at a location two kilometers down river from here. Tomorrow morning, I will take you via boat on the Crystal Run to the auction."

Constance laughed. "And just exactly how do you propose, Jin, that we get into the auction?"

Jin smiled. "I will provide a cover story for your merry little band. You will pose as…revolutionaries who are looking for a little something extra for their cause. I will provide the necessary backgrounds for all five of you. For a fee of course."

I glared at him.

Jin shrugged. "Fine. I will throw it in, free of charge."

Matilda shook her head. "I thought you said that you didn't deal in 'erroneous' information."

"I did," Jin replied, "The backgrounds are for real humans; they just won't be there tomorrow, you will."

That was splitting ethical hairs, I thought, but hey, I am not one to look a gift horse in the mouth. "Fine, that's acceptable. Now we just have to figure out how to get the Hornet once we get there."

"That will actually be the easy part," Jin replied, "I can transfer phantom funds into your bank account. All you have to do is be the highest bidder. Once the funds are transferred, you will have one hour to get the Hornet and leave the planet before the funds will magically reduce to zero in the arms dealer's account."

We were stunned. I finally found my voice. "You can do that? And not get caught? I didn't know that was even possible!"

Jin nodded. "Yes, I can do that, no, I will not get caught, and yet it is possible. No, how I do it is not for sale to anyone for any price."

Jin noticed our worried looks. "It will work, I guarantee." He clapped his hands. "But enough of that. We have some time left today so come into my humble home and I will fix something to eat for all of you. Then I will get you up to date on your new identities." He turned and stepped inside the cabin.

Eclipse followed him. "Hey, Jin, what's with all of this old-fashioned routine?"

Jin's the beginning of Jin's reply floated back through the open door. "Eclipse, I am so happy that you asked. It all began when…"

THE RETURN OF THE EHHAD WILL CONTINUE...

Dennis Gallemore

THE MYSTERY OF CHRISTMAS
A COLLECTION OF CHRISTMAS SHORT STORIES,
INCLUDING XANDER AND THE HORNET, PART II,
COMING OCTOBER, 2016

PARTING THOUGHTS

I hope that you have enjoyed reading these stories as much as I have enjoyed writing them! My second collection of stories, *The Mystery of Christmas*, will contain a number of Christian short stories about Christmas as well as the conclusion of *The Return of the Ehhad*. I will publish the book in October, 2016, God willing and the river don't rise! Blessings upon you and yours!

Made in the USA
Las Vegas, NV
14 December 2021

37682397R00121